DUSK TRAVELLERS

Carl Clarabut

First published by Carl Clarabut 2023
www.dusktravellers.com
ISBN   9780645309126

To my very patient wife Justine, for always being there.

1

Nathan

I always found the existence of advertising aimed at vampires rather strange, seeing as the target market is incapable of appearing in photos. Dressing humans up as vampires to sell products had no boundaries. Money talks throughout the world but especially so in this new town of ours. Throughout history we had never been able to record vampires on any type of media. This made having any sort of formal identification for vampires a nightmare. That is until scientists well above my pay grade, and intelligence, discovered that vampire's canines are, like our fingerprints, completely unique. Governments were taking photos and moulds of vampire's teeth and adding them to a worldwide database in order to put society at ease. Luckily that job didn't sit with our department.

Waiting to meet Gillian on the train platform was made more difficult as I had no idea what he looked like. The description some insightful intern had sent through, a male vampire of average height with black hair and pale complexion could describe more than half the population of this place.

It hadn't taken long for this formerly quiet station mainly used by freight trains, and the odd Sydney shuttle, to transform itself. It was once surrounded by old weatherboard houses with rusty tin roofs that at the time were inexpensive to own so once the rumour of a vampire prison coming to town had leaked, they had been swiftly bought up and knocked down. The train station now had six platforms, four of them new. This was the last stop before heading off to the prison.

This city had an old port that was used for transport of coal and once steel, but it was yet to be adapted for cruise ships, which the new populace preferred. That was still based in the south, as we liked to call it, but down there they were barely holding on to their dominance. Everyone once wanted to live in Sydney but the dramatic rise in house prices had pushed people out of the busy cosmopolitan city. Now humans and vampires were swarming north.

The council of the local area was reaping the rewards and much of the new money being earned was being relocated into infra-structure, as well as their own pockets of course, as quickly as possible. Most of the buildings around here were heritage listed and couldn't simply be knocked down to build cheaper more ef-ficient buildings. You could still see the remnants of these old buildings though with their iron arches and exposed sand stone brick now infused with glossy blackout windows and cutting-edge high-tech equipment. The train station looked like a modern-day airport rather than the old suburban terminus.

Now there was a reason to move to this rapidly growing city, we were taking the glam away from the south and we were glad to rub it into their smug faces, as they had to us for many a decade. It may have once been great to have an opera house and harbour but it couldn't complete with the world's first vampire prison as an attraction.

Our city airport was only a forty-minute drive out of town but wasn't prepared for international flights yet, but don't worry, they were already charging a small fortune for a small weak coffee so they were ready in some ways.

As the sleek ten-carriage train slowly pulled in to the busy station I was reminded how quickly we all adapted to the new ways of living. Half of the train windows were blacked out to accommodate travelling vampires; it was how people like my new partner could travel safely throughout the state. I still remember when the middle carriages were where the guards used to be stationed to help commuters in trouble; the vampires however needed no such help.

Change always seems to cause an uproar, and vampires travelling on trains, or any transport, was no exception. People eventually adjusted though, just as they had in the past when drink driving was made illegal and when smoking was banned indoors.

People quickly saw the effect of having vampires as part of our small city and they liked it, mainly for the money it generated. A city of steel previously in slow decline now had a new revitalised prison, which was generating millions of dollars.

The city where I had honed my skills now had new lessons to teach me, and one of those was discovering how to be a detective with a vampire for a partner. Meeting a new partner was always an anxious experience; Gillian being a vampire upped the ante.

I stood in the designated vampire waiting area on the platform sipping a tepid flat white. Drinking coffee at night wasn't unusual for me. It helped me focus and with the intake of new business we were experiencing the ability to buy coffee twenty-four seven was a welcome addition.

The blacked-out windows of the train door opened and vampires began to pour out of the carriage. Just like humans, vampires come in all shapes, sizes and colours. I searched the crowd trying to imagine what Gillian might look like. Turns out he was the last to disembark.

Gillian's age was what set him apart from the more common vampire, especially the vamps that were living out in the desert near their food source, the prison. Not that vampires aged in the same manner as humans, rather they developed more skills and grace as they matured, and as a result of this Gillian appeared as if he was gliding down the platform.

"Gillian, I presume," I said. "I'm Nathan, your new partner. Good to have you on board." I noticed Gillian had exited the train carriage with only a single small-wheeled suitcase. I reached out my hand, but he didn't do the same, as he seemed distracted by the bronzed statue of a figure sitting on a bench on the platform. The statue was in memoriam of a man who had worked there, I think.

Hundreds of people were streaming past us now as we stood there in the humid evening air, which meant it was game night. Blue and red scarves decorated the local rugby team supporters who were pulsing through the newly revamped train station. Even though it was still warm at 9pm the people loved their local team so the scarves were out regardless of the weather, the result of a city that was a one-team town. This attitude summed up the city's taking to the new prison. People from here loved, and rooted for, people who called this city home.

Feeling somewhat awkward as I slowly drew back my hand he spoke, "Gillian is my name, pleased to meet you, Nathan," he said in a working-class London accent. We shook hands and I gestured we make our way towards the exit.

Gillian moved over to the statue, placing his hand over the statue's head as he gazed at this piece of metal with soft eyes.

"The pain this bloke has been through, the mocking, the ridicule. Why would you immortalise that?" asked Gillian.

This confused me, "Not sure mate… maybe it's time for me to take you to your accommodation, I can take you for a drive around town on the way if you like? Must say not much luggage for someone moving to a new city Gillian?"

He turned around looking tired and slightly sad. "Not knowing how long I will stay I thought it best to travel light. I can always have more belongings shipped over if need be."

"From England?" I said, "That won't be cheap, anyway if you need anything let me know. For what it's worth I'm hoping you'll stay for a while, considering the situation." We moved along the platform. Vampires were now able to travel any way a human could but most didn't like flying in planes. So good old fashion trains and cruise ships were the transportation of choice and were no longer dominated by the elderly.

Raising his head, he said, "Well a city tour first would be nice mate, lead on."

2

Nevaeh

Working as a prison guard doesn't sound glamorous but with our new kind of inmate my pay had almost tripled. I've never been the academic type but I wasn't stupid, I didn't want to be like most girls round here; pregnant with no prospects at eighteen. Just being pretty and popular didn't interest me either. What was the point in being what is considered beautiful if you're breast-feeding all day and can't leave the house? I could often see a situation unfold before it ever happened, which is how I've managed to stay out of trouble. Now I'm saving money and planning for my future.

Not being afraid of vamps was a big bonus for me. Lots of the old timers had problems making eye contact with vampires let alone mopping up the blood they spilled. Vampires had in the past existed in the shadows of society, which most people could accept as long as they weren't being eaten. Working with and for vampires was a different scenario for humans, it took a while for most to think of this as the norm.

I also found it easy to converse with the vampires, they didn't intimidate me with their aura, size or age. From these conversations I had learned their power and speed were linked to how old they are. It wouldn't be considered normal for a human to feel comfortable around vampires but for whatever reason I had no issue with it. I could cut right through the bullshit with vampires, they could be dickheads just like humans.

I was instrumental in setting up the prison procedure for vampires to feed on humans. From an early age popular fiction leads us to believe that vampires suck blood from our necks to kill or petrify us but this turned out not to be true, rather they do this to feed and survive, like we all need to do. Coming up with a way for vampires to obtain blood from humans in a less aggressive, and easy to stomach, way was key to making the procedure a success.

Now let me be straight, in the beginning there were mistakes. When the law came to pass that vampires could feed on prisoners no one quite knew how it would work. Fucking bedlam it was at the start, humans weren't supposed to die, it wasn't meant to be a death sentence but that's how it was in the beginning, messy, really messy.

I remember my first day watching as a vamp tore into a prisoner's throat, I didn't realise blood from an artery could spray that far across a room. As bad as it was watching a human die I couldn't help thinking; I know who's going to have to clean that up.

Laws now stated vamps were allowed to feed but not kill. Money needed to be made out of this somehow so they had to pay a fee in order to feed off humans, and they were willing to pay a lot. Contracts needed to be drawn up stipulating if any vamp got carried away, they would be instantly destroyed and all monies paid would go to the prison.

Due to vampires' dislike of the sun, the prison instantly turned day and night cycles upside down. My shift was from 10pm until 6am, a full-on eight hours of crazy. The whole area outside the prison changed due to the influx of vamps, 1am was more like the old 9am. Prison tours, restaurants and cafes were open all hours now to accommodate the influx of vamps that were housed at specialised overpriced hotels.

To extract more money from the vamps we set up two ways for them to feed.

1: Blood transfusion from human arm to vampire arm, clean, crisp, efficient and quick. New needles were developed due to the toughness of vamp's skin. Ten bays were set up, each housed a vamp and an inmate on side-by-side recliner chairs. It was all very clinical and in a strange way seeing this happen on a daily basis reminded me of Mum's cancer treatment and helped me deal with her death.

2: Mouth to neck, as I like to call it, good old-fashioned vamp sucking on a human's neck. We worked out that a pint of blood took roughly a couple of minutes to inhale. This method is messy and incredibly scary for the inmate. We make double money this way though. Vamps pay extra for it and inmates try to bribe the security staff to get out of it.

The first way, which was my idea, helped me move up the prison pecking order, but I still knew my place. The idea came from seeing my Mum go through chemo, which was confronting for me as a daughter but seeing first-hand how our health system worked inspired me in this job.

You might think of all this as inhumane but the authorities were smart. We import the worst of the worst prisoners from around the globe, no one has a problem with watching a paedophile going through this process again and again. And just so we're clear, it is very painful having your skin ripped through repeatedly by sharp pointy teeth. The marketing wing of the prison went into overdrive, pitting the immoral perpetrators against the gallant vampires that were helping us punish the evil no one else wanted to deal with. How roles change, from the eerie pictures of Nosferatu or Dracula to vampires that on the surface look and act like us, only with a need for more extreme dental care.

Once we adapted the old prison for vamps it went from a

historical museum visited by tourists to a fully functioning modern gaol. As a result, we had an influx of new staff, whom, unlike myself, struggled at times working with vamps.

The inner sanctum of the older guards could be fucking ruthless and a lot of them didn't like having new blood like me on the scene. There was too much change going on as it was without a younger, fitter, more tolerant and efficient female there to show them up. The new role of setting up the feeding area had been allocated to me though, but I wasn't the boss of this profitable section, that job fell to Dave, I still had to keep my head down and not mess with the hierarchy of the prison guards. I learned the hard way how to fit in and I was trying my best to do that. In the past I would have choked on the idea of appeasing people I was smarter than, but my surrogate father, Maury, taught me patience, and here at the prison I was drawing on that skill, I admit it's a challenge but I'm doing the best I can.

As I walked down the brightly lit corridor my earpiece was going crazy. I was in the new, cleaner part of the prison that had been built in the last five years. It resembles an airport hangar with its' concrete floors, high ceilings and windowless walls, it was in stark contrast to the original architecture and sandstone brick of the old prison.

There had been many trials and tribulations during construction as nothing like this had been built on this type of scale. It created a blueprint that helped build other places safe for vampires to visit such as airports, hotels and ports. All I knew was that all the equipment in this new area always worked without fail, just like the clinical laboratories you see in movies. Although there was also no character, unlike the old prison, which oozed gritty charm, but

back there I always felt I was fighting against the threat of something breaking down.

Too many investors had ploughed billions of dollars into this
high-tech prison/hotel for it to fail. We were bombarded with an
advertising campaign that resembled a presidential race in its intensity. Faces of rich white benefactors who told us how lucky we
were to have a building like this in our hometown. I had heard
empty promises from their type before, it sickened me a little that
it was working out so well for me so far.

"Nev, are you there, Nev?" there was panic in Dave's normally
low voice.

"Yes boss, I'm on my way to the feeding zone now."

"Only now, Nev? We are double booked and you're only just on
your goddamn way. Move it, on the double, it's going off down
here."

"Yes boss, I'm one minute away."

Dave, my boss was all bark no bite. He couldn't handle the sight
of blood dripping off a vamp's fangs. Looking into their glowing
frenzied eyes sent him into a similar spiral. He had also forgotten
it was my fucking day off. He would remember when he saw the
triple overtime I was going to claim though.

As I scanned my security pass to move in through the final gates
of the feeding zone, I could hear screaming and shouting coming
from down the hall. I quickened my pace knowing what it meant.
As I moved past the observation deck where paying customers
had come to watch the feed, I heard Dave shout down the headset.

"Nev, we've got a squirter. I repeat we've got a squirter!"

3

Thomas Malcolm

Humans kill and go to jail. Vampires kill and are destroyed, such a waste. The pain of seeing a loved one dead or taken away from you was always hard to take. Gut wrenching some might say, but in this I had seen an opportunity. Humans are not punished adequately for their sins anymore; it was too easy for them to escape incarceration and to be free to reoffend. Then there are vampires who prefer their blood warm and spraying freshly from a human neck, pouring into their mouth alongside sweat, tears and fear. My extremely successful business combines the two into a boutique and exclusive revenge service, at a cost of course.

Not all vampires wanted to rip blood from humans and watch them die. I was one of them. There was just no class in it. It was all rather messy. I preferred to drink blood that had been donated from humans, or animals, either would suffice, I wasn't fussy. I found it degrading to gnaw on something that still had a pulse. I didn't like the lack of control or precision it came with. It felt powerless.

My service was simple; find a grieving family who had lost someone they loved to a horrible crime; inform the family I had a well-paying client who would be more than willing to devour the perpetrator in front of them. They would be given the chance to see the pain in the criminal's eyes as their drains away in front of them. There of course was one catch. The family could not press charges against the accused.

I had a team of trackers who were able to hunt down the accused. We had to be quick and we had to be right. If we got the wrong person a family would not be impressed to discover they had paid to watch an innocent person die. This had happened once before and we were very keen for it not to happen again.

Putting a team together hadn't been easy, there were teething problems (Oh Thomas Malcolm, you do love vampire jokes). Finding Jonathan, my now head of security ten years ago was a godsend. My team needed to possess certain skills in order to effectively hunt down human or vampire killers. Those who took pleasure in murder and torture were not the characteristics I required. Who was the right human or vamp, what was their motivation? Once I fine-tuned the team, and set up the right location the money from rich high-flying vamps gushed in. I may spend the days watching aloof vampires lick blood off the floor and where was the class in that? There was none, but that's ok, I had their money and that's where the real power lies.

4

Jeff

"Help... where am I?"

One minute I'm picking up rubbish as I do on Friday mornings, then I'm stuck, frozen. People keep passing me by day after day. Frozen, time moves slowly around me like a heavy fog. No physical pain but I'm sad, helpless and alone. Trapped inside this resting place for pigeons.

———————

I don't regret helping out. I've lived my life through the good and bad. It's important to help out no matter how small the gesture. And to be honest I was bored since I had retired. All the early starts I had in the army carried on throughout my life. Early bird they say, but when you live in a small town what is there to do?

After my wife passed away, I lost my focus. After being set in my ways for so long it was hard to reengage with society. It didn't help I hailed from overseas and Australia was my adopted second home, I was finding it even more isolating as I got older.

Mary and I never wanted kids and we were happy with our very small family. When we were young and fancy free, it was awesome, there was nothing to tie us down. We moved freely from one country to another. Mary being a nurse easily found work no matter where we travelled. The anticipation of not knowing what would be on offer at each new city or place we visited dwindled over the years. We found it less exciting to discover what food or museums a city had to share and instead found having routine more enjoyable the older we became. I loved the local coffee shop knew what time I would turn up each day and that they delighted in small talk as much as I did.

After being a nomad for so long it was good to finally find somewhere that felt like home. Even though in my youth I had only lived in Australia for a few weeks at a time I had always liked the culture. My accent made me stand out from the locals around here, which I enjoyed. We had bought a hundred-year-old bungalow, full of vintage features. It sounds quaint and beautiful but in reality, it means throwing as much time and money at it as possible. Like having to look for one hundred-year-old door handles to suit the now warped original timber door. I love hunting through second-hand stores, you could spend hours hunting through doors, windows and knick-knacks to help restore the character to an older style building. I thought these places were wonderful and had lots of treasures to unearth, Mary thought it was all just crap.

The three-bedroom house was enough for Mary and me and on the rare occasion an army buddy from overseas would pop up from Sydney when they were on their travels, we could accommodate them. It was warm here, which suited me, but it wasn't like the humidity of North Queensland or Vietnam. I didn't really miss home back in the States too much, well, maybe I missed the crab cakes, they were delicious and the very idea of them took me back to being a kid playing in our sweltering yard while Mom was in the kitchen making the tastiest crab cakes in the whole world.

I have always related food to my travels. I may not remember everything about a country but I could tell you what food I had partaken of in any place I had visited. When I smell or taste one of those dishes now it will instantly take me back to somewhere Mary and I have travelled. The look on her face when she found out what was in black pudding when we were in London or the way she held on to the brass railing in an underground bar in the Czech Republic that looked like a granny lounge and the peach schnapps seemed to burn a hole in her chest as soon as her lips touched the glass.

The seafood up here on the coast is good and fresh, and even though I was never a fisherman it was always nice to sit in the sun with Mary and chat while we cast our lines and caught nothing. I loved prawns and mud crabs but the oysters never tasted right to me unless they were covered in cheese then put under the grill, something Mary used to scoff at.

I got myself a job as a mechanic when I left the service and Mary worked at the local hospital. It all seemed to fit rather well. Everything was very close to where we lived, it was either a fifteen-minute walk or a ten-minute drive to almost anywhere we wanted to go, which was very convenient the older we got. There was always a lot to do. Walking along the pier, cycling, swimming and even kayaking. I like to think that we were both content and happy until one day Mary's body just stopped working. I remember asking her if she was ready for her morning coffee and slice of vegemite toast she loved. But beautiful pale Mary just lay there. I thought she was asleep. I got up and went to get the paper from the newsagent.

They said it didn't matter. She had passed peacefully during the night while I slept beside her. An aneurysm they said. Shit I thought. We were so busy living our lives we never prepared to get old. It just crept up on us.

Then I was alone, sitting there in my single green upholstered armchair. Spending my mornings looking out my window across the road to the local shopping centre while drinking a well-sugared instant coffee.

That's when it started. First, I no longer felt welcome at the mechanical garage I used to work.

"What are you doing here Jeff, get out and live your life. You're disrupting the young apprentices. They don't need the distraction of a chatterer like you. You've done your time, go enjoy life."

It was said in good jest but that was the problem, where could I go? Keeping fit and active was helpful for staying alive but I missed the chitchat. I liked to talk to people and even more I liked to listen. I didn't like being annoying and I always knew when I was getting that way. I could feel people's eyes gazing through the back of my neck. Work at the Salvation Army shop they said, or help out at the hospital, but it just never took my fancy. Too static, I thought. Not enough buzz and excitement.

Early each morning the sunlight would pour through the window directly on to my old comfortable chair. It was nice sitting there warming up my bones to just the right temperature each day while I drank my coffee. But what was the point in doing it each day if I had no purpose, no drive, no goals?

I observed the women who worked at the open-air mall the locals referred to as a village and knew their routine. Every morning without fail they would set up the promenade with chairs and tables for the bakery. You couldn't quite smell the meat pies and sausage rolls from my house but each time I crossed the road to pick up my paper the aroma would hit my nostrils.

Come on Jeff use your tablet to get on the web they said. You don't need a newspaper they said. You can stay home and read about the world online. They didn't get it. Getting the paper was a way for me to do something, I knew how to use the internet, I was old, not stupid.

At first Jenny and the other bakery girls found it a little strange that I started helping taking the curved steel chairs out from be-hind the front counter and setting them up with the tables out front for people to enjoy their hot cuppa and baked treat of choice, but they got used to it. You got all sort of customers during the day and you could set your watch to what time they turned up.

The council workers or builders would turn up at 6am in their high-vis tops for early sustenance to get them though their busy day. Then at 8.30am the school kids in their dark blue t-shirts would turn up for sausage rolls and a cheeky finger bun if they could get away with it. I often wondered where they got the money. I resisted telling the loud kids that 'back in my day' we never had money to waste or behaved in such a manner, saying that truly would have meant I was old and there was no turning back. I'm sure I was just as chaotic as these kids back then. After the kids left for school the oldies arrived, I love that expression, like myself, they would turn up for a chat and coffee. Such a variety of different people visited this little shopping village each day and it truly felt like a community. I sound like a council poster trying to promote togetherness in our area, but I really loved it.

When I first approached hard-working Jenny, who always seemed red faced from either the heat of the bread oven or the heat of summer, she was cautious. As both the owner and front-line worker of a small business she had no time for messing around. Jenny's light brown hair was always pulled back into a bun to keep it out of the way and her well-worn white trainers and gym pants meant she could move swiftly around her bakery. She was a lady who never sat still. If she wasn't taking orders on the phone, or pies from the oven, she was putting out the bins or talking to her loyal frequent customers.

Jenny had a welcoming aura at all times. If it was all going pear shaped in the kitchen you would never know. It went down well with the locals, talking to people and genuinely meaning it goes a long way in this town. People had worked hard in the mines and the steel mills; they could see straight through a liar and wouldn't tolerate it. As could Jenny, she could see right through a lie with a quick glance.

I remember being nervous when I first asked Jenny about helping out at the bakery. I had one thing going for me though, the fact that I already volunteered at the train station on game night. I was always there every other weekend when the local team played at home. I wore a reflective vest with 'Information' on the back of it. I had seen the job in the paper. I stood under the well-worn station awning giving advice to supporters from out of town on how to get to the game or where they could go to eat. The job meant I was entitled to free tickets but Aussie sport never took my fancy, instead giving out those tickets to others always made me feel good.

"Ehh ... excuse me," I said to the fast-moving Jenny. "I was wondering if we could have a quick chat?"

"We can, but while I work as I have things to get ready," Jenny said slightly confused and out of breath.

I slowly walked closer doing my best to hold my big frame together. "My name is Jeff and I live across the road and I was wondering if I could help. You might see me around most mornings getting my newspaper? I've noticed that you're always busy each morning setting up."

In the time I finished the sentence Jenny had managed to take out three tables.

"I've seen you around, but I see a lot of people in this job. I don't want to be rude but I've got a lot to do, what is it you are after Jeff?"

I could tell I was losing Jenny and the window for getting my point across was closing; I had to do something I was unaccustomed to, which was to talk fast. I normally liked to take my time.

"I have nothing to do in the morning anymore and I like to

keep active so with your permission I'd like to help with the tables and chairs. I don't want any payment. I'm already up drinking my coffee watching you do your job from across the way. I'm old but I'm not dead yet and I'd like to help out with this community that helped my wife so much. I already work at the train station on game night. So, what do you think?"

I ducked my large frame into her shop and pulled out two steel chairs and put them under the tables that she had already laid out.

Jenny facial expression had remained unchanged as I followed her around.

"Well, I'm here before six each morning, so if you want to help out then that's what time you have to be here. It's a busy place and if that's what you want to do, I have no problem with it, but be warned I can be rather particular."

"No worries, ma'am, I will see you bright and early tomorrow morning," I said with a broad smile. I skipped back home that morning, of course after collecting my paper.

That's how I spent the next five years of my life. At first Jenny was not convinced at all by some random old man helping out for no apparent reason. I slowly changed her mind though. It felt nice each morning to have a job to do. It only took me twenty minutes, but that was double the time it would take Jenny on a bad day.

I had no family and no real desire to go back to New Orleans. I attended the occasional meeting at the RSL club where I met up with others similar to me to reminisce about old times, but the numbers were dwindling by the year.

I hadn't realised talking to people much younger would make me feel younger and fresher. It gave me a zest of life I hadn't had for years. As someone who never had children or a close family hearing about Jenny's young daughter's troubles at school, or the other sandwich girls' issues, it was a different perspective for me. I wondered if Mary and myself would have been any good at raising children. It seemed rather draining and not so emotionally rewarding.

After months of helping out, people were used to me being there each morning. Jenny even made sure a mug of hot sweetened coffee would be waiting for me. The busy hair salon next door cottoned on to the fact that I was helping out and asked if I would do their customer coffee runs for them.

The owner of the salon offered a trim to my already balding head each month as payment. Of course, I said no but she could be rather insistent. By the end of the year, I was helping out at most of the shops. I got to know almost everyone from the cleaners of the toilets to the supermarket trolley boys. It was nice to be able to say hello to everyone. I started to stay until mid-afternoon, helping some shops pack away their tables and chairs from the promenade.

I brought a book with me, which I would read after finishing my coffee and paper. It was nice sitting there in my spot talking to people. I stopped working at the train station on game days. I preferred helping out at the shopping village instead.

As the years passed by, I noticed I was getting slower. I still went over to the village each morning but the two-minute walk had now tripled. My coffee and spot in the sun was still waiting for me on the corner but I no longer took out the chairs and tables for Jenny's bakery, or for anyone else.

Jenny hadn't slowed down; time didn't seem to be catching up to her yet. The conversation and bond grew between us, which I liked. People would offer to help me and asked if I needed the bins taken out or if I had considered meals on wheels. I was reluctant to accept peoples' help though. I wasn't becoming a grumpy old man and I did appreciate their offers but I knew if I stopped doing things for myself my decline would probably become more rapid and I really didn't want to move into aged care.

Getting the paper now was enough for me, and most of the

time it was too hard to read. The time of being able to live independently was coming to an end. The idea of leaving the village was very upsetting. It would rip a hole in my soul.

I still thought of Mary as the love of my life but the people that I had met in the last five years had given me something else to live for. But there was no denying the time was here, I was on my way out. I sorted all of my affairs. The house and the money I had left would go to the hospital where Mary had worked and to a local charity that helped homeless children in the area.

I passed away at night, like Mary, in my sleep. It was the way I wanted to leave this world. I didn't want to go to an aged care facility or cause a fuss. I hoped that I had made at least a small impact on people's lives.

Jenny collected donations from the locals to build a statue of me. It was a very sweet and generous but turns out it was the worst thing Jenny could have done. The bronze statue was placed at the train station so that I would be remembered as being a person who helped out in a small way and touched many people's hearts.

This memorial literally ripped my soul in two. Somehow the statue linked me here, I couldn't move on to Mary and the afterlife. My essence, or whatever you call it, was trapped inside the statue. I was stuck here against my will. I couldn't see as I once had but I could feel people's gaze or touch. All I could hear was voices, so many voices, at first it was too much, the screeching of the trains and the cocktail of noise as passengers vacated the platform. The noise was so loud that it made me spin but I couldn't put my hands on my ears as I no longer had a movable body. I was a cloud trapped inside a large heavy statue of myself. Helpless. There was no place for me to go. No escape. Was this hell? And if so, why?

I hadn't been perfect when I was alive but I was no way near a monster. Why was I here? I had no way of knowing the time or year. At first, I felt like killing myself but how could I do that?

I was so alone.

Slowly over time I learned to let go of my anxieties and despair and once I relaxed into my situation, I found I could filter the overwhelming noise I faced each day. I began to pick out sentences from the voices on the train station. I started to be able to tell the gender or age of the voice.

It was like being back at the bakery sitting on that cold steel chair sipping my coffee. I missed the smell of coffee. It was hard not to dwell on the past but I had to. I thought it would send me mad. Maybe I already was. The idea of going insane and not being able to do anything about it would... send me insane.

During the day I paid as much attention as I could, always listening to as much information as possible, whether from people conversing or the radio. At night I put every piece of information I gathered together inside my consciousness like a moving puzzle. There had to be a way out. Time was on my side so I had to try.

Everyone seemed to have headphones now and if I really concentrated on spreading myself out through that statue of myself, I could listen in. I didn't know what an iPhone or an android phone was but they seemed popular. Mobile phones had been around while I was alive but not to this extent. The music definitely hadn't gotten any better. Now I was sounding old. The old tin speaker used to make announcements was also used to play music. There was a wide range from '60s British rock to Aussie country music. My favourite by far was *Aquarela do Brazil*, which reminded me of my time dancing in Rio with Mary.

Normally everyone was self-focused; talking or texting about their own lives. It was hard to keep up, there was such a wide scope of stories. If there was a national election on, I would be able to tell as that would be all the news outlets would report on.

One day it stated to change. The buzz and conversation of people were concentrating on one subject. At the same time the vibration of new construction began to shake my statue nonstop for days on end. I sensed change, and not just in the many new platforms that were being added, to the pleasure of Mick, the easily excited stationmaster. I felt a different presence, one I recognised from the past. I had seen vampires during the war and also in my time in New Orleans. It was part of my culture growing up, the history of vamp lore and voodoo lore were intertwined.

Mary had a hard time dealing with vamps. They made her uncomfortable. Back then there weren't many up here really, or in the whole of Australia as far as I knew. You would hear of some vamps working out at the mines as cheap labour. Their strength and body type meant they could work long hours under less favourable conditions than what humans could.

When I first sensed a vamp at the station I felt as though I was shining straight through the statue. I couldn't see or feel myself as such but I knew something was totally different and I began to feel hope. I had to make sure that I didn't allow all of their thoughts into me all at once or I would be overwhelmed. Humans had become easy for me to track; it had been a bit tricky at first but nothing like the vamps. The chatter I heard and felt from the vamps was all centred on the prison out west. It had been closed while I was alive but now it appeared to be a major vampire attraction.

The quiet station where I used to hand out leaflets for the local rugby league team was now a thing of the past. It was always busy now. The station wasn't full of Novacastrians travelling from here to Sydney but the other way around. It was too much for most of the local old-timers. The sudden influx of vamps and all the modernisation was sensory overload for a lot of people.

I felt it was only a matter of time before one of the vamps would sense or feel me. When vamps walked past, I kept on trying to project to them I needed to get out of this prison. All I had was my own thoughts and if I carried on here those thoughts would drive me insane. What other option was there?

It was another busy Friday night, the comings and goings of fans mixed in with travellers and vamps from the south. The usual noise buzzed around the statue. I felt like a living timetable, I knew what trains were coming and going and if they were late, I even knew how full the trains were. In time the sense of vamps and humans had started bleeding into one, I was losing focus, losing energy but I tried to be vigilant.

I sensed the 8:45pm arriving from Sydney much earlier than normal. This train normally had a larger blacked out centre of the train to accommodate vampires during daylight saving. It was always packed to the rafters. Vamps looking forward to escaping their busy work lives for fun on the weekend, just like we humans. I felt myself buzz and glow, this was out of my control, but I had no idea why?

As the train pulled in to the crowded platform with the usual cocktail of noise, I had never felt so clear and focused. This arriving vampire, this being, felt different. I could feel his presence, his power from the train, like our intellect was linked. The joy of now being able to communicate to someone sent me wild. I felt myself losing focus as the outside world was beginning to become too much again. I was stretching too far in the statue. I was becoming like hot putty left out in the sun. I needed to regain control and keep calm. I had been waiting so long for this moment I couldn't let panic take me over.

"Hi there guv. I'm here to help, I started to feel you from about half a mile away," said a voice I didn't know.

"I've been waiting so long for this moment; I'm lost for words."

"It's ok," the English sounding voice said. "I can help but you need to breathe slowly or whatever you do to relax inside this bronze cage of yourself."

I started to regain my composure, my glow, my being. This communication is what had I waited so long for. It was not the time to blow it now.

"Good work Jeff, it must be hard to be yourself with all this going on."

I hastily interrupted, probably making no sense. "I'm so glad you're here. Can you help me? Can you get me out? How can we talk? What am I?"

"Breathe Jeff, in my time as a vamp I've seen this before, I will answer everything in good time, but first let's introduce ourselves. I can already see from your endearing plaque that your name is Jeff Harris and you've been here fifteen years. I'm Gillian and I'm very pleased to meet you mate."

5

Nathan

Driving down the freeway to the prison in the evenings was a different experience these days, you could now see the lights of the city in the cold dark sky from miles around. The quiet, narrow roads that once took you to quaint vineyards had been replaced with this super slick highway. The traffic was beginning to get busy, there was no down time now. With the explosion of people everywhere, weekends didn't count anymore. Every day was peak hour.

I liked working nights as the lower temperature suited my body type. The days could get so hot but the nights were slightly cooler. The unrelenting sun during the day made everything slower, like walking through sand, and there was plenty of that around. Sleeping during the day vampire style was the only way forward if I wanted to work with Gillian as my partner. I had a choice of what time of day I could work, he did not have that luxury.

It was a relaxing forty-minute drive to the prison and Gillian's first time heading out here. In the past we would have been surrounded by wildlife like possums and kangaroos. I used to always see their carcasses on the side of the road but that wasn't as common these days. Even the animals seemed scared of our new guests.

The city was a mixture of old and new. Modern swanky apartments circled it, their sharp edges glimmering in the night promised new opportunity. I liked the contrast of driving through the main street past the sandstone buildings and weatherboard houses. I had gotten used to the old pubs and rundown shops after the prison and the mines shut down. When investors began looking for a new enterprise, this city had been on top of the list. An aging prison in need of a major facelift and a city that could grow with it was very appealing. There was a sudden boom, those who had stayed thought they had won the lotto. The rustic hotel that sold cheap beer and food was revamped. Hipster cafes were popping up everywhere selling smashed avocado toast for twenty-five dollars.

With the new money came new kinds of trouble. There had always been issues here but not on the scale we were seeing now. The city was turning into a vampire Las Vegas. We were struggling to keep up, vampires and humans lived well together but like any mass gathering of people it became harder to control. There had to be regulations but we had no idea how to implement them. I was tasked with this role. I didn't know how to solve vampire crime so I knew I would need assistance from someone who did. Vamps were physically different, too fast and strong. They also had a way of seeing the world that I and other humans couldn't grasp. I wanted to learn as much as I could and fast. As a result, Gillian and I were the first vampire and human detective partnership in the world.

In the UK a small vampire team had been set up in North London, Gillian had worked there. When he saw the posting we advertised he was the only one to apply. Vampires and humans don't congregate with each other naturally, mainly because of the not insignificant fact that we have historically been their prey. Vampires see life through a multifaceted lens that we simply can't comprehend. The thought of a vampire sucking on your neck wasn't everyone's cup of tea. I never understood the sexual appeal to it either, but then again, I didn't understand being choked while sucking on a lemon so maybe I wasn't the right demographic.

I wanted Gillian's insight on the murders going on around here. Human instigated crime was on the decline. Vampire instigated crime was another story though. Vamps setting up humans for crimes they didn't commit so they would be end up on the prison buffet was a nightmare to investigate. Gillian could help with that.

Vampires in the modern world didn't need to kill humans as much as in the past. Not all vamps wanted human blood, there were other ways for them to feed. Yet the idea of feeding on a human for a fee was very appealing to most.

"It's a whole lot busier than I thought," Gillian said looking out onto the federation buildings that lined the old, but new again street.

"Maybe it's because night time is our new day time, businesses have all changed to maximise profit, apart from the schools of course," I replied. Schools had been banned in the prison town and no one under eighteen was allowed. With the new system in place, it was deemed safer if there were no children. It was one of the reasons why the town was so transient. People preferred to fly into the main city and drive up.

Families didn't live here. It was against the law. This also helped to stop certain groups from trying to shut the town down, whether that be the school board or a religious group. There was no point in building family homes so apartments were key. It seemed like the council was taking ideas from busy cities in countries like Japan and South Korea.

As we got closer to our office in the town I felt a sense of eagerness, the dream was becoming a reality. The hard work, the sweat and the shouting I had to do to set this up had finally paid off. For me the lack of a personal life was a fair trade-off as the idea of working with Gillian and getting to learn how vampires investigate crime was a real thrill. Vamps had always intrigued me. Immortality was top of the list but I wanted to know how the mental aspects of their existence affected them. How you could keep in touch with your sense of self if your self was four hundred years old?

"Gillian you were the only vampire to apply to my post which I'm grateful for but can I ask why?" I asked as I pulled in to the too small police station carpark, a design afterthought that had us cops fighting to find a space.

"I'm a bit of an oddity among vampires as I enjoy working with humans," he said with a wry smile. "I've never been in the southern hemisphere before and I thought it was high time, also the prison city is the reason I'm here. I've never seen so many of my own kind in one condensed place, even for someone like me it's rather unsettling. And, of course, I'm here to give you a hand with these murders. It's a myth that we feed then kill, any vampire worth their salt knows instinctively how much blood we can take before our prey might die, whether human or not. It's built in, like a gag reflex, you just know. Vampire murders, like the majority of murders, are rash, impulsive, unplanned and mostly committed by someone the victim knows. Like a serial killer Nate, a planned death by a vampire is much rarer than TV shows and films would like you to think. And the reason I'm here? I don't know, like anything I guess, I saw an ad at work and applied. It was time for a change and I've pissed off most of the human cops I work with. Dickheads," Gillian said without humour.

I was put back with his comment. "Don't like human cops? You know I'm one, right? I'm a little surprised by your comments, you got a glowing reference from your superintendent."

"Yeah, I'm sure I did," Gillian said with contempt. "That fucking stuck-up governor wanted me out of there as quick as anything. He's not prejudiced to us vamps or anyone else, he just doesn't like anyone with an opinion that's not his own. The setup I had at work was going well but the governor likes to control it all, I don't do this, like most of the vamps I work with, for money. As corny as it sounds, I like to help."

"Well, I appreciate your honesty." I said, realising that Gillian was eyeing me up to see what I was made of. He seemed completely at ease until he said the word, governor. It felt like he was checking all my indicators by looking at my every movement, like a vampire truth detector test. He could tell that his last comment had rather unsettled me; I didn't want or need anyone on my team who wasn't fully on board.

"I'm glad to have you here Gillian, with the skills that you can bring to my squad, but I have a really efficient well-trained team free from bad eggs." I don't know if I looked angry but I felt it.

"Look mate, I've just travelled halfway around the world, you're going to have to give me a little grace on what I say." I got the feeling that he was testing me to see if I, and my case, was a waste of time or not.

"Is this how you wound your boss up in London?" I said and that bought a little smile to his face. "Are the rest of the vamps you work with as charming as you? I'm looking forward to us working together Gillian. You probably won't get scared like the rest of us, will you?"

"You're right Nate we don't get scared but we do know when we are in a dangerous position. I can't quite explain it. I don't really remember being a mortal too much but the closest I can describe it is like butterflies in your stomach. In regards to your second question I do not know why no one else applied and I too was surprised to hear that. We generally like to travel and explore although we can be a little closed off at times I suppose. The unit I worked with in England consisted of dusk travellers like myself which meant we were quite suitable for the night shift," he said with a sharp laugh. "We don't complain and the brass don't have to pay us too much due to the lack of work options. They used to leave us alone to investigate crime at night and there was not much effort put in to integrating us with the non-vamp cops. Everyone was courteous and civil but I was sure they would rather not have had to deal with us."

"Dusk travellers?" I asked.

"Some of us have been around a long time, unlike the majority of the vampire populous of this time and place. In the early days I remember feeling vulnerable and weak as we travelled all over the world seeking refuge and safety. When we made it past dusk back then, it meant we had made it for another day. Not like now with these fucking exclusive vampire apartments and travel hotspots. You'd really have to be a dimwit nowadays to die as a vampire." I couldn't help but admire the emotion he was showing. I had never met anyone who had lived as long as he had. As I listened to him talk of his past, I could see flashes of the large white sharp weapons that were hidden under his thin grey lips.

The police station was right in the middle of the old town, adjacent to an old red brick fire station that didn't seem adequate to deal with the growing town. There was only the original small entry that could barely fit the new fire truck. Our office was just a ten-minute drive from the prison, which was an advantage. I lived a short walking distance from the station in an old but charming cottage originally built for the help that worked at the prison in its so-called glory days. Gillian, however, would be stationed on the outskirts of town in the new, fully serviced apartments designed for vampires.

These apartments without windows looked like giant concrete blocks from the outside. Inside some of the more lavish apartment buildings, of which Gillian's was one, there were gardens, pools and coffee shops. There were two types of vampires these days; the ones that could afford to be looked after like they were mightier than gods and the ones that sold their bodies along The Vamp Strip. It was in stark contrast to the police station we were entering; a two-storey sandstone building with a red tin roof. It had been updated recently to accommodate the changing needs of the population, but I feared it wasn't long before it would be replaced with a more functional station that would not embrace the heritage features of this old building.

We scanned ourselves in through the staff entrance, which led directly into a small cloak room that was staffed by an officer at all times. This was to ensure that only authorised personnel could access this area to ensure their safety. Each day and night we would sign in and gather our new expensive vampire equipment for our shift. We never took any of this gear home with us after work as it had to be accounted for at all times.

As we made our way from the check in area to the changing room, I heard the buzz of chatter coming through the door, which probably meant Sam and Charlie were on shift. Sam was a very bubbly character, she liked to speak before thinking which was a trait many of us shared in the past but Sam wasn't in her early twenties anymore.

I knocked on the door and led Gillian in to the changing room, which I thought would be a good way to introduce him. The smiles and chat stopped as both Sam and Charlie saw Gillian. He looked so imposing in such a small room with low ceilings. He seemed broader than the old grey lockers we had.

"Evening all," I said, "This is Gillian, the station's new vampire detective."

As Sam and Charlie introduced themselves to Gillian, I noticed they seemed a bit nervous. I found this strange, as everyone knew Gillian was coming. I had been very clear in my communication with the station officers, as well as the local stakeholders.

"How was your shift? You ok Sam?" I said trying to gauge the temperature of the room.

"Yes," she said. "Wow Gillian, what big fucking teeth you have."

Gillian gave a big smile that showed off his full range of teeth. Winking at her, he said, "Yes I do Sam, yes I do."

6

Thomas Malcolm

I enjoyed living near the beach. In all my privileged years of being a vampire I had only ever settled in cities. Beautiful cities like Barcelona and Vienna had charm and history, which was only enhanced by my presence. It was tranquil and peaceful here; I could feel the breeze of the ocean across my old leathery face but the sensation was dulled in comparison to my younger days. I've been alive a long time now and have seen so much but had never lived in the southern hemisphere. My kind finds languages easy and I wasn't above learning them, I particularly enjoyed Germanic dialects, a reflection of my love and obsession with Vienna.

History oozes out of every building in Vienna. There are benches there that are older than the whole of this country. This place was only two hundred years old so there was no architecture like that here in this sun-drenched land. I still remember the smell of a Viennese cinnamon mustard wiener, the smoked sausage wafting through the air of the church square then rising above the gargoyles perched on the gothic buildings. But where I was now was the most serene places I had experienced in a generation or so.

I liked to amble along the fine sand of the beach and listen to the waves roll in before meeting a new client, this time it was a woman named Claire. I had read her full dossier back at my desk.

I always liked to meet the client and fully research the accused so I can provide a truly specialised high-end service. I charge a hefty price and believed that it is my duty to fulfil the promise of justice. I had learned the hard way that you have to set firm boundaries. Just because I am a vampire doesn't mean I don't care or have a heart. I probably care too much. I really didn't do this for the money. In fact, being a vampire of my age, it was hard not to be wealthy.

Depending on who your maker was, information could be plentiful or scarce. Most makers taught self-maintenance (that's what I like to call it). If you are going to live and survive you need substance to grow and thrive. It's easier now of course that we are more accepted. It took time of course but like money I had plenty of that too. I had places throughout the northern hemisphere, places of note. (Thomas Malcolm you are so up yourself). I became far too materialistic, in art, houses, clothes and the like.

I still liked fine company and fine things but not as much as my new venture, as it had given me a reason to exist. You need worthwhile goals to live a long life. That's why at one point I worked with people with mental illness. Suicide to me is tragic, when you are able to sense humans' or animals' veins pulse with blood you feel how precious life is.

When I first encountered human politics I realised, politely said, it is bollocks. I learned that word in London. I tried to help humans who were in strife but no one will listen to somebody who can pierce your fragile skin with their teeth. That's what led me here. I saw an unjust law system that never really worked or gave closure to either party. When I first started my venture, it was naïve and crude, but it has developed into a smooth operating machine and even though I am more modest and erudite now, I still can't turn money down.

I have a beautiful apartment overlooking the beach in an

exclusive area. There are five floors to the apartment block. I bought the whole complex of course; I like my privacy and it was convenient for work.

I meet clients on the second floor in a rather lavish apartment, if I do say myself. Its décor seemed to settle the demeanour of my usually nervous clients. The idea of humans meeting vampires at their home could be intimidating, and frightening them was the last the thing I wanted.

I needed to be my graceful best at all times. Being charming was a natural gift and something I enjoyed (Oh, Thomas Malcolm). Humans are easier to understand. They think they can play mental games but considering the human brain functions consciously for only eighty years or so it isn't really fair to compare them to us.

My skin couldn't tell or feel the temperature any more but it looked like it must be warm out by the faces of joggers passing by on the promenade. The moon that reflected on the ocean also gleamed on the young active people passing by, trying their best to starve off time. I lived in a young affluent area that was vibrant and busy night and day.

Living in a warmer climate did seem to generate happier humans, though during the day it could reach scorching temperatures. It didn't matter how hot it was, the sun was the sun. It could always kill my kind even through angst ridden cloudy skies.

I generally met my clients at 10pm, a much safer time for me and I did like to have a lie in. Tonight, the beach area was still active past sunset. The bustling noise of the restaurants and pubs filled the air and it was nice to see people dressed to impress, even if it was in ridiculously overpriced designer singlets, although I had to admit they suited the hot days and warm nights.

I crossed the road that separated the beach and the promenade. My apartment was the penthouse of course. On the first floor was an open balcony where customers could enjoy the view and the salt air on their faces. There were two restaurants, Claude's and Sails. Claude's was a classic French restaurant with only the best ingredients from around the world and Sails was a contemporary Australian restaurant that specialised in using only local produce. Away from the entry to the restaurants a single blackened glass door faced the promenade, next to this door was an intercom where new clients buzzed to be let in upstairs.

There was no signage above the door. Thomas Malcolm didn't need to advertise. I let myself in through the door to a large marble floored reception area. To my right Frank sat behind a desk filled with monitors and other such equipment that helped secure the activities of the building from unwanted eyes. It was Danni's night off. Frank was great but I liked Danni, she had a good temperament and was very understanding with clients. Frank was excellent at slamming people's heads into walls and with those arms why not?

"Hi boss, looks like it's busy out. Your new client has been checked in and is waiting on the balcony," Frank said pleasantly.

"Thank you, Frank. Is she as nervous as most of our clientele?"

"No, not really. I find it hard to believe that she's a kindergarten teacher from her file. Her demeanour makes her seem steelier than that."

"Well, that's what grief can do to you my dear Franky. Even the gentlest souls can crave destruction."

I had a hard-working team that I trusted. I paid them well and had a great leader in Jonathan who set the tone for a professional yet friendly environment. You would never know that there were at least ten security staff around at all times throughout the complex. There were a number of metal detectors and other security equipment hidden throughout my home to ensure my safety, unfortunately you couldn't scan for wood. The designers I used had set the right welcoming tone to the building. You wouldn't know that no product in this building was made of wood. A precaution Jonathan had strongly recommended.

I walked to the lift that would take me to the second floor. It was a peculiar feeling every time standing in a lift that was floor-to-floor mirrors where you couldn't see yourself. I never got in the lift anymore with clients. It was just too disturbing for them to be next to someone whose reflection they couldn't see.

As the doors of the lift opened, I sensed Claire's unease waft over me from down the wide hallway. The large stone paved hall spilt to an open dining area with an L-shaped couch in the right corner. On top of the quartz counter there were canapés prepared to the client's liking. My office, along with my sleeping quarters, was down in the basement, dark and hidden away from prying public eyes. Unlike this beautiful relaxing apartment where human clients felt at ease but was the last place a vampire would want to be during the day. I had panic rooms on every floor to take me straight to my safe zone. It was fun to test them out. I hadn't gotten to this age without being thoughtful. Some called it cautious but I don't care what you call it as long as I am alive. Light jazz was playing through the ceiling speakers to make the evening as calming as possible. As I walked closer to Claire, I felt her heart beat intensely. It would only grow faster once she gazed on me.

The softened dim glow from the downlights made the apartment almost seem serene. Once I got to the balcony doors, I always let myself be known. It was never a good idea to sneak up upon a human you didn't intend to kill. I had learned my mind's ability to manipulate others from a lovely fellow in Austria. I could gently encourage humans to do things like to turn around and look at me the precise moment I was stepping on to the balcony through the light cream curtains.

She stood up from her chair and I gave a hopefully caring small smile to show the gravity and understanding of the situation.

I reached out my hand, "I am Thomas Malcolm," I said softly placing my left hand gently onto hers. I knew the spiel of how to gently introduce my intimidating self to humans. It was all about the right amount of sincerity, too much and you are a condescending patronising aloof vampire monster. Too little and you are an evil soul yearning monster; you can see the fine line I was expertly balancing here. "Claire Spencer," she replied.

Claire was a gentle caring human on first impressions. I had become very good at this. She had excellent posture and was smartly dressed, her blouse tightly tucked into her grey sharply creased trousers. Her fingers tapped nervously on the armrest. I am sure that she was young for a human, perhaps around thirty-five.

I looked into her tired turquoise eyes, no doubt tired from all the crying and hate burning in her body. I had seen similar countless times. Hard working people who existed to live and help other people. They didn't harm anyone else. They would work, have some fun and pay their taxes until a loved one was cruelly ripped out of their happy coexistence.

We sat down, I always let the client sit closest to the door, I never wanted anyone to feel trapped or pressured into this situation: they didn't know it but they had already decided they would be going through with it. Once they came this far, they never backed out, never. I was waiting for that day but I didn't think it would ever come. The populace think of us vamps as scary beings but humans can be worse, and they don't even need to drink blood to survive. Living through some of human's worse escapades during the Great War in Europe I saw the pathetic will of humans wanting to live, and how they could be manipulated into doing atrocities to continue their insignificant existences.

"Claire thank you for coming in today, have you had a chance to look at the catalogue of services I provide?" Claire nodded her head as I spoke, her fringe falling onto her face. "We are now at the pointy end of business Claire. Of course, you can always pull out, but once you sign today, the fee will be transferred directly to your account, less deduction of whatever punishment you choose, once this occurs the decision is final. Once I have your signature, this case will be closed," I said in my sincerest low voice. One colleague said I sounded genuine but I thought I sounded like my old friend Claude from Paris, completely up my own ass.

"Thank you, Thomas you have been really helpful throughout this time," her voice was quivering and a bit shaky but I sensed there was something else there. "I know what I want, I want to see that motherfucker absolutely obliterated." And there it was, Claire was a lovely human being but the chance to be paid to see a loved one's murderer being killed the way of your choosing was too good to turn down. The venom and anger in her voice filled the room.

The catalogue of choices had been the idea of a former client. He had wanted his wife's murderer and rapist to suffer and said that he didn't want any money even though they needed it for their three kids. He just wanted to see the convicted man hurt most foully.

The catalogue explained to the client what revenge options they could choose. Would they prefer the perpetrator to be castrated, made to beg for their life or maybe just a good old-fashioned beheading (Thomas Malcolm's favourite)? The price was next to the picture and description and would be deducted from the total fee the vampire would pay to carry out the chosen deed.

At the back of the catalogue was a tasteful list of memorabilia that they could choose. You could watch them die again and again on a commemorative film, or maybe keep a piece of their hair in a locket. It was a way for the client to feel empowered in a situation where there was none.

Claire had chosen no such thing. All she wanted was for the guilty perpetrator to be punished. She didn't want or need to gloat in the death of another human no matter how despicable that person had been. Claire, like most people, wanted closure.

My human psychologist estimated she would feel the guilt for six months to a year. Once this time had elapsed the human mind accepted what they had done and could justify it to themselves and they would then feel elated. They would think of their murdered family member and know that they could now rest easy.

My service was the only type that I knew of in the western world and I intended to keep it that way through hard work and diligence. If anyone did muscle into my business it would be impossible for them to live up to my impeccable service. People from all over the world came to me for what I could do. I was not beneath kidnapping the right person and having them shipped, flown or driven here. I insisted on being here for every revenge, or closure killing if that's what you prefer to call it.

To ensure secrecy and confidentiality clients had to allow us access to their social media accounts. As we operated outside of the law all accounts were monitored for breaches by my team day and night.

For the most part the clients didn't mind signing away their privacy, as usually they were upstanding citizens. You wouldn't believe the number of crooked politicians I had to turn down or scorned lovers who wanted a lover or rival killed.

"Ok, Claire, thank you for your signature. Everything has now all been taken care off. A member of my team will be outside your apartment at 10pm to collect you. Please remember to have no personal belongings on you at all. No jewellery, no cash and, of course, no mobile." I kept eye contact at all times with Claire and spoke concisely and to the point. Claire's breathing was slowing down, her clasp relented from the chair's armrest. She was starting to feel more relaxed, not fully relaxed though, that would be unreasonable at this time.

I continued, "A white blacked out SUV will pull up outside your house and the door will open. Once inside please put on the head-set that will be left on the seat for you, the headset will prevent you from being able to see where you are going and it will have music playing to calm your nerves. Once again this is non-negotiable. The car will take you to a location where you will witness the ter-mination. Once the action is over, expect to be on edge, when you begin to regain your senses, we will return you to your home. No one other than my team will be aware of what happened Claire. Our staff will help you into your house and we have relaxation medication available if you require it. I must say I think you are handling the situation very well." Humans loved it when vampires compliment them – they lap it up. "Are there any questions?"

Claire was relaxing into her chair now and her breathing was less shallow. She was adapting to what was happening a lot better than most. I wouldn't say that I thought Claire was beginning to enjoy the idea of what was to come but maybe Claire wasn't the meek school teacher I had thought.

Leaning forward and clearing her throat Claire said, "Will I be able to hear him scream when the termination is happening? Will he see my eyes at his final moment?" Her voice was strong now, determined.

"I'm afraid no one from inside the room can see out of the room, it's a one-way mirror. It is to protect you from the vampire," her eyes dimmed a little when I said this. "Claire you will be able to hear his last gurgle as he clings to his miserable depraved life." A small smirk appeared on the right side of her mouth. Well, fuck me I thought. In all my years I had never misjudged a human. Maybe I was getting old, but I guess you don't know what humans can keep hidden deep down inside.

"Is there anything else that I can help you with Claire?" In my head I was thinking I should have offered her the gore package.

"No Thomas Malcolm, I think I'm going to be fine after all, you have been most helpful and I do not have the need for any additional packages."

I suddenly had the strange sensation Claire knew what I was thinking. What other talents was she secreting away?

Standing up, I placed my hand towards Claire's ready to end our meeting "Once again thank you for coming in Claire, this may be the last time you see me so I will wish you luck with your future endeavours. You only have only one life to live and it is very important." Maybe that was a bit pretentious I thought to myself.

Claire stood and gave a small courteous smile as one of my staff appeared and escorted her out of my building and out of my life. This was how I lived, simply and elegantly. I helped people as well as helping myself. My empire built on trading one death for another was increasing rapidly. I didn't have to be the figurehead anymore but it was the only thing that gave me joy, well that and cricket.

I'd never liked cricket in my mortal days but now with plenty of time on my hands I began to enjoy every slow detailed gesture. The only problem was, for obvious reasons, I couldn't watch it during the day. I was overjoyed when night cricket took off. A small deviation on the pitch could alter the movement of the ball and make a batsmen's life a nightmare. I was hoping that it wouldn't be the case with Claire. That smile and her presence worried me.

Life could be smooth and round with no complications. Then a small divot could alter your well-planned life sometimes for good or for bad. I was hoping the exhilaration I glimpsed in Claire's eyes would not come back to haunt me, but I had a feeling our paths would cross again.

7

Nevaeh

"Hey Heaven," she said in a patronising voice, "How's your mum? Are you going to go home and cry? You fucking loser. Enjoy your spacious caravan." She walked off laughing while the other kids either smiled in solidarity, or to protect them from also being picked on.

It was already warm, even at this time of the morning. Small beads of sweat were running down Helen's face. It was a small and quaint coastal town secondary school. Six buildings sat on bare brick columns. These were our classrooms and there was only one class for each year so I was stuck with fucking Helen for the whole of my time at school. The grass surrounded the class rooms was brown from the unrelenting sun. There was one concrete playground court that served as our basketball, netball and tennis court. It was a charming school from the outside but a shit place to be looking out from.

I wanted out of this town. Mum had gone and so would I. I couldn't wait to leave. I didn't care where I went. I knew if I could get decent marks, I could get out of here even if it was only to a crappy job at the prison. It wasn't far from here and I'd heard the pay was ok and they were looking for women to fill some sort of quota.

I didn't have many friends at school. Coming from a family without much money, kids knew how to be cruel. Mum being sick didn't help matters. She still went to work but going through chemo and looking after me and the house was a lot. My school wasn't wealthy or exclusive it was just that we were below the income level of most families in this area.

Not only had the chemo robbed me of time with the only person who cared for me it had taken away her smile, her cheery disposition. Mum was awesome and always tried to do the right thing. She was completely biased towards me and saw me through a lens the rest of the world didn't see me through. She really thought I was an angel and that she had been blessed to have me. Mum had good intentions when deciding to name me Nevaeh, which of course is heaven backwards. Fuck me did I get teased for that. But this combination of poverty, living in a caravan, dark skin and a trashy name made me who I am.

Helen was a tall pretty girl with bronzed skin to go with her long wavy blonde hair. Her slight build was deceptive as she was strong from surfing all the time with her older brothers. That's why I had to be quick when I kicked her in the back of the leg as hard as I could. Her body buckled backwards as she fell to the ground, she yelped out as she hit the concrete deck. The school ground was busy with people getting dropped off.

I leant over her, my face right in hers. "Fuck you Helen," I screamed as I slapped her in the face. "You leave my Mum out of this or I will rip your fucking hair out, you stupid mole."

As I was being pulled off her, I smelled the coconut sun cream she bathed herself in each morning when she went surfing. The right side of her face was red from where I had slapped her. Helen's blue eyes glistened as adrenaline pumped through her body, boy she looked really pissed.

It wasn't the first time Helen had sledged me at high school or when I was on the way past the local surf shop her family owned. But it was the first time I decided to fight back and I was promptly led to the principal's office. I had been there plenty of times, with the principal and teachers talking to me about my mum and the dire situation I was in and how sorry they were. I didn't believe them; they didn't care about the bills that were piling up at home. Not so much the medical bills as the government and Medicare paid for that on the whole, rather the rent for the caravan we lived in and the daily costs of living were an issue. We had no savings as my dad disowned us when I was around five. That wasn't really anything to complain about as that happened all the time with the mineworkers, fly in then fuck off.

I had an after-school job at the fish and chip shop down the road. It overlooked the beach and was a prime location for the locals. It didn't pay much but I got free food at the end of each shift. I was lucky I didn't smell like fish and chips. The oil from the deep fryer felt like it seeped into my hair and skin. But I was getting tone in my arms from lifting those twenty litre drums of cottonseed oil. The family owners, like most in this seaside town, were nice enough but had no issues with young girls working their guts out for ten bucks an hour.

As I walked with my year advisor into the principal's office, I could smell the lavender in the courtyard outside his window. Its perfume filled the old and weary room and made being there not quite so bad. I sat on a brown leather couch that was cold from the air-conditioning, waiting for that cow Helen to grace us with her presence, while the principal sat nervously on the end of his table trying to look like he was in control. He was nice enough; he didn't generate any fear though. I talked to him like I would to a neighbour, or like the people who came from child services to monitor me and see how little I had, with their big sad eyes taking pity on me. The principal was another one in the long line of people who tried to help but always ended up sounding patronising and not at all genuine. The only time in my life where I didn't feel judged was when mum was going through chemo. People at the hospital reception were so used to seeing busloads of people in all shape and sizes coming in for their treatment that they didn't judge. Their passionate eyes never looked down at us. They must see all sorts trying to hang on by a thread.

I would prefer to be treated like that now. Don't judge me; I don't need your help; I'm doing just fine. I go to school, work, pay rent and best of all I'm not fucking pregnant from some local wannabe pro surfer who has a golden tan and streaky light hair, even if some of them are hot.

It wasn't that I wasn't interested in boys, I just always felt guilty if I left Mum. I remember getting ready for a swim meet, which I had spent months preparing for. Mum and I were so excited, then her temp went above thirty-eight, a common occurrence, and we had to go to hospital. It wasn't far if you could drive, but when you had to take two bus trips it was tiring. Public transport is only for the poor and the crazy.

I tried my best to keep busy and not feel sorry for myself but it seemed every time I took my focus off the situation with my Mum, maybe even crack a smile, something jarring happened that dragged me back down to earth.

Helen entered the principal's office, gracefully moving across the cheap nylon carpet and sat opposite me on a metal-framed office chair. Her bronzed legs were crossed as she gazed at me with hate. She looked unsettled for once in her perfect life. It wasn't often someone confronted her for being a bitch.

The principal began to speak but I wasn't even listening, all I saw were nameless adults opening their good intention traps. Up and down, up and down, nonsense. I knew I was going to get in trouble and to be honest that was fair enough. I just wanted out of there, I had things to do.

Then I noticed Helen flinch and sit upright, I came right back down to earth. I left whatever happy place I was in. Turns out Helen's dad Maury had been in touch and decided, with all the wisdom that came with owning a surf shop in a small crappy town, that instead of me being suspended from school I would be helping out at his shop twice a week. Helen and I would be fucking helping set up the surf program that they ran for local schools around the coast. I would be paid of course and, in their privileged wisdom, we would come to understand each other and lose our mutual contempt. We would become fucking friends… as if.

8

Alfred

That's all they want. Is it clean Alfie? Is it safe Alfie? How much does it cost? How will we sell it efficiently? How much impact will it have on the environment?

All these questions are buzzing around in my head all of the time. When I answer one question as quickly as possible, ping goes my inbox. Ping, ping, ping. It's becoming too much. I can't even have lunch or go to the bathroom. If I block out a lunch break so I can eat upper management overrules it. Great wages, they told me, great package, they told me. Well, done, Alfred, great problem solving but can you also take a look at this. Fix this, figure this out. Is it clean? Is it safe? It simply wasn't good for my nerves.

Back in England; cooler, greener and less intrusive England, I always made sure I knew what I was getting into. I hadn't done my research this time had I? For the first time in my life, I jumped in with both feet. The idea of that infamous prison, the thought of being away from my mother's prying eyes helped me make those decisions. A new way of life on a new continent, I thought. The great outdoors, I thought. Brand new adventures on your doorstep sounded intriguing and fascinating. Time to embrace a different lifestyle, different seasons and foods. But what's the point when all the outdoor creatures can kill or seriously hurt you? Even the cockroaches can fly. That is just not fair.

Feel them crawling up my skin. Oh, it makes me shake just thinking about it. I signed up for this though didn't I. Saw the big round zeros on the contract and signed on the dotted line for three years didn't I? For a member of Mensa, it seems I wasn't so smart.

Ping, ping, ping. Free mobile phone, laptop, apartment, smart car, free everything. Everything paid for, all food, all drinks. But it cost me my privacy. I saw you had a curry, someone would re-mark, at that restaurant, around 7pm last night, Alfred, early mark? They'd say with a sarcastic smirk.

Looks good on the CV I kept on saying to myself. Go anywhere in the world now and live the high life. Only a year left now Al-fred. The project deadline was approaching faster than anticipated. I hadn't realised the complexity of the task at hand and how hard it would be to implement the payroll and accounting systems. The power stations infrastructure was set to a time before I was even alive. I had to be ready as my bonus was relying on this. Push for-ward I would.

I could hear my steel heeled leather shoes ricochet off the con-crete walls around the gigantic power station. For a place that could produce enough power to service the entire east coast of Australia, a place that employed thousands of people who worked around the clock, how could I feel so alone during the day? I was starting to feel sorry for myself again but deep down I knew I was lucky. I had a job that paid, and paid well enough so that my fan-tasies could be enacted. It made what I wanted to taste and touch and feel throughout my body a reality. No longer did I have to sit on the side-line, watching humans and vampires having fun, I could now participate. In this town I had found somewhere I was made to feel as though my tastes are acceptable.

If I wasn't walking for five minutes to a meeting through these impeding vast walls, I was driving a golf buggy to the other side of the complex. A golf buggy! That had always seemed surreal to me. I had only ever travelled briefly to attend conferences and training courses before, I had never resided overseas. I had thought new country, new me. I was wrong. I was just as shy with humans in Australia as I was back home in Essex. But at work I could be feisty and passionate and I fed off the energy of those around me, and despite the job's constant claims on my time that's what worked for me. I suppose you could call my behaviour annoying, but if I'm right and passionate is that annoying? Why spend money to see a psychologist when I already knew that I was socially awkward? Except with vamps, they made me feel alive, how ironic that a being without a beating heart was the only thing that made me feel alive.

Then the intrusive thoughts would start running around in my head again. I would get flashes of sharp pointy canines being dragged down my skin. I was shaking again; my small wiry frame made me agile and quick but I could be overpowered. Was it really being overpowered if that's what I liked and preferred? That was the real reason I was here, I loved vampires.

Vampires were a short train ride from the coast of Essex to London, but here in Australia it's different. They are right on my doorstep. I could almost taste them in here. I didn't realise how much I liked the Aussie accent, male or female it didn't matter to me. Back in England they made me feel like I was worthless, wouldn't put me out if I was on fire. Everything was so rigid back home, just like my exterior. I grew up in a confined and mentally unhealthy environment. I tried to conform to my mother's expectations as much as possible, always neat and tidy. My thick black hair had always been uncontrollable though. That's why I used hair gel to control the beast on my head, I was presentable but I still never felt my mother fully approved.

Renewable energy is a job I love and enjoy. It's always a challenge trying to make corporate giants like power companies go green, countless media campaigns continue to try and convince the public it's achievable though. People above my pay grade thought that turning the power station green would help the dying eco structure of the east coast, as well as being good for public relations. We could use the profits from the vampires to help restore the area to its once natural beauty. Having vamps here will improve and expand this once little country town, even though they could kill half the population if they wanted to. Their presence here would revitalise the town through travel, hotels and entertainment, that's how I, and the mayor, saw it.

In the two years I have been here and made this town my life there were always people trying their utmost to derail this idea. I was on the power company's community consultation committee and had been at plenty of town hall meetings demonstrating the benefits the power station could bring to this tired old long forgotten town. Implementing new programs would save the company millions and enable us to be more efficient and in turn greener. We could then pass the benefits on to the community. I could see fear and distrust on the faces of the locals and I worked relentlessly to open their minds to how much the power company could regenerate the wild life and the area with new skills and industry. The residents knew this dusty red-tinged town was dying but still they clung desperately to their memories of the past, it must be hard for people to let go of the only job they'd ever had even if that was dying too. At first, I didn't care about the ramifications for those who didn't want this to work, now I could understand why a worker who'd been at a company for twenty years on a massive bonus structure was scared that their job would cease due to new practice, but it was like this throughout the world. Being here on the front line at these small red brick buildings, that were full of opinionated workers and farmers, it was hard for me not to be swept away by their demeanour. Initially I judged county folk far too quickly but over time I realised they knew the land and the local wildlife much better than myself and they gave me the knowledge I needed to get the go ahead for the power station project. I had tried to please everyone with my proposal but I'm not sure if I will ever get all parties to a happy middle ground.

I was constantly aware of the threat of being outsourced or replaced, which is why I was always doing refresher courses and self-improvement classes. The added bonus of traveling around the world and acquainting myself with different vampires added a certain spice to my private life too. I consider myself open and curious, race and gender are not important and adding vampires to the mix only upped the excitement level, not only sexually but also in other ways physically and mentally that I could never even fantasise about with a human.

There wasn't much about me to intimidate vamps, or most people for that matter. My small frame and quiet voice made it hard for me to be heard, this was one of the reasons why I had thrown myself into my work. I could be quite scathing on email but I never really backed it up when it came to face-to-face interactions. Maybe I was a coward in some respect but then again some of the things I let vamps do to me would frighten most people to their very core.

In England I had grown accustomed to my weekly pilgrimage to London to meet vamps, the money I was earning there afforded me this privilege. My colleagues and family were not aware of my fetishes, and I never really fitted in with anyone in my local area. I made an effort though and always went to the Dog and Duck pub after work on Fridays to try and fit in. That's what's good about England, if you look a little odd or are socially awkward, people just smile and nod. Unlike in Australia where teasing was socially acceptable: "Alfie you party boy, what you up to this weekend, eh? You up for some fun at The Strip this weekend?"

It wasn't called bullying; it was just the banter some of the long-term employees used to help 'settle' me in, but I didn't like it. Anything they could use to make my pale skin go red with embarrassment they would. The sledging I get when England loses at cricket is unrelenting.

'Just having a laugh Alfie.' I wasn't impressed by the banter as it can hold a measure of sins within its context. I didn't like to be called Alfie either, why on earth do the locals like to abbreviate every word to something shorter as a form of nickname.

I'm whining again, I need to snap out of it. It's Thursday night, almost the weekend, which means pleasure time with the vamps. What concoction could they come up with next to make me shudder with bliss? Thursday was a big night in prison town, schnitzel night, or, of course, schnitty night to the locals. I had never heard of such a thing until I moved here. It originated from Austria, lightly crumbed veal hammered thin and cooked in clarified butter. Here, they use chicken, throw it into a deep fryer, serve it with hot chips and call it a meal.

I hate this town! Or do I? I don't even know anymore. Maybe I should spend more time with some living, breathing humans, try and blend in. It sort of worked in England. But did I want to go back to England and leave prison town behind?

Maybe I was just homesick. The heat, the lack of social activities and the pressure of work was probably getting to me. Maybe I should join the work social club? I was okay-ish at playing cricket back home in Essex. A nifty little spinner I was once called. Obviously, I couldn't play in the heat but there was a night competition I could join.

Mum might miss me if I decided to stay here, or would she? Maybe she'd only miss the money I send home. We never really got on; she never threw her opinions in my face though, rather she'd do it behind my back to her church group. We weren't a house of shouters or screamers, which simply wasn't our way. When Mum was angry, she would just shake the newspaper incredibly loudly. Pent-up emotion was our family motto. You never really knew when it would release and show its ugly face.

Once I unthinkingly left a tea bag in a cup while adding milk, when Mum noticed I thought she was going to spontaneously combust. I copped an earful for the teabag and then for the next hour I had to hear what a disappointment I was to her and me not having a child was breaking her heart. When I said I thought I was being considerate for not wanting to bring an unwanted child into an overpopulated earth I thought she was going to throw the milky Earl Grey tea in my face.

I didn't enjoy arguing with Mum and she wasn't used to me back chatting her. There was no point to it. People think what they think and it's unusual to be able to change their mind. Instead, I studied hard, did my best to keep her off my back and got the hell out of that house.

Maybe I'm only happy when I'm whining. I'm not sure I really know what I want, well apart from one thing, no scratch that, two things; I love vamps and I love the environment. Perhaps I could get different work up the coast after this. Of course, the pay wouldn't be as good but people say that's not everything in life. Maybe I could learn to surf and even get a spray tan. Alfred stop complaining there is always something to look forward to. If I can just get through one more schnitzel night, there'll be a weekend of joy and then I can plan my life.

I was so lost in thought that I didn't realise I had already reached my next destination within the power station. The pleasant hum of the electric golf buggy I was sitting in was a result of my suggestion to introduce more energy efficient modes of onsite transport. As I left the buggy and headed towards the glass walled meeting room,

I could see people waiting for me, ready to discuss the next step in the roll out of the project. It was going well but it was arduous. I would not be the lead on this project forever, I was only here for implementation so my role would need to be passed on at some point and this meeting was held to ensure a smooth transition.

As I was walking towards the door big loud mouth John stood up and opened it for me. I felt the cool air-conditioned air hit my neck as John slapped me hard on the back in a jovial way, but I could feel the sting of his hand through my white cotton shirt.

"Hi Alfie how you doing today? Looking a bit pale today aren't ya," he said with a smirk.

The aroma of the Earl Grey tea Linda was preparing, as per my request, wafted through the room. I took my seat at the top end of the table. There were six people, which was normal for a team meeting. As I was about to start the slide show, John raised his large hand and leaned back in his chair, which creaked in protest.

"Yes John," I said trying to hide my impatience at yet another example of his interruption of anything I ever said. "How can I help you?"

"Well Alfie before you start your intriguing and enlightening slide show that is sure to galvanise us as a group, I was thinking that maybe…"

He had a really annoying way of drawing out words and sentences in his Aussie drawl. I sensed thousands of dollars going down the drain as he took another laboured breath.

"That maybe we should all go out tonight at the local pub and have a schnitty on you of course…" His long breaths were doing my fucking head in. I'm sure he knew it.

"That's what most team leaders do when we approach the end of such a long project…"

I was fuming as John was trying to derail yet another meeting. I needed to take back control. I ran my hand through my gelled back hair as I looked back at him defiantly.

John went to open that rather large trap of his again.

"You know what John," people looked up from their laptops, breathe Alfred, take control, don't be weak. "That's a great idea, I don't know why I didn't think of it sooner," I said as calmly as possible.

He began to open his mouth, again.

"In fact, Johnno, I will even pay for the meat raffle tickets to-night, it's time we let our hair down."

I could tell that I had slightly rattled him. Not that I was being super smart or aggressive rather that I was saying more than two words to him and I wasn't letting him finish his sentences.

He tried to open his sweaty mouth again.

"You know what Johnno?" I said looking at him with a light in my eyes. I was beginning to enjoy this now; it was fun being on the front foot.

"What?" John looked around the room for sympathetic eyes to help him regain his balls.

"I was thinking it's time we start that cricket team you're always going on about. It's time we bonded together. It would be good for team morale. Wouldn't it John?"

John started pulling at the big black tie that was wrapped around his fat wrestler shaped neck. It wasn't even hot in here.

9

Nathan

I don't like seeing injustice in this world. I have always been this way, seeing people being abused or taken advantage of twists my stomach into knots. That feeling of integrity and fairness has always been there. One of my early memories was on a night bus trip to Auntie Fay's house with my Mum and my sister. Mum and Dad had had a row over his constant drinking after work with his so-called friends. Dad would say sorry and then Mum would shout and we would make the short trip to Auntie Fay's. It wouldn't take long but this particular time it was Friday night when everyone liked getting hammered. I remember the scratchy tartan cloth of the bus seat against my skin. Colours of brown, black and yellow were patched across the seats. Most of them had holes in them from wear and tear or cigarette burns, which made travelling on a bus late at night smell awful to my eight-year-old self. This was, I suspect, one of the reasons why I never smoked.

I enjoyed looking out the window to the flashing of passing headlights and the glow of neon shop signs. It was raining which made the outside air cooler and easier to breathe, although the air-conditioning of the bus was cranked to the max no matter the temperature outside. The raindrops drizzled down the outside window glass and I tried to catch them impossibly with my fingers.

I liked to sit half on Mum and half off and would lean into her soft fluffy coat in order to sneak a cuddle. My sister would be on the other side and because it was late, we were half asleep. She was too young to remember any of the bad times and only saw Dad in a good light. Mum always felt safe and warm to me. No matter what time of year, she always smelt of citrus, this was due to the fact she could devour an orange in half a minute. The smell was reassuring.

At one stop the driver shouted at one of the passengers that he wouldn't be let on the bus as he was too inebriated. This wasn't unusual as there were often commotions from adults outside the pubs, but something about this man made me feel sorry for him. He seemed old to me at the time but was probably only in his early forties. I remember him arguing with the bus driver and he couldn't even get change out of his pocket without dropping it on the stained grey floor. As he stumbled off the bus, he fell back into a group of young guys who were out on the town, this prompted them to start teasing him. One of the young guys swiped the drunken man's worn-out baseball cap, the man then lost it and slapped the young guy in the face. They all jumped him in retaliation. Small jokes can often escalate into violence. As I watched the attack unfold, I heard the gas pumps close the double doors of the bus and it pulled away. As we left, I could hear the screams of the man as he was being kicked on the ground. I still remember the hopelessness and pain in his eyes. The helplessness and the fact there was nothing I could do about it stayed with me.

I never wanted to see eyes like that again. It's one of the reasons why I became a police officer. I was thinking about this as Gillian and I pulled up to investigate the latest murder in prison town. It was Gillian's second night here and his first out on The Vamp Strip, as the locals called it. Bar after bar were stacked together on both sides of the paved road that was now closed to traffic. It was easier to close the street off at night to vehicles, except emergency services, otherwise it became just too crowded and dangerous.

Like many a classy location throughout the world like Ibiza, Vegas or the Gold Coast, most of the bars or strip clubs were themed. It wasn't very new and hip: you could get that on the other side of town in the high-class hotels but vamps on holidays and bucks and hens parties loved The Vamp Strip. Different music genres poured out on to the street, one minute you would be listening to an *Abba* song from a '70s club, the next to the '80s music of *Depeche Mode* or *Duran Duran*, my favourite. I often knew where I was on the strip just by listening to a few beats of a song. A beat of *Donna Summer* and I was at the bar *Glitter Ball*, any *Guns & Roses* or *Poison* I was outside the pink signage of *THRUST* with people wearing bandannas and tight black spandex. The most popular bar was one with the highly imaginative name of *The Under*, an Aussie hangout where *INXS* and *Men At Work* played constantly on a tiresome loop; it was always full of cashed up bogans and trouble. Some of the new vamp bars like *After Dark* have staff dressed like Grace Jones in fluorescent coloured short bob wigs like the movie of the same name. The club *Sucked* plays with satirising vampire life, the patrons all look like Dracula or Elvira, it's a stereotype people find familiar. I think some of us find it easier on the whole if vampires are evil bloodsuckers with a lust like thirst. It's simpler to compartmentalise them like this than face the cold hard reality that they are more like us than we care to admit. It's true that certain vampires can perform powerful acts but I know that we have caused more killing than the small number of vampires on this planet.

The Vamp Strip itself was only half a mile long but with all those bars and the mix of events and opportunity for humans and vamps to mingle and party it could get rather messy. Brothels were legal here, which made The Vamp Strip very male heavy. Greyhound bus after bus poured in, it resembled downtown Las Vegas

I was told and every business and owner had adapted to ensure they maximised their profits.

You always had to be ON when working The Strip and as Gillian and as I left the vehicle we were met by Sam, a trustworthy constable on my team.

"Hi boss," her nasal voice penetrated the sounds of The Strip with ease, the glow of *Smash* nightclub's neon colours flashing across her face as she spoke. I never had a bad shift with Sam, who was always open to learning and was an extremely hard worker.

"Hi Sam, thanks for getting here so quick and setting up the perimeter on such a quiet night," I said sarcastically. I didn't need to look at Sam's face to see her large blue rolling eyes.

"Of course, boss anything for you and your new partner. I'm glad you didn't have to park too far away, wouldn't want you to walk too much in this heat." Sam's humour was dry and no doubt helped her cope with all the sordid goings on here.

"I'm a partner am I now Sam?" Gillian said playfully. "Would you like me to get you a coffee or maybe do your laundry later luv?"

Sam looked taken aback. We were all slightly surprised to discover that Gillian had a sense of humour. We'd all presumed he would be posh and uptight like a vampire from *Pride and Prejudice* but instead it seems we found ourselves with a very intelligent and cheeky vamp who also looked and sounded like Billy Idol.

"I'll drop my laundry off after shift and for God's sake try not to get any blood on it," Sam replied quickly.

"God has nothing to do with any of us."

"Gillian… why are vampires so unpopular?" Sam said playfully. She didn't wait for an answer.

"Because they're a pain in the neck."

Gillian stood there staring at Sam. "Oh it's on Sam, you will be sorry you've opened this can of worms," as a smile stretched across his face. Sam was excellent at making everyone in the team feel like they belonged and apparently that skill stretched to vampires as well. I noticed Gillian had a silvery chain round his neck that I didn't think he was wearing yesterday.

"Right," I interjected, "let's curb the banter until after shift."

"Sorry boss," Sam said, almost put off by Gillian's jesting. "We have one male in custody who is on his way back to the station. The victim upstairs is a young human male who at first glance resembles the victims of similar previous murders. His identity is being verified as we speak."

"Thanks Sam, let's head on up."

It was always busy along The Vamp Strip but tonight seemed more intense. Even where I was standing with our team, I felt slightly claustrophobic. It was only 11pm and we were already beginning to struggle with the influx of people tonight.

As Sam, Gillian and myself readied ourselves on the pavement outside the nightclub, we checked our specially designed belts that we had been testing and modifying for the last year. How do you protect yourself and others when you can be so easily overpowered like putty? Having specialised equipment was my answer. UV lights, holy garlic water (this only worked on religious vamps), three wooden stakes, silver infused batons (works on both humans and vamps) and specially designed guns.

The guns were more like mini shot guns; the range was terrible but we found that once a vamp with menace was within a three-metre circumference of yourself all bets were off. They are simply too difficult to hit from that range due to their fluidity and speed of movement.

We stood outside the nightclub, which was now closed, but we weren't here for the club. We were here to investigate the apartment above, the location where the murder had taken place.

Mel, the owner of the nightclub, was a cluey old-timer who through thick and thin held on to this previously rusty row of houses that were once falling apart. Once it was apparent prison town was about to take off, he took out a massive loan, begged the local council to become a licensee and voila he had one of the best and most profitable bars, nightclub and hotels in town.

From a young age Mel had only known hard work and debt. He felt that the local steel and coal mine had smashed the earth to get what they wanted and then they simply left, hence the name of the club.

It was quite a deep meaning for a bar that broadcast sports from across the world twenty-four seven, and also boasted being a topless bar on Friday nights. He was a tall slender man who only dressed in red and black flannelette shirts. He either had ten shirts of the same type or washed the same one daily. Mel appeared un-assuming in his jeans and long-sleeved shirt but always looked and smelled clean. His tanned face was covered in wrinkles that hinted at the tough times he had endured during his life.

He walked and talked slow, unlike his mind. I couldn't quite tell what his angle was. He owned five high-end apartments above the club that he rented out. He charged a pretty penny for these places, and they were in high demand. You would never know you were above one of the busiest places on earth. Time stood still in these apartments and that was the point. The outside world was blocked out due the excellent insulation and surround sound that was in each room. It also made them an ideal location for a killing.

I tried as hard as I could to get on with Mel, and all the own-ers of new establishments on the strip that seemed to pop up on a monthly basis.

I was aware that it might appear as if I was trying to 'kiss every-body's ass' but I needed all the help I could get. Time is of the essence when there is a murder where the evidence is often not visible to the human eye. I didn't take bribes or do anything ille-gal, my moral compass wouldn't permit that, but in times like these it did help that I had a rapport with Mel and the other business owners.

Some owners would be highly annoyed if the police closed down their place of earning for a couple of hours but Mel just took it in his purposeful slow stride. He stood near to the entry of the apartments on the boardwalk, looking disinterestedly into the flashing night sky as he slowly sucked on the apple-flavoured vape. His fingertips were still stained yellow from the years of smoking twenty a day but the vaping had helped get that addiction under control after smoking was banned in public. We were now discovering it wasn't much better but it seemed more acceptable on The Vamp Strip and it added additional aromas to the smorgasbord of smells. Mel had his own favourite fragrance of cinnamon apple and it helped me identify him in a crowd.

Sam was letting me know that no one had heard or seen anything. If you were up here partying, why would you bother paying attention to anyone that wasn't helping you get laid or get high.

"Hi Mel," I said as I walked over to him putting out my hand for a firm handshake.

"Hi Nate, how's it going?" No matter what happened in the world that was his first question to everyone.

How's it going? I thought. How the hell do you think it's going. For starters a human in one of your apartments has been murdered and another gullible human has been tied to one of the beds, sedated and set up for the crime.

"As good as can be expected Mel," I said, "I know it's a pain closing down your club but we won't be long. As always, your assistance is much appreciated. If you give Sam the details of who was staying here for background checks that would be a good start."

It was the same spiel I always said but it was needed to grease the wheels so I could get my job done.

"No worries detective, I always appreciate your candidness and efficiency," said Mel matter-of-factly as he shook my hand and left. He didn't need to be here; he could have got one of his staff to do the interview but Mel was hands-on with everything in his life. Not just the nightclub either, he still picked the grapes on his farm in the Hunter Valley, which produced a rather good sav blanc. The Hunter is full of quaint small wine cellars and local cheese and chocolate shops. Now these picturesque places found themselves joined by the main attraction of the prison and The Vamp Strip. I hope if I ever make it to his age that I have even a fraction of Mel's wealth and work ethic. Despite being rich he paid on time and didn't screw his employees, an anomaly in the world of hospitality.

Sam and Charlie were conducting interviews at the surrounding businesses with their patrons while other officers canvassed the area for evidence. Gillian and I made our way up to the apartments. Mel had really outdone himself with the renovation on this old sandstone building, instead of gutting the entire building he leaned in to the history of the area and added small contemporary touches.

Staying at a place like this was a little beyond my reach. Upon entering the building, you never would have thought there were nightclubs and floods of noisy people outside. It was calming in here and made you feel as if you had been transported to somewhere luxurious; the décor and the smell instantly made you feel you had stepped up in the world.

The human who had been set up for this crime must have money to be able to indulge themselves here for the weekend. Mel's apartment made the guest feel anonymous and pampered, like they could get away with anything. Tonight though, the guest we had in custody would be feeling the complete opposite. As I walked up the polished wooden floors, I knew Gillian was behind me but he was silent as he moved, no footsteps, no heavy breathing, only the gentle jingle of his key chain, it was strange to say the least. Why did he even need a keychain? I was pretty sure that the hotel he was staying at used swipe cards. Did he have this item so as not to scare people on approach? I needed to focus and get my mind ready for what I was about to be confronted with, dealing with death was never easy and I didn't want to lose my sense of empathy. I never wanted to become numb to the rigors of the job, I was determined to remain connected and be in touch with my human side as much as possible. The idea of losing oneself through life experiences must be something that vampires deal with for the whole of their existence, something I wholeheartedly knew that I could never do.

The strip bought with it many choices and one of these was sexual freedom. Introducing vamps into our society broadened people's minds and altered sexual preferences. Often with non-vamp crime in the suburbs a police person would find patterns they would become accustomed too, maybe become even a little lazy in their analysis of the predictability of crime. The Vamp Strip was a completely different ball game, the training I'd had in the early days back in Goulburn couldn't prepare me for what my team and I were about to see. The physicality of vampires made it hard for our human brains to adjust to what is, and is not, possible. Vampires had always been in the shadows of society and now with the introduction of the species into mainstream life we were learning quickly what they can, and cannot, do in real time, and not what the movies and literature would like us to think for dramatic effect. It took some getting used to. It also made the motives of crime difficult to predict. Since I had first been assigned here the learning curve had been steep.

The recent murders had a distinct pattern in that there would be two humans at the scene. The victim would also have lesions on their body that would match the attacker's fists. The victim would be dead from a snapped neck, which could not be matched to the accused attacker. There would be drugs on the kitchen counter or coffee table. Bottles of beer and wine would be scattered throughout the apartment. The victim would be a working male or female which made it easier to find out their details as by law they had to be registered with the Red-Letter Allegiance, a foundation that tried to get better rights for workers in the sex industry. As much as it ever could be, sex work was now a legitimate job with benefits. Of course, adding vamps to the mix had changed everything. Did you pay more for a worker to torture you, bite you or tease you; that was up to your discretion.

I found The Vamp Strip made people desperate, chasing dreams that were never really in reach, it sounded like a cliché but I often saw the aftermath of this desperation at the station, whether that was being robbed, manipulated by scams or assaulted. The strip constantly threw up new ways for people to be at their most vile and desperate, that's why Sam chose her cheery disposition, to cope with the conveyor belt of unhappy, broken people.

As Gillian and myself entered the apartment the forensic team were busy securing the crime scene. They had the thankless task of looking for clues from a life form that left no traces, no fingerprints, sweat or any residue. Authorities around the world were starting vampire databases in order to help assimilate them into human society. Governments were offering incentives, like jobs and benefits for vampires to come forward and register. Although vampires were banned from South America, hunting them was still legal after their kind had slaughtered thirty men, women and children at a restaurant back in 1965. The legal and privacy debate of the database was top of the agenda for a lot of highly visible vampires in government and the media, such as Cole, a podcaster who relished the spotlight, I had no time for his attention seeking commentary though.

Worryingly, hate crimes were starting to pop up in small pockets across the world and it seemed all sides wanted to weigh in with their opinions and debate if these crimes were even crimes at all, as many people still considered vampires inhuman, which I found really disturbing. This question resulted in protests for and against whether vamps should have any rights, as they were not human in the historical sense of the word. I didn't like the fact that the more vampires became integrated into our society the bigger the push back there was to exert control over the vampires, it felt to me this came from humanity's own fear. That fear, for me, is not a reasonable response as our past had shown us what humans are capable of doing to people whom we are scared of. The history of Australia is drenched in blood and is an example of the hurt and suffering fear can cause.

The laws for humans in states and countries vary wildly due to their beliefs, religion or culture. The law for vampires was more of a blanket law that didn't allow for second chances. The general population was often calling us a police state, protests and rallies were banned on the grounds they incited hatred. The jobs vamps could hope to be successful in applying for were limited, jobs where they were overworked and underpaid. With their strength, ability and lack of choice when it came to working hours, they were often being exploited. On top of this the humans who were losing their jobs to vampires hated them even more.

While the international debate on vampires raged on, Australia's forward-thinking plan for a vamp prison was the first step in the acceptance of vampires. It was also the first step in cashing in on them, and caught the rest of the world sleeping. Australia passed a law deeming all vampires had to pay a significant fee to the government in order to enter the country. These funds enabled the federal government to select a prison site that could accommodate everyone's needs and the very astute Warwick, who was the warden of our prison, presented a plan that made all sides, to a certain degree, happy. Warwick possessed negotiation skills that would make politicians envious.

Walking in to the apartment I could smell the faint hint of a rose scented candle. How sweet and romantic I thought, I then took in the bondage equipment on the grey maple counter top, maybe not. I was starting to analyse the scene when I was interrupted.

"What's that you smell Nathan?" Gillian startled me a little as I was lost in thought.

"I saw your nostrils flare up and could hear the saliva in your mouth. Sorry is that too much information for ya guv?"

"No," I said feeling slightly uncomfortable. "I didn't know vamps couldn't smell?"

"We can mate but I can't, it was long before I became a vampire that I lost my sense of smell but that story is for another time," he replied, smiling lightly.

I thought, if I could harness Gillian's skills it could really benefit us as a team. So far, he was very open and seemed willing to share his knowledge.

"It's a rose scented candle, probably used to set a romantic scene. It's not often the case with these types of murders. The scenes are normally more formal. Maybe the male killer was trying to woo the victim, but we will find that out soon enough as he's at the station waiting to be questioned."

As I watched Gillian slowly walk around, I thought I saw his keychain glimmer. I could tell Gillian knew I was watching him; I was going to have to figure out a way to cover my natural human instincts as I didn't want Gillian to know everything I was thinking before I did.

I had a feeling Gillian would make me (and everyone else) up their game. I hoped he didn't think we were a sloppy team; I didn't think we were but it's difficult to look at your own self when you believe in your work and conviction so much.

Tonight's victim was a tall handsome male aged thirty to thirty-five and in reasonable shape. His lightly browned skin looked as though it could be a spray on tan. There were no tattoos I could see. His hair was dark and his brown eyes were staring out through the one-way window that over looked The Vamp Strip. He was almost naked save for the designer underwear he was wearing. His head was tilted slightly to the right that meant I could see the bruising across his neck. I bent down to take a closer look, his well-manicured fingernails appeared to have small specks of blood on them.

He looked well kept, with a mostly clean-shaven body and toned midriff. The body was located in the middle of the room lying beside a low glass coffee table. The table was covered in fresh flowers, the red of the roses were in stark contrast to the beige of the room.

Only an hour ago this place would have been filled with pleasure and excitement, the two males engaging in whatever activities the client had paid for. The victim's client was now being held down at the station and when the shock wore off would find himself in a state of total panic. I wonder if the accused killer was married or not. If he were it would almost be easier to explain to the wife her husband was being held for murder rather than sleeping with a male entertainer.

I knelt down and tried to imagine what last thoughts had flicked through the victims' mind. I was hoping the evidence on the body or at the scene would give me some sort of clue or lead.

The pain and fear that I could see in their eyes made me determined to solve the case. The empathy I felt at violent crime scenes drove me forward. I couldn't but help put myself in their shoes, even though often I would have nothing in common with the victim. It was the same feeling I had as a kid on the bus, a feeling that never seemed to fade away.

I moved into the only bedroom in the apartment and surveyed the area. The king size bed looked as though it had seen a rigorous workout with black silk scarfs draping across the white cotton sheets. Nothing felt particularly unusual, just the regular throes of lust and passion. Everything seemed neat and tidy in the bathroom, apart from the exhausted looking person in the mirror. Even though I showered and shaved and tried to look like a modern professional, the lack of sunlight, too much coffee and not enough exercise was taking a toll on my late thirties body.

Soft jazz music was coming from the speakers set into the ceiling of the kitchen. Many settings of a sexual nature seemed to be set to jazz but I was pretty sure that no one listened to it in their normal lives, well maybe a select few. What tone was the accused killer trying to set? Music, expensive wine and flowers throughout the apartment screamed romance.

Maybe this was more than just a meet up. From the look of the victim, I was pretty sure that he was a prostitute but until we had a positive identification, I couldn't be sure. It was unusual for a working person and a client to have feelings for each other but it could happen. If this were true it would make the accused even more distraught. It might be difficult to get information out of him depending on his mental state.

According to the pattern the accused will have no recollection of what has happened. He would have awoken to see someone dead on the floor with his DNA and fingerprints all over them. After the initial jolt of pain and terror that shot through his body then would come the guilt, and the urge to flee. What about my family, loved ones, work friends and my life? The deceased person in front of them leaves their mind pretty quickly as the thought of self-preservation kicks into overdrive.

It was taking me time to get used to Gillian's different move-ment, stance and manner, and right now he looked odd. He looked like he was talking feverishly without speaking. Instinctively I knew something was wrong.

Should I go over? Leave him alone? I wanted to know what was going on but I didn't want to force the issue.

"Hey mate, I can feel you staring. Come on over, we need to talk," Gillian said gruffly, sounding perplexed.

As I headed over to Gillian, I quickly canvassed the room to see what I may have missed and what it looked like he had found. Why was he smirking? Boy his teeth looked intimidating when he did. He was looking intently at something incredibly tiny on the end of a small wooden spear, the size of a large toothpick.

"Alright Nathan, can you see it?"

"Sorry, do you the mean the little spear you're holding?"

"No, I don't, I mean the speck of dark matter that is on the end of the tip of the miniature stake I'm holding. This wooden stake is a gift for you. I have one for each of your staff members. To help protect each of you against my kind," he said rather sincerely.

I heard Sam snicker at Gillian's claim. Gillian abruptly turned round to confront her, his chain jingling like it had earlier. He gazed intently at Sam.

"Is there a problem?" he said as he moved past the dead body towards Sam. "Is something funny?" He was sounding almost ag-gressive now. Sam's body became more rigid and straight and she looked Gillian in the eye. Sam didn't look scared but I could tell she was on edge. It was not often we got questioned on our behav-iour by other cops especially North London vamps.

"Well…" Sam slowly said holding back any tinge of aggres-sion or annoyance. "I was wondering what a small stick could do compared to the equipment we're all wearing on our belts. With respect of course."

"Look everyone," he said raising his voice into a rather unsettling growl. "I know you're trying your best here but none of you have any fucking experience with a vampire trying to kill you. I have, I've seen first-hand how our breed can rip your weak flesh into bits that end up hanging on lampshades. Do you know how long it takes to clean that up? I don't want to see it again." As he spoke, he looked around at everyone in the room and we all paid attention to him.

I interrupted as calmly and as sternly as I could, "Gillian. We are all trying our best here and we all want to hear what you have to say but maybe…"

Gillian was across the room in a flash. I took a step back, he lunged at me with menace, his arms stretched out and his hands wrapped round my neck. My hands were reaching for his hands but I was pressed back hard against the wall. As this was happening, I sensed my team ready for action and I noticed that strange chain round Gillian's neck was glowing intently again.

I looked into Gillian's eyes as he pushed me up against the wall and they appeared calm.

"Look mate," he announced loud enough so all could hear. "I'm not fucking here to hurt or kill anyone but I'm also not messing around, do you and everyone else get it?" His hands still round my neck but not squeezing too tightly.

"I understand Gillian," I said, trying to calm my rapidly beating heart, with one hand on my gun.

"Well, let's see if we were paying attention shall we guv."

Everyone in the room had their guns out and had surrounded Gillian to make sure they could all take a shot at him if they had too.

"Do you all see how quick I was upon your boss here? Five more seconds and you're dead mate. I could probably take you all out within a minute, depending how on your guard you were. Never lower your guard with a vamp around, fucking NEVER.'"

He took his hands off my neck now leaving me feeling slightly sore and probably red.

"I know my little performance was a tad over the top but you need to know that if you let an attacking vamp, especially one of my age, get within fifteen feet, you're probably dead. A gun, baton, garlic spray or a wooden stake attached to your belt with leather fasteners will be useless if you are confronted on your own. You see this," he said, holding out the small wooden stake I saw earlier, "it might be small but it could save your life. Wear this round your neck with a silver chain. A vamp will always go for your neck, your heads are just too easy to pop off," he said without humour. "While you're struggling with us put one hand on my hand like this," he turned and looked at me. "Can I show them please mate?"

"Oh, I have a choice this time do I Gillian," I said jokily, trying to take the edge off the room.

"I like you mate; you don't scare easy. Right put the chain around your neck. Ok everyone, you see this," he now put his hands gently on my neck, "I've got both hands and I'm about to kill your boss. Now Nate put one hand on mine try to push me off as hard as you can."

I didn't know where this was going but I put my full body into it while he just stood there, like a rock star loving everyone's attention on him.

"Right, now grab the stake with the other hand and quickly put it right up against my chest, right in the middle there. It's easier to push through if you do that and make fucking sure that you have your thumb on top of the stake. Once there, push as hard as you can. Once we feel this, vamps will remove our hands from your neck, and as soon you feel the pressure ease you quickly put your other hand up and push the stake in as hard as you can. This could save your lives. I have enough of these to add to everyone's kit when we get back to the station. Most importantly make sure you tie them to a pure silver chain. You'll have to supply those things yourself; those shit things burn me like hell."

The way Gillian spoke and was able to change gears so quickly from aggression into calmness was an impressive skill. Some of the team management seminars that I've been on would kill to have his charisma and magnetism. Then again, I don't think the force have any vamps as educators.

"Alright everyone, schools out," he said. Gillian turned towards me apologetically, "Sorry," he said quietly "you can bollock me later for this stunt. I just need everyone to be go into this with their eyes wide fucking open."

I stood there rubbing my neck trying to ease the soreness out. "And you're sure with all your so-called experience there was no other way?" I said slightly irritated. "Hell of a way to make a point."

"Well of course there was probably another way," he said "but if I hadn't done it that way then everyone wouldn't be talking about it when they get back to the station. I do rather like the attention but after looking at the clues we've found tonight I don't think we have much time on our hands, Nate."

"What?" I said rather taken aback. "What clues? You've shown me a speck of black dirt. Is there anything else I'm missing?"

"Well, yes there are two things but don't beat yourself up, mate, I have some help, I will talk to you about that later. That dirt that I showed you is much more than dirt and the main reason for my dramatic performance is to show you vampires can be killed, just as easily as humans. The problem is, if the killer knows what they are doing and has a lot of experience with vampires they don't leave much mess. The other thing is…" He reached down for something on the floor.

"Wait!" I said shocked. "A vampire was killed in this room to-night? And help what help?" I must have said it loudly. People's heads looked towards me.

"Yes mate. It's hard to tell. Have you ever witnessed a vampire die in the flesh? We don't always explode like they do in the movies. Imagine all those years of experience in a vamp's body being wiped out. We crumble to dust, out of existence and all the repercussions that come with that. All of that can be gone with the small wooden stake I just gave to you."

"Gillian, I don't understand almost all of what you have said. Let's focus. A vampire died tonight. Help me with that. This could have happened before and my team wouldn't have noticed. This changes everything, damn it." I was annoyed with myself; this could jeopardise the whole operation.

"It's possible but I wouldn't think so, Nate, as it's not so easy to kill one of us. We also need to talk about the other piece of evidence I found." In his hand he was holding a tiny piece of shiny silver plastic in a pair of tweezers. "Do you know what this is?"

Leaning in and looking at it "It might a sequin. It's shiny enough."

"How do you know what these are, or maybe I don't want to know?" he said with a wink.

"My sister did three years of tap dancing and had to wear all sorts of loud and proud costumes. Oh, not so funny now you know my reason is pure and innocent."

"Well, well… cheeky chops you've got me there."

"Look Gillian, tonight has been eventful enough let's go back to the station and go through everything and see what the evidence tells us. After all this I need another coffee."

"Ok mate, but do you have any idea where the sequin comes from or could mean?"

"Well, it could be from one of the dancer's costumes at a nightclub, my guess would be *Glitterball*."

"I know what that means," Gillian interjected excitedly showing off that smile large white teeth again, "it means that we're going to a strip club."

10

Claire

I was on time and looking good. I liked these moments alone in the darkness of the early morning while I worked out and gathered my thoughts. The display of the treadmill showed I was keeping up a good pace and I was working up a sweat. I could hear my feet pounding against the treadmill over the wellbeing podcast I was listening to. My husband Tom had built this gym for me in the garage. I convinced him it wouldn't be a waste of money and that had proven to be the case.

More than just a place to keep fit I also used it to develop my plan of attack for the day. I would check through all the items that I needed to do in my head. I took my job and my life seriously. I had always known what I wanted from an early age and through hard work and determination nothing could stop me.

I wanted to work as a primary school teacher since I was young, I love kids and I enjoy people looking at me with appreciation when they knew they could trust me with their children. Everything I do in life has to be perfect, I like to be able to control every last detail. I know I might be considered hard work but I just have no time for people who use packet cupcakes from a shelf, I always make the effort to bake from scratch. You can definitely taste the difference. My mum always said that I took life too seriously. Others agreed. It made me come across as uptight they would say it, but that's how I relaxed, by doing the best I could.

I met Tom during a ten-kilometre run I was doing for charity. I managed to complete the run in under an hour, finishing that run in my best time was an awesome experience. I remember at the end drinking water to replenish myself while looking out over Bondi Beach, Tom caught my eye as he stood on the beach, taking in oxygen as sweat dripped down his hard, toned body.

It wasn't hard for me to attract men but finding the right one was a challenge. I had learnt from earlier experience that being attractive meant dealing with unwelcome approaches from over confident but incompatible men, but this only increased my inner strength. I had learned many ways to tell men the intentions are unwelcome. Not Tim, though. We fit perfectly together.

After introducing myself I knew in a flash that he would fit my criteria; driven, intelligent, hardworking and charismatic. Being attractive to the eye didn't hurt either but there was more than looks to consider. I wanted someone who would be there for me even if things went bad.

I had my dream job as a kindergarten teacher at a quaint primary school, being the person who taught children the fundamentals of education was beyond rewarding. Their school bags where often bigger than them, so cute. I didn't mind not being liked by some people due to my drive because the number one priority for me has always been the children, whose spark brought joy to my soul.

I was constantly going through the checklists in my head, some of the items were the daily things I had to do like workout, shopping, lesson plans for school. Then there were the larger things like earn the respect of my peers, be dependable, move up the ranks at work and maybe try for an addition to the family. Now I was sounding like one of the motivational podcasts I listen too.

At times I analysed myself, why I cared so much about having a family and contributing to society. I was in a car accident at an early age, which resulted in me not being able to have children. Instead of feeling sorry for myself I threw myself into my work, which became my life. But I didn't want to be a bystander, I wanted to take part and be involved in the community. I wanted to be someone people looked up to and having Tom by my side fit the mould. Initially I was only attracted to Tom because he ticked my prerequisites in a partner, but he was so nice, kind and funny that shortly my feelings changed and I fell in love.

My viewpoints also started to soften, but only a little. I started trying to not to take everything so seriously. It worked for a while. I didn't drop my standards, rather I started to listen to other people more, becoming more empathic and in touch with the feelings of others, and not just my own.

Tom worked hard as a surveyor. It was a good job and he was very accomplished at it, although he never bragged. Even when he played sport on the weekend for his local footy team and was awarded man of the match, he didn't gloat, just smiled. People loved being around Tom, he was naturally likeable and never really seemed to have to do much to attain admiration and attention.

I couldn't help myself. I got myself on the committee of the local AFL board. It was too hard to resist not organising a down on its luck and not well-funded club. I made sure I was always front and centre for fundraising, whether that was selling cupcakes or on the sausage sizzle, I'd even added vegan sausages to the menu. When I was helping there, I was happy.

Tom eased my anxiety and neurosis, to the point where over time taking a more relaxed approach became enjoyable for me. I was seduced into his carefree view of the world and his belief that people would stick together and be kind.

Growing up in a white middle class family I had certain privileges that I didn't appreciate until work experience took me out of my comfort zone and opened my eyes. I'd been placed in a small local school in an isolated coastal town. It was there I saw the hardship of poverty, sexism, lack of education and racism, things that I had, until then, only seen on TV and even these depictions were often made and presented by people who looked like me.

What a shame, my inner monologue used to say, like many other white people in a similar position would do. We would all agree gently that the local community was going downhill as we debated over what smart watch to buy or whether almond milk was superior to oat milk in a coffee. I used to give ten dollars a month to a charity to help indigenous people just to make myself feel better than other privileged white people.

A well-intentioned family had raised me, but work experience in these small towns educated and changed me. The sanctuaries of cities in Australia were merely a bubble where we were all free to be liberal and believe the rest of us are the same. It didn't take me long to realise that a short drive out of that bubble racism, homophobia and sexism ran rampant.

The culture of gambling and drinking there made me realise that my fundraising efforts didn't even scratch the problem of abuse young indigenous children received not too far down the road. My intention was never to be patronising but I could now see how it could appear that way.

When I left work experience, I realised how wrong I had been. I need to wake up to myself. And I did. When I first started talking about fostering children from abusive parents or similar situations people smiled and nodded. I knew they were humouring me, probably thinking "That's nice but Claire won't follow through."

Well not only was I not full of shit, Tom wasn't either. We started off with one child but this quickly became two young girls, it wasn't easy though. We made mistakes, as we really had no idea what we were doing. We could never fully understand what it was like to be judged every time we walked into a shop and feel every-one's gaze because of the colour of our skin.

Those lists in my head of someday owning a beach house, a fancy car and a platinum gym membership were replaced with making sure the child we were looking after had love, a safe place to sleep and an education. My Mum had never put any pressure on me to have children, unlike the constant complaints I listened to about my brother still being single and not showing the small-est sign of ever giving her grand-children. My Dad was making more and more appearances in my life and was trying his best to not be as big of an asshole as he had been in the past, which was difficult for him at the best of times. Although the introduction of our first small beautiful brown-eyed baby girl melted my dad's rough edges instantly. The support and love Tom and I received from both set of parents was beautiful and invaluable, it made us feel like we were doing the right thing.

While the lists in my head continued to become less self-absorbed and materialistic, I still enjoy life's little luxuries like my home gym but that is all I need for now. The importance of par-ticipating in sport and the local community, as well as teaching, can be a lot of hard work but the sense of satisfaction I get from it all is rewarding.

I sometimes asked myself was I just doing all this for to feel good about myself or was I doing it for my family, I don't really know. I hoped my motives weren't selfish but I still liked to ques-tion what I was doing so I could become a better person for the children, even if I had to do it without Tom.

Tom... oh Tom. Our lives were so intertwined and my love for him was deep... but then Tom was ripped away from me one night at the whim of a vampire. He was out with his construction com-pany celebrating the signing of a new contract. It was a night on the town he was paying for, as usual he was thinking of others. The staff loved Tom and were loyal and hardworking but they also liked an all-expenses paid night out, and what better place than The Vamp Strip. No rules, time to let your hair down, time to party.

A lot of humans don't have a brain to bless themselves with, as I found out through the flawed foster care system, and there were just as many fools amongst vamps as well. It's just that when a vamp is intoxicated and they have a friendly pushing match with a human, the human ends up going through a bar's glass window at the same time a truck is delivering beer. The truck hit Tom at full speed and I was told that he died instantly. There were three vamps at the bar the night Tom died. The police thought it was just unlucky but perhaps they could charge the vampire that pushed Tom for affray. I snapped; my inner strength and my innate kindness began to turn that night. The bubble I had created where I thought my family was untouchable had not taken vampires into consideration.

The change Tom's death caused in me was swift and powerful. I didn't know really what the word vengeful felt like until then. A tragic accident one night changed my whole life for the worse. Our friends, the club, our local community were devastated. They were so in awe of Tom, for him to simply vanish from our existence was hard for us all to take. Our foster children were of course devastated, to finally have someone in your life who is a caring and positive influence suddenly taken away hurt their hearts and souls deeply.

During this time the pounding of my feet against the base of the treadmill became more and more aggressive. I started hating everything. The lists in my head took a darker turn. I became fixated on the circumstances around Tom's death and I wanted revenge. I still might have looked serene like a swan, but underneath I was ready to explode.

The anger changed and consumed me. My old nature of

kindness and helpfulness evaporated and my patience at work was paper-thin. Mrs Spencer the children said, can you help us. Of course, I can help I replied, but inside I wanted to run away from the responsibility.

I was horrified at these thoughts in my head. At first there weren't too many to manage but soon there was an avalanche of negative emotion, I could not stop. What was I to do? I was too far-gone for lists to help me now. But I wasn't going to fold and let the anger win. After all, I had worked so hard, Tom and I had both worked too hard for this life.

How could tiny me get revenge on a vampire anyway? I didn't know but I would try. It was the only way forward. I would kill at least one of those smug murderers or die trying. Even if I just lopped off one of their ears, something they would remember me by. I knew it may prove fatal or result in my incarceration but the repercussions would be worth it and I would leave the money we had saved to the girls.

I wanted to do it in front of the same bar, there was no turning back. I thought long and hard about it, no matter how much I ran on that treadmill there was no release for me. I was drowning in the weight of grief and the expectations that I had put on myself.

The police had been in contact to tell me one of the vamps was in fact going to be charged with third degree manslaughter. When these words funnelled through my head, I was left questioning my revenge plans. I started to feel some positivity. Maybe society did work, witnesses had come forward to make a case against this vampire. I couldn't believe this was happening. Maybe there was a way through this, maybe I would no longer imagine squeezing the hands of kindergarten kids who trusted me.

As the days wore on, I received updates from the police as to the steps they were taking to bring this case forward to trial. Case number 292987a, as it was known, the way the police spoke about it was detached but for me it was still painful. Although I began to enjoy the treadmill again and the outside world become less of a blur, my life was refocusing. There was still anger and pain but my therapist was telling me these feelings were to be expected. I could breathe again, I was back in my stride, I was almost happy. The last three months had been hell but running now in my makeshift gym I was able to control the anger so it coursed down my legs and out through my toes.

It was humid in the garage; I ran on the treadmill after I had put the girls to bed. This was my treat to myself. To run with just the music from my new smart watch, why not I thought. The soft vibration of the watch tickled my arm while I ran. Someone was calling me; the number was blocked and I didn't really know anyone that would phone this late, 9:30pm on a school night. Instead of declining the call my hands slipped in the sweat and hit answer in confusion of how to operate this new gift to myself.

"Hello?" The voice on the other end sounded like an old distinctive gentleman of European background.

"Hello this is Claire," I said hesitantly, rather out of breath.

"Oh, my dear... I'm sorry if I've gotten you at a bad time. I was wondering if you would have some time to discuss a rather sensitive matter this week if possible."

I was quite confused and a little irritated. I was in the workout zone and this rather pompous sounding man had brought my pumping heart rate down to earth.

"Look, I think you might have the wrong..."

"This is Mrs Spencer, isn't it? First name Claire, occupation primary school teacher. Is that correct my dear, do I have the right person? I have heard only good things about you."

The hair stood up on the back of my neck as he rambled on. I was standing with either foot on each side of the running machine as the belt ran through a cycle beneath me making a thudding sound each time it completed a lap.

"Hold on one sec," I said and turned the machine off. I wiped myself down with a grey towel. "Look mister, it's rather late and I don't know anyone who would call at this time…" I was just about to hang up.

"Well, my dear this is breakfast time for me, as it is for most vampires, my dear Claire. I can tell you would rather be done with these pleasantries, as your time is your own. I have a rather luscious proposition for you. Would you like your revenge Claire, to see the vampire who killed your husband Tom die a horrible death?"

"Pardon? What did you just say?" I shook as I heard the words, but most of all I was beginning to feel slightly excited, which concerned me. I began to tremble.

"Claire my dear are you still there?"

He knew I was still there. He could hear my breathing, "Who the fuck is this?" Adrenaline was pumping through my body; I was losing control as the confusion spread through me. I had spent my whole life maintaining that control and some fool on the phone had thrown me completely with his words about Tom and revenge.

"Well, Claire, how rude of me not to introduce myself. I am Thomas Malcolm," he said in a rather smug tone.

11

Nevaeh

I was standing in the prison auditorium, watching it fill up with journalists, paying tourists, and general gawkers who had come to observe the feeding. Cole, the infamous vampire podcaster, was even here today to see this next victim. Of course, the swine was here, he wouldn't miss a prized viewing like this one. It was hard to keep the audience engaged with proceedings people had seen hundreds of times before. Having pretty or well-known victims increased our viewer numbers and fuelled the gossip Cole laundered on a daily basis. They all took their seats on the steel pews (it was easier to clean than wood). In the early days, before we had a solid system for charging attendees to watch the attraction, all sorts used to come. Back then people would be so shocked by what they witnessed they would often vomit or piss themselves; others would cause trouble by throwing fake blood and yelling abuse. In comparison it's like being inside a laboratory now. There were no windows, and the bright fluorescent lights and smell of disinfectant in the air created an atmosphere of sterility. The idea was to make it more pleasant for people to visit. We even sold t-shirts, pencils and photo packages so visitors could take a memento of the experience home. Simply watching a vampire suck warm blood from a live human in front your eyes wasn't enough anymore, it had turned in to a controlled and well-paying circus.

The showcase feeding area was shaped like a funnel. At the tip of the funnel was a steel door that led into a white-tiled room, inside two chairs were bolted down to the clean, shiny floor. Medical equipment hung on the left-hand wall, for treating any mishaps that may befall the human prisoner. On the right-hand wall, next to the fire alarm, was the vamp alarm and also equipment to sedate or kill a vampire if they lost control. We had stringent protocols to follow if a vampire did go off the rails but this had never happened, and I was glad for that. Emergency equipment included wooden stakes and garlic infused nets to trap vampires. The vamp alarm opened a hatch that was directly above the vampire's chair, the hatch admitted direct sunlight, which could destroy, or at least hinder the vampire if their feeding got out of hand. All showcase feedings were scheduled during daylight hours. The night feeds, which vampires preferred, weren't for public viewing.

The room was only five meters long and ended at an impenetrable two-way glass wall. The viewing room on other side of the glass, where I now stood, was much bigger. Two large steel double doors were the only way in for those from the outside world. These imposing doors led into a more relaxed room with couches and a TV. There was even a bar to calm your nerves or numb the pain if you were watching a loved one being fed upon.

Standing in the viewing room was unusual for me. I was normally inside the critical feeding zone as the PR team liked to call it. I could feel the buzz of excitement as people filled into the room and moved into their allocated positions. There were no people working the cameras in the viewing room anymore instead they now operated them remotely. The tiny little black dots that scattered the ceiling and walls were the lenses of high-tech media equipment that allowed spectators to almost feel the blood splatter and taste it on their tongues.

I found it disturbing that people revelled in watching one being hurt another being. No matter how far we have moved forward in this so-called modern world we still enjoy seeing people being killed or hurt. As the room filled, I could smell the sweat of the crowd wafting through the air. With the prison having no windows and excellent temperature control I always forget how unforgivingly hot it can be outside during daylight hours.

I tapped my hard leather regulation boots nervously on the floor. I looked around the room canvassing everyone and the overall mood of my surroundings, being out of my normal work zone I wasn't as focused as usual when the buzzer started to ring throughout the auditorium to hurry people into their positions. I felt my breath becoming shallower. I was trying to be professional and not show any emotion but inside I was worried.

The door within the feeding zone opened and the guards on shift entered the room. There she was in all her grace and beauty. She even made the green prison garb look hot with her toned brown body inside it. The guards closed the door and led her to the feeding chair. Her tall frame visually distracting as she slid into position, it was hard to look away.

I looked at her intently as my body felt like it was going to explode with pain. The guards carefully and gently strapped her arms and legs to the chair. Her long hair was hidden under a clinical green hat, worn to prevent hair being soaked in blood during the feed.

The guards put their hands on her head and gently moved it towards the pole that would hold her in place. They were strapping her in at a right angle so her neck would be exposed. That's when she looked up in the direction of where I was standing. I looked into Helen's beautiful blue scared eyes and my heart sank at this helpless situation.

I didn't often go to the prison during the day shift and would not usually visit on a planned day off. As I pulled into the staff car-park, I realised I had forgotten how quaint the old part of the prison looked. Four three-storey limestone buildings stood grandly around the lush green lawn. The sun was shining brilliantly down upon me. I was reminded how hot it could be during the day. It was very rare for me now not to be in an enclosed, air-conditioned room.

These four original buildings were where the human prisoners were now housed. It was more modern inside than the exterior suggested. Only the outside of the buildings hinted at the crimes of the past. The limestone building on the far left had pink trim around the iron doors as this was where during the depression women and children were housed as they had nowhere else to go. The rooms within delivered their own type of torture. The cells were only two meters long and wide. Tight and cramped, four wooden single beds hung from the walls and back then the inhabitants shared a bucket for a toilet. The squalor and disease in this hellhole of the past often killed people before they were hanged.

Who would have thought that each cell would now house only a single prisoner, and be fitted out with his or her own private bathroom and smart TV? No expense is spared when a rich vampire has you earmarked for their dinner.

Alongside the four prison blocks sat a small tinned roof infirmary and a massive tiled shower room where all manner of unpleasantness had once occurred. It felt surreal being here in my plain clothes rather than the uniform I'm used to.

The showers had recently been transformed into a tourist information centre with a canteen and gift shop attached. Paying visitors could see how the prison had changed from the 1900s when it held people who were mainly immigrants from England or poor people living on the bread line. It then became a tourist attraction for school kids and educators, before becoming a small correctional facility for men. During this time only one of the four buildings was used to hold male prisoners, with the others left as part of the history of the area. But now the whole prison had been turned into a glossy modern attraction that facilitates vampires feeding on criminals. I was sure the founders would have never envisaged that.

I sound like one of those information prison pamphlets that I used to hand out. I had heard the spiel many times before. When the local heritage association got involved, there was no way the new development could move ahead without certain concessions. In the past they allowed school groups and children to tour the abandoned prison. But it wasn't the old days anymore. Now adults wanted to come to see the gore and the action. At first, I thought the idea of a viewing deck in the new part of the prison was repulsive and absurd but tickets sold out for that sideshow as soon as word got out. As far as I knew, the warden and the investors never contemplated having a tourist and media department as part of the prison. But there was such thirst for information and morbid interest on what was going on in here the prison realised it was something they could capitalise on. They could not have known that the prison would be such a phenomenon, once the money started to roll in religious and political groups were constantly looking for donations in return for their support. Then once the Warden got the media department up and running with the right staff, such as our consummate public relations professional Lucy, the prison's popularity went into overdrive.

I rarely visited this section of the prison any more since my promotion. I still knew some of the old faces, like Trevor and Tracy who worked in the ice-creamery, I waved at them as I walked by.

I turned at the gift shop and made my way to the visiting bay. The warden had obviously heard about my visit and asked me to see him on my way out.

As I walked along the dark grey cobbled pavement, I worried about what I was going to say to Helen. It had been a while since I'd seen her. My god I had loved being part of her, and her family's, life. They took me in when I was scared and alone, I still had some of that fear left but not as much thanks to them. They didn't care what I looked like and they never judged. Helen's three brothers were dicks but loveable dicks.

They were always getting into mischief but nothing that Maury couldn't sort out with a cuff around the head or a few shifts at the family surf shop. I never knew what I wanted to do, apart from surf and party, but Helen always knew, she wanted to be a lawyer. I think she might have watched too much *Law and Order* when she was younger, she would have looked good in high heels and shoulder pads though. When we finished school, Helen left for uni down in Sydney while I stayed and worked part-time at the surf shop. I didn't want to live here forever but I still had some of Mum's family to help out. They were my only link to her. Auntie Carol always told me stories of the mischief they got up to when they were younger. It sounds silly but for me it kept parts of Mum alive. Even though there were only a few bad years with the cancer compared to the many good the bad stuck in my mind. It was difficult for me to push those memories away and remember the good times. That's why I saw Auntie Carol often, not only did they look alike with the same beautiful brown eyes but they had the same laugh which was both infectious and naughty at the same time.

Helen had thrown herself fully into the life of a student, not only was she studying hard and achieving the marks she needed to progress her career but she was also figuring out who she was, making new friends and listening to new music. Bands regularly toured the uni circuit so as well as opening herself to new music she opened herself to the alcohol, drugs and partying that went with the scene. I think Helen found it freeing to be on her own and living her life away without the eyes of her family, and maybe even me, upon her. At times I found myself looking at Helen and feeling jealous of her perfect life but I never let her know what I was thinking. Sometimes I travelled down to Sydney to party with Helen. It was these times I knew I was losing her; we were still best friends and no one could fight like we did but I knew she wanted more. I could tell Helen had her eye on a life away from where we grew up. More than anyone I had reason to leave our small coastal town but I wasn't going to run away on a whim.

I had finished running my Saturday morning surf lesson for the local kids when I saw Helen's Dad waving at me from the shop up on the cusp of the sand that overlooked the beach. I must have been about nineteen and I loved working there. As I walked over, I could see he looked rather perplexed.

"You ok, Maury?" I asked flashing my best smile at him, trying to gauge if I was in trouble for anything. "The surf class seemed to go well, no complaints I hope?"

"It's ok Nev, save that lovely smile for when you truly need it, you're not in trouble today Nev, well not at the moment," he said.

Maury's sense of humour and good nature was infectious, when he first came into my life, I just thought he was some old prick who had raised a spoilt child that was trying to make good with the local community. But I was wrong about him being fake, he turned out to be one of the most generous men I'd ever met. Maury was never ever angry with me, or anyone for that matter, for longer than a minute or two. Oh, save maybe when the Knights were playing footy against Manly, he fucking hated Manly.

He wasn't a tall man, about my height, five foot six, which was a surprising as he'd produced four tall kids. Helen's Mum had died when she was young. Maury never complained though, that wasn't his way. He had a freckled face and sun-bleached hair that only served to highlight the ginger streaks. His boys were a spitting image of their dad, but unfortunately none of them had his charm.

"I've got a postcard," he said.

"Great Maury, from who? One of your many girlfriends?" I teased.

"No, it's from Helen, she's in England apparently."

Maury must have seen me mouth the words motherfucker as I stood there in bewilderment.

"I take it from that filthy reaction that you didn't know?" He hated people swearing. He should have been used to it as us beach junkies swore profusely at the best of times.

Taking the postcard from him I saw it had a picture of Buckingham Palace on the front. I turned it over and instantly saw from the style and grace of the writing that it was indeed from Helen.

It read: *Hi dad and bros and I'm pretty sure Nev. SURPRISE I'm in London. I just couldn't help myself, don't worry I've just put uni on hold for a year, I'm having a lot of fun. I must admit it's hard to look awesome in these heavy thick clothes as it's so cold but I manage it. Anyway, much love see ya soon, H.*

I let my brown arms fall by my side and a mixture of sweat and water ran down them and started to soak the edges of the postcard. The first thought I had was; fuck me, I'm truly alone.

"Well Maury its looks like it's just you and me looking after the shop for the summer months for a while," I said, thinking maybe now was the time I should move my life forward.

"Don't forget the boys as well, Nev, you forgot the boys. They can be helpful... Nev don't look that way... they do mean well... Nev stop laughing"

"As I said Maury it's just you and me and I wouldn't have it any other way," laughing I hugged him so tightly he flinched away from the cold of my damp wetsuit.

And I wouldn't. I would forever cherish these moments I had with Maury. He'd taken me in when I was confused and angry.

Maury ended up getting taken by a heart attack. I'd had enough of watching people who I loved, respected and felt safe around dying. When it happened, I was doing fewer shifts at the surf shop as I was also working part-time at the prison in the gift shop, mainly because they paid really well. The boys and Helen took Maury's passing hard. Helen had forged a life for herself in England and while we chatted on the phone with each other it wasn't the same. She came over for the funeral and was happy enough to leave the surf shop to her brothers while she worked hard on becoming a lawyer and living her best life. It was the worst decision she could have made, but no one could have foreseen what would happen to her family. The brothers were old enough to make their own decisions, how bad could they be?

It all spiralled out of control though, the brothers fell in with the wrong crowd, making dodgy deals with bikies and drug dealers. All three of them thought they were the gangsters of the coast but they couldn't help shooting their mouths off at every opportunity and pretty soon this ruined the surf shop as a viable business. Maury had mainly kept them out of trouble but with him gone their gambling, drug taking and bad investments left two of the brothers in jail and the third, Bruce, was in wheelchair, the result of a bad beating at the hands of someone he had screwed over along the way. Helen's fledging career in the court system had just begun to take off but she had to leave it all behind to return home and pick up the pieces. Helen's attempt to build a life of her own overseas on her terms came to a crashing halt.

The world is vast and full of potential, it's your oyster, as Mum used to say. Helen's lust for life had sent her to South London and this meant she visited places and had experiences I could only dream of. Guilt, lack of self-belief, my heritage or even that I was slowly growing proud of this small town had pinned me here. In the past it was like a collar slowly tightening around my neck and I was jealous Helen had broken free of that, even if it only ended up being briefly.

But now Helen's collar was tightening around her neck, the blood of which was being used to pay for her crime; a charge of murder she had been found guilty of. She was being held in one of the rooms where countless women and children had been held in the past. Her love for her dad and her stupid fucking brothers had now destroyed her new life in London and now she truly believes her existence and soul are worthless.

Helen had become a commodity and the blood that pumped through her beautiful elegant body was paying for past mistakes that had resulted in someone's death.

Where was I when this happened? I was there. But I didn't know any of this was happening. I cried with Helen at the funeral not knowing the trouble the family were in after the death of Maury. I was in the full swing of work and didn't notice what was going on. The surf shop was in debt because that her brothers had managed to squander all the money. There was nothing left.

One night I drove down the freeway after finishing a twelve-hour shift, it was only thirty minutes to my old stomping ground. The drive at 6am was quite beautiful, I left the sandy dry surroundings of the prison with the night at my back and drove towards the sun coming up over the ocean, feeling it graze over my skin and warm up my bones. I felt my body relax with the thought of the ocean crashing around me and catching a wave.

It kept me sane, kept me wanting to work so I could eventually move away and do my own thing. I pulled my old hatch back into the carpark trying not to hit the small crowd that had amassed, I was hoping that nothing bad happened. Sometimes there were shark attacks or maybe some young idiot had broken into one of the shops? When I left my car, I heard the noise of the crowd heckling someone who was being led through the local onlookers by the police. I looked up and I saw a tall beautiful woman being led to a police car. It was Helen. Dried blood was on the right-hand side of her face and had matted into her hair. Her face was red from crying. Her white elegant blouse was covered in blood.

I tried calling out her name but it was lost in the surrounding kerfuffle. As she was pushed into the car, she stooped her tall frame and turned around, looking lost and confused.

I hadn't seen Helen since, until a week or so ago when she was put into the viewing deck for the first time. With my roster and the media frenzy hovering around Helen I was, as usual, way down the pecking order. The fact that Helen was beautiful made her appealing clickbait for the tabloids. And now I was waiting to hear Helen's version of events. I had seen Bruce. What a sad fucking soul he was. He'd been sad even before the recent tragic events, an expert at blaming the rest of the world for his faults. Nothing was truly ever his responsibility and he always blamed everyone else for his problems. Another privileged white male skirting responsibility made me sick all the way down to my gut. The way he'd dumped all the blame for his fuck up onto his younger sister made me want to smash his head against the brick wall of the halfway house he was staying at. It was Bruce who had set up a meeting between Helen and a potential buyer of the surf shop. Selling the surf shop would mean they could start paying of the enormous debt the boys had amassed with the local gangster loan shark. This guy was just as dumb as Bruce but had even fewer moral scruples. There was no proof he had tried to attack Helen, in fact her own strength and grace made it easy for her to overpower him and smash his skull into the wall. The fact that she repeated this movement twenty times would suggest that Helen had lost control. Each skull crack against the wall was her crying out for the pain that she suffered and her guilt over what happened after Maury died.

As I walked into the visiting bay, I had a nervous feeling in my gut. I thought back to when I had worked on prison door duty before the vampires came, it was a lot less glamorous back then. It was my second job in this complex, after the gift shop, and after I had shown that I was capable of holding my shit together. I had applied for the job on a whim; I knew I'd have a chance as the government had incentives for women to apply for roles that in the past had always been jobs for the boys. The HR department lapped me up during my application process, they were glad to be able to tick a box that proved as a company they were embracing diversity. Gaining the respect of my fellow workers was the exact opposite though, I'd say maybe three times as hard. Most people out here have only one opinion of indigenous people and none of them would dare say out loud what they really thought in front of human resources.

The hallway split the prison in half right down the middle, but now it looked like, and had the graces of, a secured hotel rather than a traditional prison. The soft grey paint on the walls was visually appealing and the carpet on the floors stopped the awful echoes that filled the prison in the past. The smell of sandstone and dampness had long gone. In a bid to sell the idea of a vampire prison to the world no expense had been spared. It was a lot like the opening scenes of *Jurassic Park*. I only hoped the vampires wouldn't end up wiping us out like the fucking dinosaurs did in that movie.

As I stepped into the hallway, onto the thick carpet I felt a sense of awe at how much this place had changed. Where I worked now resembled a hospital more than a prison due to all the body fluids we encountered, mainly blood. I now hated the word fluids. Every time I heard that word on my coms, I knew that I would be cleaning them up with a lot of elbow grease and bleach.

There were three floors and each flight of stairs had a guard on duty. The guards in here were just highly trained porters really. There was never any trouble in this part of the prison where the prized assets live. The ones considered the tastiest of the meal tickets. The downtrodden and less attractive, in every sense of the word, were housed in my area. This building however was more like the VIP section of a nightclub, something I had never been invited to as I never knew the right people.

Vampires have the option to choose the victim they wanted to feast on. When this occurred, the victim would live here so there was no damage to the livestock, so to speak. There was a high monetary cost to picking your favourite human meal but it came with benefits. Not only could you select the person you would like to feed on but also you could dictate what the human of your choice must eat in order to ensure their blood has your desired taste. If a vampire preferred say, cinnamon or the taste of lemon we incorporated those particular ingredients into the prisoners' diet. This gave our most lucrative clients a sense of ownership over their victim. It made the prisoner feel like a slave. Of course, the prisoner had the choice to go back to the shithole where I worked, where they had no private room or Wi-Fi and also had to endure the abuse of other inmates and guards. My moral compass found it difficult to turn a blind eye to the goings on of some guards, who had no problem in helping the inmates obtain little benefits for exchange of money or favours. I knew that my boss Dave, had an idea with what was going on but there was no way I was going to get involved in any of that. I just kept a watchful eye on everything going on and who was taking what. You never knew when that information would come in handy.

I arrived at the waiting bay and added my details into the tablet given to me by the guard, necessary even though I worked within the system. I was also searched, as per standard procedure. As if I could hurt Helen but there was no way for them to know that. The top brass wasn't exactly happy I knew someone who was being housed here, even though with the constant flow of inmates it was bound to happen once in a while, but the warden agreed I could see Helen seeing as I used to live with her family. I was surprised I was allowed, considering it was a different department and section to mine but Dave said off the record the warden liked me. I was a little taken aback to hear that, as I didn't think he even knew that I worked here, why would he?

I had no idea how I would react when I saw Helen. I knew I had to keep it reasonably together as everything was recorded in here. Would I cry, scream, hug or fall down on the floor in a heap. There was only one way to find out.

I walked through the metal detector and was searched thoroughly for weapons or contraband. The staff were a lot kinder here than the police I had encountered growing up, I had flashed back to the treatment my cousin and I received when we lived in the caravan park. I had forgotten, or put away somewhere deep inside myself, the racial abuse I used to cop as a child, it happened so often when I was younger it was almost like the rain, you knew that it was going to come eventually.

The influx and spread of vampires had transferred this innate racism to another kind, one all the racists in the world could get behind and hate in solidarity. This repulsed me even more, as I could somehow see myself in the vampire's situation, I presumed it was one of the reasons why I wasn't scared of them.

Usually, you never got to see an inmate alone in their quarters, as the cells were small enough already you would move downstairs to one of two family rooms. We all knew that was not needed in this case and I didn't want to bring any more attention to Helen's case as it was.

Upon arriving on the first level, I noticed how civil everything was. There were no inmates screaming blue murder or throwing excrement at each other. Everyone in their cells had a smart TV or music, anything to make their lives more relaxing. It was a far cry from the other prison, which was more like a youth hostel with four bunk beds to a room, a small bathroom and a TV that they all shared. The alpha inmate got the remote, the modern-day symbol of power.

But even within this small set up there were power struggles big and small, whether it was someone taking food from a shared fridge or a guard trying to fuck up an inmate. The prison was a complicated beast and there were secrets being passed around throughout the whole system. It was difficult for me not to get involved and not take sides. With Helen though I didn't have a choice. When I think of the hatred, we first had for each other, mainly due to our lack of understanding, it was amazing we had become best friends. I don't think the town could believe their eyes when they saw us together. Helen had always been confident and headstrong and she found it very hard to cope with any racism I received whether it was underhand or just blatant. It gave myself more strength and belief in seeing Helen and her family go to bat for me, even those idiotic but well-intentioned brothers of hers.

Helen didn't know I was coming. I had tried for weeks to talk or see her but to no avail. In the end I went to her lawyer for any information about what happened and to see if I could help. Her lawyer was completely up front with me, "My client does not under any circumstances want any contact with you." When these condescending words came out of his fat mouth it hurt, but more than that I was confused. Helen obviously thought that if I got involved, it would only make trouble for me. But there was no way I was going to let a sister go down the road to hell by herself. Arriving outside the door to Helen's cell I looked up at the camera and gave a gentle nod to the guard behind the lens, whom I knew would be watching from the expensive control suite where I now spent most of my life.

The door buzzed softly then clicked open. Helen was sitting upright on her bed underneath the only small square window in the cell, she was reading a book, from the cover it looked to be a legal text. Even in this situation it seemed like she had her shit together. She was wearing expensive ear buds and hadn't heard the door open. Her long hair covered most of her neck but I could still see some bruising on the left side, the puncture marks barely covered by a plaster.

Helen must have sensed my small frame move nervously in the doorway. She looked up and into my eyes. At first there was love and joy as we gazed at each other, rather than annoyance. In a flicker of a second she placed the book face down on the bed and removed her ear buds.

"I knew you would come. You were never any good at following instructions," she said sadly with a slight English accent, which just made her seem even more posh.

Trying to remain calm and to not let my emotions overtake every word, but also knowing I would fail, I said, "Even glamorous in those prison rags aren't we." It was a poor attempt to break the ice. "I have no idea what has been going on but I want to help. Look at me, Helen, I'm here for you."

She sat there silently looking down at the floor and I couldn't work out whether she was ignoring me, laughing or crying. It was the first time I'd seen her hunched. She appeared incredibly tired, even fragile. Her body trembled slightly, then there were deeper and deeper movements. Helen was crying and soon she was sobbing uncontrollably. Putting her hands up to her hair she pulled it back so I could see her face and the tears rolling down it.

Turning slowly while still sobbing, she looked at me with

sadness and desperation in her eyes, "Where have you been, Nev, where have you been?"

12

Alfred

"You know I can hear your heart beating you little fuck. Squirming away in the corner aren't you my little worm. Wait until I pick up your pathetic little slimy frame, you're going to fucking get it like never before."

He was right. My heart was almost popping out of mouth. I couldn't see him as I hid as small as I could behind the single armchair that was in the bedroom of the very expensive apartment.

Being a vampire meant he could be as graceful, noisy or loud as he wanted to be, and tonight, I was in trouble, I had no idea what he was going to do. Peeking my head out from behind the large armrest I could see the destruction of the room. Broken chairs, tables and ripped clothes lay scattered on the lush carpeted floor. I couldn't feel or see him, this was my moment to run, to break free. I tensed my small wiry frame, ready to burst across the room to the freedom of the front door, but then I felt the jolt of cold fingers dig in against my neck.

He had me; I was being pulled up from the ground by one very powerful vampire arm. As he lifted me up in one motion he slammed me hard against the wall, knocking the air out of my lungs, his long nails digging into my neck as he did so. My face was pinned and squeezed against the wall and I could feel his tight muscular body move closer against my naked back.

He learnt in close, his lips next to my ear, "I fucking have you now, you little runt, there's no escape for you now Alfie, I'm going to destroy you." His Aussie guttural voice, his power, his coldness turned me on like I had never been turned on before. He was right, he did destroy me, and it was exactly what I wanted.

———

Scott and I lay together on the bed damp with my sweat due to our physical activity, I had never been happier. This was the fifth time I had asked for Scott; he was exactly what I had been looking for, which was funny since I hadn't known what I was looking for to begin with. I had presumed I would desire a female vampire, when it came to human partners I had only ever been interested in women, but when the catalgue was laid out in front of me, in the velvet curtained selection room, I instantly chose a male. As I was new to the scene and had extra cash available, I decided to splurge on one of the more expensive vampire brothels, a place where being discreet was their promise.

Blush was just off the nightlife's main strip, a big square looking building with no signage or lights to bring it to anyone's attention, it wasn't easy to find. The setup and booking process on their secure app showed me they meant business and they were well funded.

In the home of my birth, I had been ridiculed for liking vampires, but *Blush* made me feel like a VIP. Of course, I was paying for this service but it was nice to feel accepted and free. The only problem was after I selected Scott for the first time and then experienced what it was like to be with him, I of course began to fall for him. What an idiot I was, I just knew I was going to get hurt.

On entering the premises, I hovered my phone onto the door

scanner to gain access. The red lighting reminded me of Twin Peaks. The whole place felt otherworldly. It felt like the perfect escape from my mundane life. The first time I was there I was shown to a small, expensively furnished, black-walled room where a digital catalogue sat perched on a table, this was where I discovered Scott.

Weekend after weekend he found out more about my likes and dislikes. He was starting to get inside my head and drag out all my sexual fantasies. At first, he followed my lead. I was never good at telling anyone what I wanted, unless of course it was to do with natural resources and how to save the earth. Scott soon learned what I liked but he also knew if he went too hard, he would kill me. I had to sign a waiver that would protect *Blush* and their employers. The Red-Letter Alliance had helped set up policies for all vampire sex workers and make the industry just as legitimate as the power company I worked for.

There would always be people like my sad lonely self. I knew my place, my niche, it wasn't shagging people for money. Luckily for me there were others, like Scott, who excelled in this industry. I think I would have died if I had no one to be intimate with. Being stuck out the back in my small, but neat, room in my mum's house has taken most of the light out of my soul, and even though I knew that paying for sex was wrong, it gave me a reason to live.

The more I encouraged Scott to talk, and most importantly the more I listened, I became aware of how hard it was to be a new vampire of his age. Like in our society, being young and without money, influence or an education is a struggle. No matter how beautiful I found Scott or his kind they struggled to look after themselves just as much as a child does. I understood that no one chooses Scott's line of work without doors constantly being shut in their face.

Scott told me how real the fear was of being burned alive by the sun was for the first few years of his life. Being turned into a vampire is illegal but that doesn't stop it happening and Scott was just another victim. His fiancée, his family, his career as a medical professional had ended. It was like turning a life support machine off. He was left with nothingness, silence, with no assistance from anyone. Where do you live when you're kicked out with no money, no help and no shelter?

That's why Scott, if that was his real name, moved here, like so many vampires he had no other choice. It's a story of the ages. Why did wannabe actors move to LA, New York or the like? Why did I want to get a job in London away from my sleepy town in Essex? There was nothing there for me anymore. I was pulled there in search of my own inner freedom.

Within a few short weeks of telling loudmouth John at work where to go I started to really enjoy myself. I finally joined the local cricket team. It was strange at first playing at night, the heat during the day was just too intense and made most outdoor activities feel arduous, but everyone really enjoyed it and seemed to have fun.

My sexual awakening had lowered the inhibitions I had around talking to people. I wasn't super Mr Popular, but I was on my way. I was even beginning to enjoy schnitzel night a little.

Work was going as well as I could expect, no one likes change but I think my small team of co-workers were making an impact. The work I was doing was starting to gather recognition. I had to travel more to the other power stations as they too wanted to be seen as making a difference for the future of our kids and country, it was all PR fluff but if I could make a tiny change, I would take that.

I woke sleepily from one of the best nights of my life, stretched out my arms I rolled over towards the middle of the bed to see Scott staring contently at me. At first this used to startle me but what did I expect, this was his daytime, his work time, his new normal. There was always interesting bed chat between Scott and I, that's how I found out how he became a vampire. At the time he was happily engaged to a woman called Emily. One night while at a nightclub a female vampire tried to seduce Scott, upon him gently turning her down, Emily laughed in the vampire's face. This resulted in the vampire attacking Scott and turning him into one of her own so neither she or Emily could have him. In doing the right thing he lost his love and life as he knew it. Of course, Scott could be lying through his beautiful white teeth to me but something made me feel he was sincere.

As I woke, Scott reached over and tucked my slicked back hair behind my ear.

"You do wear far too much gel in your hair Alfie," he said playfully. "To be honest mate I didn't realise they still made gel. That's from the '80s isn't it?" he said while sitting up against the headboard completely naked. "I'm sorry if I hurt you during our escapades but you sure do bruise like a peach, my cute little man."

I loved it when he lay there playing with me. He has been one of the best actors I had ever met as he made me feel as if no one else mattered. Luckily there was no one else here to see how feeble I looked lying next to him.

"Thanks for tidying up Scott, you do know that I love a clean room after passion. Just so you know," I said as charmingly as I could with my squeaky nervous voice, "my gel is environmentally friendly and for every dollar you spend…"

"Yes, yes I know," Scott interrupted while lifting his beautiful head aloft in a teasing way. His voice adopted a posh English accent, which he was terrible at, "the money goes to children living on small farms with no running water or electricity. Ain't life grand," he said in his best Mary Poppins.

"Now come on, I don't sound anything like Dick Van…"

"Well, the dick bit might be more appropriate." He jumped out of bed as I lunged forward and then chased him as he skipped gracefully across the room. I pinned him up against the cold full-length mirror in the bathroom. As I was shorter, I placed my arms on his elbows and positioned them above his head. I learnt in closer, my naked body pressed firmly up against his clean-shaven body. He was up right up against the mirror but there was no reflection. It was almost like kissing myself. I closed my eyes and banished the thought, there was no one else I would rather think of than Scott. As I kissed his firm lips, he pulled my head back playfully. He looked into my eyes, "Times almost up guvnor," he said in the worst chimney sweep accent I ever heard.

"What's that now Scott, Oliver the musical?"

"I don't know Alfie it all sounds the same to me."

He was reaching for his clothes now. I knew how the business worked, there was a short turn around between each client. The cleaners would come in like a military outfit, they had only ten minutes to turn this place round and sanitise everything within an inch of its life. I was happy I wasn't there for the moment they used the UV lighting.

This cold process brought me right down to earth; I was getting too attached to Scott, I should set up a meeting with someone else next week. It wasn't hard to do, all I had to do was swipe left or right on the app.

I had always tried to behave like someone my Mum, or society, would see as more acceptable but I couldn't even eat yoghurt without spilling it on my cotton shirts, so I had little to no chance of that. But there was no doubt when it came to my work Scott had put a bounce in my step, if only a small one. I wasn't going to get above my station though. I had been burned before in work situations where people only pretended to be nice and say they would like to meet up for a drink when in fact they didn't.

In my heart, I was already married and living with Scott on a yacht on the Whitsundays. Dreams never made any sense. Why would Scott want to live with a small little runt like me in a yacht on the ocean in the middle of nowhere, under the hot sun, where he would burn to a crisp? Still, I smiled at Scott as I left, there was no need for sadness, as I had more than I ever dreamed of. I closed the door and walked silently down the wooden steps; I retrieved my navy blazer from the cloakroom. I know that it was strange to wear blazers but I had worn one since school and it was my signature style, good or bad.

As I approached the doors that led out to the anonymous side street, I felt good. I felt as though in a couple of months, maybe even weeks, I might finally be able to take a breath and settle down in this place. How quick ones mind-set changes when you're getting laid on a regular basis, even if I was paying for it. Hopefully that would change over time and I could meet someone who just liked me for me.

I felt like unwinding with a drink before heading home. I didn't usually do this, but I decided to spoil myself with the fanciest martini on offer along this vulgar but alluring strip. The drink app on my phone said the best place for a classy cocktail was *The Great Gas*. I had never visited the establishment before but its jazz music from the roaring '20s poured out onto the strip infectiously.

The dress code was smart casual and I was told at the door my attire fitted in perfectly, which I don't think was a compliment. I was led to a table for one by a lovely waitress who was wearing an expensive looking pearl necklace and an incredibly revealing outfit.

The noise inside was deafening, music blaring and people dancing, it was an attack on the senses. I couldn't help but smile. They were going for a classy 1920s feel, but to me it was more like my favourite kid's film *Bugsy Malone*, I loved that film, I was expecting the next set of sequinned dancers to be children. That would kill the buzz in this room. No one here wanted to be reminded in any way of their home life or day-to-day routines.

I couldn't care less; I was happy and really looking forward to my drink. I was in control at long last, doing what I liked and answering to no one except myself. As I brought the chilled passionfruit martini to my mouth, I noticed a smudge on my glass.

As I placed my right hand into my blazer pocket looking for a handkerchief, I felt some paper in there. It wasn't mine. Who used paper anymore, such a barbaric waste of resources? I pulled the paper out of my pocket, and unfolded the small square in my hand.

The handwritten letter read;

Dear Alfie

I know this is inappropriate and rather straight forward, but this is Samuel (you know me as Scott). This is of course totally against the rules of Blush, but I was wondering if you would like to go for a drink some time. Just you and me in our normal lives, that is if your name is really Alfie. I understand if this is too much and you don't want to see me again, but I feel as though there is something between us. It would be nice to meet up and see if there is a connection.

Yours S

First of all, I thought to myself, wow what lovely writing and second, fuck me Samuel, you're going to break my heart.

13

Nevaeh

The fifteen minutes with Helen went quickly. After the tears and the hugging stopped, I managed to calm her down. I hadn't seen Helen since she had first sat in The Chair, the first time she had the blood sucked out of her. Seeing her scream and flinch as a small, repulsive, but incredibly rich vampire, sank his fangs into her long slender neck made me feel violated too. I would never tell her I had been responsible for the design of the room and feeding chair.

I wished she had reached out before she tried to wrestle the surf shop back into her family's hands all by herself. Helen thought she could protect me by keeping me out of the loop, knowing if she had involved me, it could jeopardise my job. But being such a close part of her family, I thought I would have been the first person she'd call. I wish she had called but we'll never know if it would have led to a different outcome.

Everywhere I had worked since the surf shop seemed a lot harder than it had to be. The fish and chip place almost tore my back out, the gift shop at the prison almost drove me crazy with the pointless questions that spewed out of the paying public's mouth. With this prison cell job, it was the human scum we had here that got to me.

Maybe that's part of the reason why I loved Helen and her family so much, the surf job was the only job I'd had that I'd really enjoyed. If people caught a wave for ten to fifteen seconds out of a ninety-minute lesson, they were stoked, you could see the buzz and excitement in their eyes. Unlike now working at the prison, where I see trepidation and fear in people's eyes.

Don't get me wrong, nine times out of ten they deserved it, but I'm still human and I don't like seeing people, or vampires in pain, I never have. I couldn't just flick a switch and not care about others, unlike the guards that I worked with who said, "Burn them fucking all."

The amount of time I had spent with the prisoners, and vampires, setting up the prison procedures meant it was hard for me to turn that off. It was ok for fucking Bill to shout and brag how masculine he was when he wouldn't even go in the transfer room with the vamps. There were a lot of loudmouths in the crew I worked with. Only time decided the tough bastards from the show ponies. I put on my game face as I walked through the courtyard to see the warden. I didn't have much of a relationship with Warwick, which was the best way to be. He was far too busy arranging sponsors and advertisers for the prison to talk to the little people such as myself.

The prison liked to put me in their brochures. Good to have a pretty woman for that. But once that was over, I was back in the shadows keeping my mouth shut.

The real person who ran my section of the prison was Dave. It was hard not to love Dave. A man in his mid-fifties he was always in a rush and never on time. Being the boss, you would think this was a problem, but it had the opposite effect. Everyone in the prison knew he was here all hours of the day and that he had no time for small talk. He always made himself available and his employees had total respect for him and his ways. He breezed into rooms unannounced, adjusting his jacket or tie and asked questions regardless if people were mid conversation or halfway through a job. Dave was always polite but forthright. He had his finger on the pulse and didn't miss a trick. No matter what clothes he wore, he always appeared frazzled, like he had been through a tumble dryer. He took too much on but there was not another with his experience or his personal touch. I was sure that he partook in all the prison gossip, which was his way to keep his finger on the pulse and track staff morale. The amount of team seminars we attended about having a safe and happy place to work drove me insane, but Dave was very insistent on this. I could understand the reason why there were safe work practices on how to lift a heavy box the correct and safe way, but how the hell can you protect yourself against a vamp with a wooden baton and a taser that often had no effect on more powerful vampires. The longer I worked with Dave I was beginning to think that his friendly and approachable exterior was really just an act to hide the fact that he was always watching. Dave had no problem shepherding inept staff out of their job before most of them even realised, there were no issues finding a replacement, as the list of people from all over the world who travelled here hoping to get a job was long. The job was high-pressure and took a toll on you mentally and physically, but the money I have earned and saved has transformed my life. You would be crazy to jeopardise this, even with the random drug tests and psych evaluations. When I first started here at the prison ninety percent of the staff were local Australian men. That had changed rapidly, and for the better I thought. Back when I was working in the crappy gift shop selling tacky stubby holders, I could not have envisaged the diversity around me now.

Most of the staff here had a healthy respect for Dave so they all called him David. I don't know why he never intimidated me, maybe it was the pencil moustache he thought made him look regimental, I reckoned he looked like he was from old re-runs of

Monty Python.

His cheeks were always red from either shouting on the intercom or from the pies and red wine he consumed in the staff canteen after a stressful day, of which there were many. Aside from a portly midriff, which he hid by tucking in his tailored striped shirts, he was in good condition.

Dave always had my corner whenever there was a dispute between a staff member and myself, but that was a very rare occurrence.

The prison had to appear as though everything was hunky dory from the outside even if it was rotten from the core. I presumed that's why I was here to see the warden, Warwick. I had told human resources about my relationship with Helen as soon as she arrived. I knew that a guard having a friend in here could be a conflict of interest, but I was always above board, I had to be squeaky clean.

Walking out of the prison cell building and back into the hot unrelenting sun, made me realise how refreshing the temperature in the prison was.

While I stood outside the warden's reception area, I gathered myself together, hoping that I wasn't going to get a roasting on ethics or anything worse. Despite the prison's sordid history over the last two hundred years, the heritage style of the warden's office building somehow managed to make it look like a cute cottage. It oozed charm with its sandstone walls and green timber trim on the windows and doors. The longer I worked here the more I noticed the attention to detail that was paid by the heritage societies and volunteer workers of the past while maintaining this place. The more I looked the more I noticed that emerald green was not only on the windows and doors but also on the wooden benches around the grounds. It was also the colour of the font on the information brochure and of course the colour of the uniforms, I'm sure it was meant to be soothing or something similar. I knocked courteously on the door as I entered and as expected saw dependable Jane sitting on the right-hand side of the room typing ferociously away on her computer.

Jane was the warden's receptionist, an often-surly woman in her mid-sixties, if you dared to call her that you would be sure to feel her quiet wrath. Jane was a highly intelligent and capable women, the quieter her voice went the more dangerous she became. There were no airs or graces with her, what she says goes. Jane had gone from job to job with Warwick, from his time as property developer, to mayor and now warden. I never got the feeling that she followed him, his success I truly believed was due to a professional partnership they have both worked long and hard at.

Jane had the power to silence the most powerful person with a single glance if she chose to look up from one of the many tasks she accomplished each day. Both sets of prisons were run by a sophisticated computer system, with every high-tech gadget that was on the market, in order to help our guests feel at home and keep our inmates in their cells. This room, however, had only minimal updates and had kept the style of yesteryear.

I always thought that Jane had the waiting room and office designed to the look of *Shawshank Redemption*, which I found rather unsettling. Jane was a baby boomer who didn't seem to sympathise with people dissimilar to herself. When Jane wanted something in life, whether that was a report or a slice of tiramisu when the kitchen was closed, she got it.

As I walked into the room I looked over to Jane and smiled to say hello and was about to take a seat, as the warden always liked to keep people waiting, but Jane waved me in without a word rather nonchalantly. I didn't like the feel of this.

Taking an assured breath, I knocked and entered the room and was surprised to see the warden sitting in his chair behind a desk full of monitors and paper notes and seated opposite him was a man that I had never seen before.

"Hello Warden," I said. "I didn't mean to interrupt… I can wait outside until…"

"Good afternoon, Nevaeh, thanks for coming," he said confidently. "You're not interrupting at all. In fact, Gary is here to see you."

To see me, this didn't seem right, and who the fuck was Gary?

"Don't worry Nevaeh," he kept using my full name keeping this as formal as possible, "this is a friendly chat between you, Gary and I. Please take a seat and we will begin."

I took a seat in front of the warden. His desk looked more expensive than the contents of my entire flat, Gary sat adjacent to me. He was a tall, slim, good-looking man in a black suit with matching cufflinks securing a confident salmon shirt.

"Let me introduce myself formally Ms Jones, I am the prison's lawyer, Gary Wilkinson. We are here to discuss a sensitive matter in regard to how we manage our financial transactions and database. We wish to implement a new process that will track expenditure of our most exclusive clients. Only five people will be involved in the trial; myself, the warden, Jane, Lucy from PR and of course, hopefully, now you."

Gary had a very calm disposition, which put me at ease even though my heart was racing. I was beginning to believe I wasn't in trouble. Gary was as posh an Australian as you could meet, his accent was very mild, it was there if you listened really hard but my guess was years of North Shore boarding schools had taken the edge off it.

Growing up where I lived not even the teachers sounded like Gary, money from birth moulded people like him. Education, money and a sense of entitlement that usually made it hard for him to talk on the level of someone like me. I was intrigued by his genuine charm. As yet he didn't sound like a dickhead.

Maybe I was starting to move up in the world? Moving up in this prison sounded good to me and I started to relax in the hard-wooden chair. Mum had raised me to work hard and do the right thing. I'd sworn to myself while caring for her during the cancer that I wouldn't let the hate building up in my soul change and destroy me like it had countless others.

"We want to develop a new reward scheme for our vampire customers. As you work in the feeding bay and have an excellent reputation and appear to have a rapport with the vampires, we thought it would be a good idea to bring you on board. The higher the bank balance of the scheme's member the more privileges they would be entitled to." He was in his zone now and on the full charm offensive, I didn't really know why. It's not like they needed my permission, I would do as I was told.

"We would like you to approach the most elite vampires first and educate them on the benefits of being part of the program. In a crude way it's similar to an awards program with perks and bonuses for our most influential clients. It would enable them access to bars, hotels and chauffeur-driven limousines, it's an easy sell." He sat back in his chair and reached for his tablet.

"This is only a small sample of what we plan to offer and who better to introduce this new form of VIP status than someone they trust like yourself. Please read over the position description and the contract carefully before you sign. As I said earlier, we don't want you talking to any other staff members about this program. Of course, you will be well rewarded for accepting this role as I, and the team, are very confident it will be successful and profitable."

I always hoped for a pay rise, but this was something that I could never have imagined.

"You do have to sign a confidentiality clause and please take time looking over the finer details, but we would like an answer in the next day or so as we are keen to get this program out into the masses. It's a lot of information, Miss Jones, but as a whole what do you think?" Gary excelled at asking questions he already knew the answers too.

Throughout Gary's wordy spiel the warden had sat there staring with no expression, a look I'm sure he'd relied on countless times as Mayor, he sat quietly fidgeting with his black and gold pen.

I took a large breath, "I … to be honest, I'm relieved. I thought I was here about my friend who is being held in the prison." They both gently laughed as I said this.

"No," said the warden "you have always been exceptional in performing your duties, and sooner or later it was bound to happen that one of the guards would have someone they know here. The world as we know it is so small these days."

I never knew that Warwick the warden had this much charm, he had never needed to use it on me. In fact, why was he using his charm, he could just tell me what to do? That made me feel slightly uneasy, but I'd always felt uneasy around the top bosses.

"Warden and Gary, I'm very happy to be involved, I didn't realise anyone really took any notice of me to be honest, I just try to keep my head down and do my job the best I can."

"Please call me Warwick, Nevaeh. First of all, don't be so modest with your own ability. The changes and strict procedures that you have put into place in the feeding zone have been more than a success. You have shown great initiative and knowledge, David has told me of your improvements and your ability to communicate with humans and vampires alike. I like to be kept informed and everyone I speak with has only praise for your high standards and work ethic. Your inventive ideas have impressed us all."

I had never been so flattered in my life, and definitely not by a couple of middle-aged white men who weren't just trying to get in my pants.

"So, Nevaeh, what do you think? Do you think you might be interested in this opportunity that we are offering you? We are going to be going ahead with this enterprise but having a rising star on board would be our preference. What do you think?"

"I am really flattered by both your praise and ideas," it took all my inner strength to not say fuck yeah, I'm all in. "Yes, I would like to start this project. What are the next steps? What exactly do you need me to do?"

"Well," Gary interjected, "it all comes down to legal I'm afraid. Read through the details and when you're ready to sign and commit please call Jane to set up a meeting with myself to go through the finer points of how the membership works. Does that all sound ok Nevaeh?" I smiled and nodded while looking at Gary as he leaned closer to me.

Words came smoothly to Gary, as smooth as his well-moisturised face. Everything about him screamed, 'I am extremely well looked after and knowledgeable'. Let's see how trustworthy he could be, it would take more than an expensive suit and smile to win me over. It hadn't always been that way in the past but I had learned my lesson and raised my standards.

"Well, that's settled then Nevaeh," the Warden said bringing the attention back to him. "Thank you for your time and we will be seeing you soon for weekly updates." As he was talking, he walked over to shake my hand.

After shaking the Warden's and Gary's hands I left the room, tablet in hand and in a slight haze not really sure what I had agreed to. I must have been in my own world thinking to myself as I heard Jane call my name for maybe the fourth time.

"You ok Nev?" she asked without a note of genuine care in her voice, she was all business this woman.

"Yes, I'm fine thanks Jane, just a lot to take in but I'm good."

"Just before you leave, there are some documents and samples that you need to sign for and take home," Jane said in a way that meant right now thank you very much.

Half an hour later I was packing a couple of boxes into the boot of my small car. I had been informed that I would be on leave for a couple of days off while I researched the new equipment, they wanted me to sell and I had more than a few manuals to read up on. The more I thought about it, the more it seemed they just wanted a glorified salesperson that wasn't afraid of vampires. Well, fuck it why not, I thought as I started the car, I put on my seat belt and quickly cranked up the air conditioner. The generic pop music that came out of the tingly car speakers reflected my upbeat and happy mood.

If I still managed to be in control of the feeding zone with the added bonus of being on a manager's salary with all the perks it came along with, I could live with that, as long as I kept myself prepared for the possibility of a catch. I didn't know what yet but there was always a catch. Being talked at by powerful older men who thought they knew what place I belonged wasn't new for me, but for once I reckoned, I could put all of them in their place.

14

Nathan

The previous day at the precinct had been tiring and a total waste of time. After interviewing the male stripper's killer and thoroughly researching both their backgrounds I hadn't come up with a strategy that could link the murderers. The suspect we had in custody was on a business trip from America. He worked for a government department in New York and was in town for a meeting with head of operations at the power station, and while he was here decided to have some fun. Things didn't turn out as he planned and he couldn't offer much information to us that would get him out of this situation any time soon. He'd refused a lawyer; men like him find it hard to release control of their lives and to put trust in any sort of legal representation.

The only common trait the killers share is that they are highly paid business people from all over the world. An extensive search showed none of them had met or even crossed paths before. But the murders were too clean and organised to be a mere coincidence of chance. Maybe I was looking for a link that wasn't there? No. New clues were turning up, even if they weren't always obvious, but with Gillian assisting, I was adamant we would get to the bottom of it.

I was still waiting on the test results from the sequin Gillian had found that night and reeling from the fact Gillian was one hundred percent sure that a vampire had been killed that night. After a long night of interviews and research where no new information had come to light, Gillian wanted a day to himself. He wanted to have a few hours walking around The Vamp Strip, to become accustomed to his new surroundings. Sam commented that she thought Gillian just wanted to see all the strip clubs, of which there were many, this brought a small smile from Gillian which seemed to suggest she had hit the nail on the head.

I didn't know how funny Gillian was, I wondered if even he knew. It was pretty obvious that Sam and Gillian were becoming buddies. Those two were already giving each other a ribbing on a daily basis. Even with the on-going murders, and the pressure from the mayor and the council weighing heavily on my back, I began to believe now, more than ever, we had a fighting chance to solve this case, a case which had slowly embedded itself in my thoughts, both waking and sleeping. Murder in any form was repulsive and difficult to digest but as the killings increased, I was becoming more and more uneasy and couldn't help but think there was something bigger and more sinister at play.

Charlotte, the fast-rising liaison from The Red-Letter Alliance, had been in touch. In the past few weeks, they had received numerous complaints from sex workers who felt victimised and unsafe in their jobs, much more than usual. I agreed with Charlotte when she said this was serious, but the increasing workload made it harder and harder to prioritise the order of my days. I was starting to feel swamped.

Waking up in my cottage I should be counting my lucky stars. I didn't know which I enjoyed more, the expensive coffee machine, which was paying itself off day by day, or that this old cottage had ducted air, which made me less cranky. The sleek Italian designed chrome coffee machine stood out from the rest of the rustic looking house, which I kept neat and tidy enough, but I lacked the time to bring it back to its former glory. As I stood at the kitchen counter glancing at my emails and making bircher, the doorbell rang. On the security screen I saw Charlotte standing at the door looking rather frazzled, this was unexpected as usually she had a professional demeanour, her stylish black-rimmed glasses always made her look like she meant business.

I unlatched the door and poked my head out.

"Hello...?"

Charlotte was clutching a rather large folder. "I need to speak with you detective," the words burst out of her mouth, she leant forward and placed a hand on the door to show her intention.

"I can see you're under a lot of stress Charlotte but showing up at my house is quite out of the ordinary," I said sternly. She nodded, her eyes wide and anxious under those glasses.

I let Charlotte in and gestured her through to the kitchen.

"Would you like a coffee, it's strong and I always have one before I go to work. We both know this is very unusual and against protocol, but I'm assuming you wouldn't be here if it wasn't important, right...?"

"I have been trying to reach you for days but I'm beginning to think you are not interested in what I have to say..."

"Surely Charlotte you don't want to start the conversation on the offensive after coming to my home, right?" I interrupted, hearing my voice rise in annoyance.

"Look you have a point but I'm the wrong type of person to apologise when I'm trying to help you save lives. Unless officer... tax paying sex workers aren't your priority."

"Ok, Charlotte I can see how important this is to you. I admire your passion but this is the wrong way to go about things. I can give you five minutes now and then you need to call my office and make an appointment for a time when we can over the situation in detail. And just so we're clear I care about everyone, I'm disappointed you would suggest otherwise, especially if you want my help," losing my cool would get both of us nowhere. Charlotte stubbornly set a five-minute timer on her watch, steely determination on her face as she laid photographs of eight victims. Scanning the pictures, I knew four of the faces, one of them I recognised from last night. I already didn't like where this was going.

"Ok Charlotte what are you here to discuss, what is the significance of these pictures?"

She looked me in the eye. "You do know why I'm showing you these files right? Surely, you're not that far behind the eight ball? If you don't know what these are then I'm just wasting my time aren't I?" she reached out to take back the pictures that were on the counter.

"Calm down Charlotte, I've let you into my home uninvited, I've made you coffee, do you expect me to just open up all my files and show you everything? Take one step at a time Charlotte. Tell me your theories and I may be able to meet you halfway with some of what I know."

"Do we have a deal? Time is ticking and there are other cases I need to get to."

Pushing my hand aside she quickly spread out eight photos, the four individuals on the top line I recognised and four on the bottom line were unknown to me. "The top four hopefully you recognise, unfortunately they have all died in the last six weeks. They were all killed while providing paid services. All of them had regular clients and regular work. None had debt or any family issues as far as I know. The four you won't recognise are sex workers who have gone missing over the same period of time. From what I know they all also seemed settled within their working life."

Hearing this new information left me with an uneasiness that only came when situations didn't add up or feel right.

"So, these four people haven't been seen around at all. Have they been reported missing by their…?"

"Of course, they have officer," Charlotte was worked up, she wasn't hiding her contempt for me or the situation at all. "The families of the missing have reported them to the police as well as the Alliance, of which they are all part of. That's why I'm here. We as an organisation are used to being ignored at the best of times but this is too much. We add value to The Vamp Strip, up to fifteen percent of all trade there is sex work. Sex workers are the silent money makers yet they are being used, stretched and pulled in all directions for fun, pleasure and pain. The clients that I fight for and protect are from all races, religions, genders and species. Of course, there are some elite workers that are lucky and earn a good living but at what cost? Imagine being wined and dined for one reason only, knowing your life experience and knowledge is irrelevant and all you are is a tool for someone else's single moment of pleasure and titillation." Even though this felt like a well-rehearsed speech, the passion from Charlotte was real and somewhat moving. "Once the lust for pleasure is sated the client has no further need for you, instantly you can feel the force of them pushing you away, repulsed. As a sex worker you feel that again and again each night and day, the rejection, the loathing and the looks of regret. You're supposed to smile and forget, as if it never happened. You gather your mind and soul and go through the same motions over and over, trying to imagine yourself in a better place, but you can't escape. Even though you and your client both know that it's all a lie, a transaction. I'm not asking you to feel sorry for the workers Mr Police Officer, while you sip your expensive coffee, but respect them and what they do. They deserve that, they need that just like the rest of us."

"I'm listening now Charlotte," I sipped on my coffee not looking away once. I felt her words and I felt her pain. "Do not judge

me on your past experiences with other members of law enforce-
ment. We all get off on the wrong foot at times Charlotte, but I
promise that my team and I are paying attention to the wellbeing
of everyone who visits The Vamp Strip, no exceptions."

"You seem to be," she said, although her tone sounded like when
it came to me, the jury was well and truly out. "Now as you know
in both our lines of work there are always rumours and innuendo.
It's hard to know how to separate the truth from the lies, but in
my research, there is one name that keeps on coming up and I've
had no luck in trying to find out what it means."

Charlotte had my full attention. "What is it?"

"It sounds silly, but the name is *Blush*. Apparently, it's some
high-end exclusive club they all worked for. There is no record of
it anywhere I can find, it must pay well as they have better places
to live than me, and clearly you too," she said looking around my
cottage distastefully.

"And you're sure they all work in this same place? We haven't
been able to link any of the clients or the victims to each other in
any way whatsoever yet. If correct this could be important, I could
start to put some of the jigsaw together. It's been difficult as the
victim's profiles don't match either; different backgrounds, education, sizes and ethnicity. The only thing they have in common is
their wealth, but considering they are able to pay for sex, there's
nothing new there. So, who is your source on *Blush*?"

"Well, that's your job officer." the alarm on her watch went off.
"Right, I'm off, just in case you've misplaced my details or forgotten who I am here is my card again." Her voice was dripping with
sarcasm as she slid her card across the table and stuffed the rest of
her belongings in her bag and left. I stood there drinking my coffee, the empty eyes of the victims staring up at me, haunting me
for help. I got changed and headed in to work.

I could see Gillian waiting outside the apartment we had temporarily put him up in. He was standing against a lamppost looking at his phone, casting no shadow. These new apartment blocks and area were known locally as Newfound Land. It would take a while for me to get used to seeing apartment after posh apartment scattered around this area. None of them had windows and all had the same grey rectangle concrete shape, which made it almost impossible for anyone to tell the difference between them.

Until now there was no real need for me to come out here and see how all the wealthy vampires that came and stayed in the Hunter lived, it was eye-opening to say the least. The only thing that stood out about Gillian's living quarters was the tourist information office underneath, which even at this early evening hour was already full of vampires buying tickets to shows and attractions created especially for their tastes and particular needs.

As I pulled in front of the kerb, I saw Gillian look up and smile. I couldn't tell if it was just a front or if he was truly being himself but Gillian always seemed to be having a good time. He opened the door and jumped in. "Alright guv, I'm surprised you're a little late for our first proper date I didn't think you were that type of officer. Usually it's no swearing, looking tidy, keeping your cool. It's only been two days and you're already breaking that visage."

"Well Gillian I wish I could say the same about yourself, what '80s punk character are you trying to look like tonight? The only thing that is consistent about you is the jingle of your key chain, and the colour black."

"I'm deeply hurt mate, there's a splash of red on the front of my Iron Maiden t-shirt representing blood, thank you very much."

"Well, enough pleasantries and I deeply apologise for being two minutes late, I will tell you why after you put your seat belt on."

"Really?" he said, "I'm a fucking vampire Nate, going through a window won't bother me, I would be more surprised if you drove above forty-k Miss Daisy."

"Yes… really. I can wait here all night if I have to."

As he clicked his belt in reluctantly, I drove off as slowly as possible.

"So… how did it go yesterday, Gillian? Did you manage to get yourself acquainted with the area?"

"You know what mate, I did. I met up with Sam on her night off and she took me out and about. It was very nice of her. Good woman Sam, good fun and not afraid of anything, on the other hand her husband, well he was a bit of a bore."

"Well," I said, "Tim is like most of us humans and completely intimidated by vampires. He's a really nice guy but in his line of work as a lifeguard he doesn't get to see many vamps sun bathing and swimming in the ocean, so he may be just a bit naïve to it all."

"When you say naive, you mean boring right?" Gillian was sitting back relaxed now in the car, looking at the light the strip generated in the night sky, like our very own northern lights, but manmade and a tad crasser.

"To be honest I'm surprised he went out at all Gillian. What did you learn?"

"Ok mate, enough of the joking," his tone instantly changing to a more work like manner, it was the first time I had seen this, a softer voice and less of a cockney accent. "It's much more tense out there than I anticipated. I knew it would be a cauldron of people from everywhere in the world but due to the close proximity of all those old buildings and how the road is built it's all very crammed. The noise on the strip is intense and it's hard for me to focus on one voice. Usually, I'm able to see humans in a different way to most where, how do I explain this; you generate heat and a heartbeat, I can sense those. A bit like a dog but using sight rather than smell. When there are so many humans in one place though it all gets jumbled together and I can lose track."

"Impressive skill to have," I said. "Any more strings to your bow you would like to share?"

"All in good time mate, what I'm trying to say is it just means that spotting a killer here will be harder than I thought and I'm pretty sure the killers we are after know this. That's a problem isn't it Nate? Especially when it looks as though there is a group of vampires and humans working together. What's your theory? I'm sure you have one, right?"

Now it was my time for a wry smile, "Yes, I do, it might be a bit outlandish…"

"You had me at outlandish, go on."

This was the first time that I felt I had Gillian's full attention. It was now about an hour or so before people would start arriving on the strip. There was a strict curfew from 4am to 9pm, no matter the season. This was to ensure the safety of vamps; it wasn't good for anyone if paying customers were bursting into flames.

There was a ten-minute drive between the apartments and the strip, enough time perhaps to share my theory.

"Right Gillian, it's only a working idea but so far this is what I have. We think that high rolling vampires are hand picking their dinner. As you know criminals from all over the world are sent here for committing the most heinous crimes, the more notorious they are the happier the media and public. Now imagine paying handsomely for the right to feed and finding out you have to gnaw on a paedophile. That's not exactly an appetising meal, right? So, I think there are vampires engaging humans to set up people they want to feed on for crimes that will get them on the menu, so to speak. Considering the prison has strict rules regarding what crimes are eligible for this prison, and tax fraud or parking fines are not on the list, the set-up has to be murder. The speck of dark matter you found at the apartment the other night is the first concrete evidence of vampires being on the scene. Unfortunately, there is little evidence of any humans being at the scene let alone vampires, but I can work with that. I'm sure I'm missing some little details but that's what I've got so far."

"Well fuck me mate, I like what you're thinking, but just to be clear you have no evidence of this at all. Am I right?" he said plainly.

"Yes, I'm afraid that's right," hurting as I said it quietly. We had arrived at the police station and I reversed into my car spot.

"Well, goodo, I like a challenge, looks like I'm going to be here a while, right mate?"

"I hope not, but yes, as long as necessary," I said coolly.

Getting out of the car, I stretched out my arms in the warm air. "Do you fancy a walk down the strip before it gets crazy? There is one lead I have that I want to check out."

"Is it that sequin? Are we going to a strip club?" he said hopefully "Am I right?"

"Half right, it's from a nightclub, not a strip club, you can engage in that activity with Sam some other time. From what I understand it matches the colour of the costumes over at the '70s club where they dance to *ABBA* and the like. Right up your street, eh Gillian." I heard Gillian groan in disappointment.

It was a quiet time of the night so it only took eight minutes to walk to *Glitterball*. At peak times, when the strip was full of bodies swarming from club to club, it could take up to an hour. The only noises now were the trucks and lorries arriving to drop off much needed food and beverages for the punters.

The workers cleaning windows and roads had almost finished their daily tasks, it was just too hot to do this during the day. Some bars and clubs already had music playing, albeit at low decibel levels.

"So, Nate, is Mel the one who told you about the sequin from the nightclub, 'cos I can see him fucking standing there, puffing away on that awful vape he has in his hand. When it's quiet like now the glow of him sticks out like a sore thumb."

"No, no, he was not informed of this piece of evidence," I said knowing that someone inside the apartment was passing info onto Mel that wasn't meant for him. From Gillian's body language I sensed that he knew I was disappointed.

As we approached *Glitterball*, I smiled and reached out my hand, if there was ever a time to channel a politician it was right now.

"Hi Mel, how you doing? I'm surprised to see you here." I knew Mel didn't own this club so I was wondering why he was here.

Mel as always shook my hand firmly. He looked like he was still wearing the same clothes from the other night but clean and neat. I noticed him glance subtly over at Gillian.

"Mel, this is Gillian, my new partner. He's helping me get more acquainted with the ways of vampires."

Gillian smiled saying, "Alright mate, nice to meet ya. What flavour is that vape. I can see it wafting away from a distance". He placed both hands on Mel's while looking directly at him. This seemed to unsettle the normally cool looking owner of most of the strip.

"It's apple flavour," Mel spluttered.

"Don't blush mate, apple used to be my favourite fruit when I was alive, yum."

"Blush?"

"Yeah guv, most people do that when they see me, that is, you know, blush."

It was this exact moment that I knew that Gillian's weakest point was being tactful, he was the bluntest hammer I'd ever seen.

"Well don't let me stop you two love birds from chatting, I'm going to have a quick look in here, dying for a fucking drink."

Gillian walked past the both of us, gliding up the stairs and straight in through the glaringly pink fluorescent doors.

"Sorry about that, Mel, he's a character my new partner but we're getting used to him, especially Sam. I think they are becoming firm friends."

"So, Mel what can I do for you, don't mean to be rude but there are certain matters that I have to attend to."

"Oh, don't mind me I was just doing my nightly stroll before another busy evening ahead and thought I would say hello. Also…" here it comes, what do you want Mel, I thought. "…I know that your department is very busy, and it was only a couple of nights ago but if there is any new information about the murder you could share that would be great. My staff are getting a little worried with what is going on and I just want to settle their nerves."

He seemed to be making words up on the spot, like he was trying to slow me down. "Look Mel, you and your staff have been incredibly helpful, especially yourself, but I'm afraid I can't disclose that type of information as of yet. You have my direct number Mel, so if you want to discuss anything please call. Look I'm sorry but I have somewhere else I need to be." Smiling, I turned to walk up the steps. I could hear him murmuring some words to himself.

"Oh, one more thing have you heard from a lady called Charlotte from Red-Letter Alliance? She's been bothering some of my hard-working staff." This was said on purpose as Mel's tone had changed. He was fishing for something. "If you see her, tell her to calm down would ya."

I didn't know where Mel got off thinking that he could give me a direct order, but it seems we had reached that point and he was waiting for my reaction. I turned around and, when he saw the look on my face, for the first time in our working relationship, he knew to walk away, which he did, slowly and pedantically.

Passing through the doors into the elaborate foyer, I got a fright to find a rather angry looking Gillian standing in the old smelly cloakroom.

"Well, that was fucking strange, I don't think he said one honest word apart from not wanting Charlotte to be hanging around. You know he's full of shit, right?" Gillian said, looking on edge.

"Yes Gillian, I do know that but obviously from your demeanour you've never had to smooth things over with the devil. Also are you worried about me? Standing right next to the door, how can you hear from so far away?"

"To be honest mate I am worried if that's the calibre of friends you have. Remember I'm a vampire and I have excellent hearing and I heard that you're a terrible liar, I couldn't tell if Mel knew too though. Time will only tell."

"Is that another one of your skills you haven't told me about and… hold on, that necklace, it's glowing again?"

"Yes, yes to both your questions," he shouted, losing composure for the first time. "You're going to have to trust me Nate, and it's not a necklace, it's a cool looking chain," he said indignantly.

"Gillian, are you going to tell me what the hell is going on? You're acting weird even for you, there is just the two of us here and by the way it's definitely a necklace and it looks very quaint round your punk neck, I like the tone of the silver against the aqua blue."

Gillian remained distracted, but he did manage a low-level snarl, which I found rather an amusing response to my joke.

"Right Nate, my companion is telling me there could be trouble ahead. Stay close to me alright?" he saw me looking rather puzzled.

"Companion?" I said looking around and seeing nobody.

"Alright, alright enough of your chatting, I've had enough Jeff."

Gillian learned his head forward and took off the glowing necklace and placed it round my neck.

"Nate, meet Jeff. Jeff for fucks sake meet Nate. How's that?" he said rather flustered. "You both happy now?"

I could feel the necklace pulsing round my neck, such a strange sensation, I didn't know what to think.

"Hello," a voice pulsed inside my head, the shock almost bought me to my knees until Gillian caught me.

I looked up at Gillian, "What the hell is happening?"

"It's ok Nate. That's who's been helping me on this case. It's a lot to take in and I can't explain it all now as we are in immediate danger. Jeff has been going crazy since I've entered this foyer. There are vampires inside this club waiting for us." He placed his hands under my arms and looked directly into my eyes, "Jeff will help you; it will feel intense and surreal but go with it. He can sense danger, as of right fucking now. Do you hear me Nate?"

It felt like a cloud was sharing my brain space.

"Nate!!" Gillian said louder bringing me closer to his face. "You ready mate?"

I nodded.

"Right, let's fucking get into it!"

He flashed his large white canines. It looked like he was flexing a muscle that he was about to use. Gillian opened the heavy double doors and we walked into the most overly decorated space I had ever seen, the carpet, chairs and décor were covered in lots of bright pinks and yellows, with some tiger print thrown in just for the fun of it I presume.

The room was expansive and circular in shape with a small neon lit stage adjacent to the doors we had just walked through. A round timber dance floor, which had seen some action, took up the middle of the room. Surrounding the dance floor were single tables with high bar stools and behind those on each side of the room were two long bars with mirrored windows as their backdrops. The harsh white lights created an unwanted clash of reflections throughout the large room. Wherever you turned your head you could see yourself, unless of course you were Gillian. Looking up

I noticed there were balconies looking down on us. The star of the show was a giant glitter ball dangling down into the middle of the room.

What made the garish colours and decor stand out was the lack of people. It was still two hours away from opening so there was no one here. Some faint music was playing through the club's sound system, but that was the only noise I could hear.

Gillian leaned in and whispered, "No one is meant to know we're coming, right? Cos, I tell ya now mate, someone knows." He couldn't have sounded more like a character from *Snatch* if he tried.

Walking to the left-hand side of the dance floor, I couldn't escape my reflection bouncing around the room from mirror bar to mirror bar, it was disconcerting. There was a door where I presumed the office and staff room were located.

"Hello, is there any one here?" I shouted out trying to sound official "This is Detective Jenkins, I'm here to see..."

And with that all hell broke loose. Someone turned the music up to ear bleed level and all the lights went out instantaneously, leaving the room in almost complete darkness, all I could see was the small reflections of the giant glitter ball bouncing around the mirrors. Without notice, Gillian grabbed me with both hands and shoved me over the bar. As I went over, I could only hope that he was trying to protect me. I crashed through cocktail glasses dangling from above before I landed behind the bar on my ribs and tried to steady myself on the broken glass. As I gingerly got myself into a crouching position, Gillian jumped over the bar and landed next to me, I jumped unexpectedly.

"Sorry mate, you ok?"

I tried to reply but gunshots started firing from all around the room, smashing into the bar and splintering the wood that shielded us.

"Nathan they are everywhere, you are being flanked from the left and from above, I think there are six of them and they are moving fast," the words pulsed into my brain instantly, making me more alert. This was surreal, how a necklace could communicate with me, but now was not the time to try and analyse it.

Gillian leaned in close, a sight that would frighten most humans. "Stay behind the bar and get ready. Get that fucking vampire gun and stake ready, mate... and tell Jeff to bring his A game."

Uncasing my gun while trying to get in a position where I could protect myself, I was shaking, I had never fought one vampire, let alone multiple. I looked at Gillian and shouted, "Don't let me die Gillian, not to 'Love is in the Air', I hate this bloody song."

Gillian dashed to his left and screamed in pain as he fell to the floor shouting, "Shoot the blue lights, Fuck!" I hadn't noticed them before; I was finding it difficult to adjust to this situation. The music was suffocating, not only could I not see but I couldn't even hear my own breath. The smell of burning flesh was repugnant and I was pretty sure it was emanating from Gillian.

"Shoot now brother, now!" the voice shouted urgently in my head. In contrast to everything else, his voice was clear and precise. I could focus on that crystal-clear Southern American accent and block out the oppressing chaos surrounding me. I jumped upwards into nothingness; my weapon ready. I felt a rush of wind heading towards me and pulled the trigger of the vamp gun. I was smashed back into the mirror as blood and whatever other body fluids landed on me. The sound of a vampire combusting mingled with the music.

I staggered back, holding my gun close. With the other hand I pulled the gunk out of my eyes...

"There are two, moving quickly on your left around mid-height shoot on 3... 2... 1," the words popping in my head like statements. I fired as quickly as I could. I heard something crashing into the wall but all I could see was the flashing of my gun when

I fired shots, and the glimpses of movement and light it produced in the darkness.

I had one bullet left. I wondered if they knew. I was trying hard to control my breathing. My back was against the mirrors. I tried to stop the sounds drowning my mind. A faraway voice persisted, "The lights, the fucking lights."

The smell of burning flesh intensified. Was it from the vampires I had shot? Moving to my right with my back against the wall, I reached towards the ground, searching for Gillian.

"You're doing good brother, move slow, stay on your feet," the voice in my head was steady.

I swapped my vamp gun for my other gun so I could shoot the faint blue lights that were hanging on the celling and balconies. As they shattered, blue dust fell to the floor

"Up... now above you."

Shooting off another round I saw a vampire lunge at me through the light of the shot. He hit me full on, his hands around my neck as he smashed me to the floor, knocking the air out of me. He was terrifying to look at. Blood dripped on me from his mouth. The flesh was falling off his burning face and hands, his eyes were black and angry.

"I'm going to rip you to fucking shreds," he screamed at me. My hands gripped at his wrists trying to pull them away, I was choking, I couldn't breathe, he squeezed tighter... I ...

"Stake Nate, now!"

I pulled down my right hand and grabbed the stake round my neck. I pushed as hard as I could at his chest. There was resistance at first, then his arms relaxed slightly and I felt a small give in his chest and pushed the stake through his heart with all my might and ... he ceased to exist.

I was covered in a ball of dust, dead vampire dust, as well as dried blood. I was panting. I felt like I'd been hit by a train, I needed to rest, but there were three more, I looked up from the floor through the bedlam I hear the words, "Lights, lights," I shot the remaining blue light, then Gillian was up like a flash, returning the vamp gun to my hand and I fumbled in the darkness trying to reload it.

"Stay here mate, while I sort these fuckers out!" There were rumblings of noise in the background as the song came to an end. My head stop pulsing, a terrifying scream was followed by a thud that seemed to come from one of the balconies above.

And with that the lights were on. My eyes blinked rapidly, adjusting. I tried to regain my composure as quickly as possible while rubbing all the flesh away from my face. Gillian was standing in the middle of the dance floor covered in the blood of the two vampires whose bodies lay on the not so shiny floor. Their decapitated heads stared up at the glitter ball.

"There's one more," I said, breathing heavy from the pain in my body, holding on tightly to the gun.

"He scampered before I could get him, didn't he the prick," Gillian shouted out from across the room.

"Oh," I said slumping down on the floor with, glass, blood and dust everywhere, feeling very tired. Even though I was wearing body armour underneath my blood-soaked shirt I knew that I would be covered in bruises from the impact of being thrown around and attacked. I had never felt power like that before.

"Nice to officially meet you Detective Jenkins, you've done a great job," the voice sounded safe and reassuring in my head.

"Yeah, thanks," I said, not knowing who, what or how I was talking to anyone at all.

Gillian looked like a rock star when he leapt over the bar to see if I was ok.

"You made it mate, well done. Stake worked a treat, didn't it? You, ok? You don't look so great, almost as pale as me," this time there was no joking in his tone.

"I'm fine apart from a vampire trying to strangle me, being thrown through glass, fearing for my life and feeling that every bone in my body is broken... oh and that your necklace can talk to me. Did I forget to mention that?" I said wearily.

"I've told you it's a chain," he said smiling.

15

Nevaeh

After arriving home from the meeting with the warden, I went through some of the data they had given me, soon after I received a message from Jane saying Gary would like a meeting tonight. I don't even know why I said yes. Don't get me wrong it wasn't very often, if ever, I got to attend a place like this. Especially with my background and my paycheque, but even for one night it would be nice to see the other side, the side of humans who aren't obsessed with vampires; the ones who don't have to work in prison town. The ones who can sit on a restaurant terrace on a Tuesday night overlooking the ocean, feeling the breeze and listening to the sounds of people enjoying themselves on the shore. Tonight, I was part of that world, I could hear the joy of children eating ice-cream on the promenade. It was great to have a night off so that I could see and feel the warmth of the sun on my skin and see the sun go down while I had a chilled glass of wine. For once I didn't have to drive, being picked up in a chauffeured car was completely unusual for me. I had been in a limo once before with Helen when I tagged along on one of her dates. I missed her, it was good seeing her today, but it would have been better to see her here.

I felt reasonably relaxed even though I had no idea why Gary had invited me. It always seemed the people around me thought they knew what was best for me. You're strong Nev, you're relia-ble Nev, you're a fuckwit Nev. Where were these people when I'd needed them the most? The fuckwits had always been there, but this was new. This was the first time I'd felt I could control the space around me. Fuck it, I couldn't fight cancer or a heart attack, but I was well up for this battle. And that was why I was sitting here in a pretty turquoise dress I had bought from David Jones that afternoon. I normally shopped at Big W but with the sud-den pay rise, why not, even if the staff looked at me extra carefully and seemed surprised when they saw me pay full price rather than putting it on lay by.

Someone with Gary's privilege had probably been warned to steer clear of a girl like me. People like him wore it all over their handsome faces. My first reaction is to tell them to fuck off but if I could make Gary find a reason to release or help Helen, I would go on all the dinners he wanted. I didn't know if he had any in-digenous girls hanging around in his circles at Kirribilli but I'd be happy to tick that box. It didn't hurt that he was charming and attractive either.

As I sat there waiting the doubt set in. What if there was some sort of sinister plot behind their wooing of me? Maybe I should just shut up and enjoy my drink, focus on the wine and the view. Gary was late. I had picked out the most expensive white wine on the menu, and while I sipped, I couldn't help notice how pretty it was here. The restaurant's terrace only had six tables, tea light can-dles flickered softly on their crisp linen tablecloths, it was all very elegant and calming. As the sun set, I relaxed with my Semillon to the sounds of the waves and the chilled music playing in the background, the dangling fairy lights began to shine down on me and the other patrons.

Even though this was a new experience for me I wasn't intim-idated. I didn't know where I belonged in life, but I knew I didn't belong in the gutter. As I looked out onto the ocean thinking about the silly things I had done on that beach with a bottle of Sambuca and a joint, I heard a suave voice.

"Hi Nev, you look wonderful," were the words that came out of Mr Dreamboat's mouth. I turned round and I burst out laughing. He was wearing white freshly pressed pants, secured with a brown leather belt, tucked in to this was a light salmon shirt which he rolled the arms up to show off his lean fit arms.

"Is there something funny?" Gary asked with an amused look.

"I've never been to dinner with a man wearing white pants before," I said jesting.

Gary looked at ease as he placed his swanky cashmere pullover on the back of the wooden chair. He sat down, looking like he belonged here. I could see that he enjoyed being ribbed.

"Just so you know I have a couple more pairs of white pants at home if you ever want to borrow them, though they might be too big for you. I can see you're enjoying the wine."

"Oh, don't worry about me Gary, I can hold my liquor, it's just helping me loosen up my lips but I'm only ahead of you by a couple of minutes," I met his eyes, trying to gauge his response.

"Well, Nev if we could stop the jesting for a minute, I'm glad you came, there is a lot to discuss."

"Thank you for asking me, just so I'm clear this is just a business meeting, correct?"

Smiling he said, "Well Nev aren't you a straight shooter. If you're asking if I take all my clients and colleagues here the answer is no, but if you want to go somewhere else, the local RSL is also an option."

I could tell he wasn't joking, that he was used to all types of surroundings. Gary was extremely self-assured, and I was still wondering what had made him want to see me. Was it really just business?

"So Nev, how did you find today? Have you had time to process what we're after and what we need?"

"I will be honest, not entirely. I've only flicked through the documents. And I'm sorry if I sound crass but it seems you want me to become a high-end salesperson. Is that right?"

"You're not entirely wrong Nev, by the way do you even know what you're drinking or did you just pick the most expensive wine by glass like I used I do as a kid…that's the first time I've seen you blush," he smiled as he topped up my glass and poured one for himself. "There is some truth to what you're saying but when you have time to look deeper into what we're attempting to do, it has the potential to change the world for vampires. Think about it, having some of the most wealthy and powerful vampires on our own database, the information we could gather and control is immense. I know that you haven't read the small print yet Nev, but I should point out you will receive a generous share package upon implementation of the project."

If this was his hard sell, it didn't feel too hard, what was I missing? What would I find out later down the line? "I'll be honest Gary I'm not sure why you and others feel that I'm so important to the program. Right up front you should know why I'm here, and it's not for a dinner date and your fancy looks," I said. "I'm here for my friend Helen. If there is anything you can do to help her or get her out of her situation at the prison I need to know."

"Well thank you for your candidness Nev, I appreciate it. It's something I don't often see, or practice, in my line of work. I admit it makes me feel a tad uncomfortable but it's a refreshing change." He was looking straight at me now, making me feel like I was the only person on this terrace despite it being a busy night.

"Let me try and make you realise the power you have here. The warden and I, or in fact anyone for that matter, can't help Helen, but you can. You're the only person in this whole justice system that communicates and relates with vampires like they aren't second-class citizens. I mean my God I have tried but I just can't let my defences down. Anytime I'm in close proximity to a vampire I want to run." Gary was shaking his head as he spoke, and I could tell that it really bothered him.

"Helen I'm afraid is out of our reach, for the moment. As you well know, once a vampire, especially one of high status has their eyes set on a commodity, there is little chance of changing their minds. This is where your skills come in. Study the inmate roster and see if you can persuade the vampires in their selections."

That made perfect sense to me. If I spoke with Lucy, maybe I could find a way in, only I didn't have a real relationship with her due to the hours she worked. Like the warden and Jane, she worked mainly nine to five in the prison's communication centre, while I worked at night and was mainly on the floor. When she wasn't at work, she could be found at corporate functions and formal events trying to entice new vampires to our offering. I had heard that she travelled overseas on occasion in order to close lucrative contracts with new clients. I couldn't think of anything worse.

Lucy was the head of the PR team and the success of the prison was shared between her and Dave. Dave made sure the prison ran smoothly from day to day, but Lucy made sure the vampires' victims would be highly sort after. Her eyes must have lit up when she saw Helen, she would be able to auction her to the highest bidder. That's one of the rumours I heard. Apparently, there were high-end groups of vamps who would bid off the books to get what they desired. There was no proof of this, but I was pretty sure it was going on, and there was no way that Lucy couldn't be involved.

Gary continued. "You laugh and joke with the vamps, help them settle in. You even do a prison tour so they can settle into their new surroundings. I also know that you're the connection with the hotels, restaurants and bars to help make their stay as comfortable as possible. I can tell Nev, you have morals when most of us don't. To be frank, all of us struggle with holding the higher ground, especially with the extreme wealth vampires throw into the mix. I … sorry Nev I haven't stopped talking, are you ok? You look sad."

"No one is a second-class citizen, Gary. I'm not afraid of vamps or anyone. I've been considered a second-class citizen my whole life. I know you mean well but the only way we can make change is by making the change ourselves. I know from experience that if you talk down to someone you can't earn their respect. Nor should you."

"I'm sorry Nev I don't mean to offend you…"

I placed my hand on his and said, "You don't, Gary, your ridiculously expensive jumper offends me more. Saying you're not a racist doesn't mean that you're not one. It's the same with the vamps. We were more than happy to see them on the side-lines or even hunt them down like animals. That's what we humans do; we lash out at the unfamiliar. Now let's be clear. They have the power to destroy a lot of us humans without even a second thought, but they don't. Do you know why Gary?" His eyes held mine. I had him under my spell, which was nice. "Believe it or not, vampires are scared as well. All you have to do is listen. The longer they live, the more they see, the more fragile they become in the face of death. It starts to haunt them. Imagine gaining more physical power but also growing more accustomed to the many ways by which you can die."

He just sat there staring at me, taking in all I had just said.

"Wow Nev," he said quietly. "So that's your power, then Nev, it's your empathy. You know you can't fake that and that's what the vampires, and now I, see you have in abundance. What I am saying is that I really want to help you. I think this could be a great venture and it would be so nice to show the likes of Jane that they can shove their condescending tone up their tight rigid arses."

That made me spit out half my wine, "How dare you make me

spill my drink, Gary. I'm not sure where you're from Gary but its sacrilege spilling alcohol. Besides I didn't know you didn't like Jane, I thought she was just rude to people who are below her?"

"No Nev, she's just a bitch to everyone. And if you truly took drinking seriously you wouldn't have spilt any."

A waitress, who had been hovering for a gap in conversation, jumped in and introduced herself while handing out the menus. She spoke about the weekly specials and expertly mopped up my spilled wine.

Gary scanned what was on offer, "Would you like to take a look Nev or shall we order the most expensive item on here?"

"You're a funny one Gary. I'm wondering who is going to get in more trouble, me or you?"

"I have no idea what you're on about Nev, I'm just here on a work meeting with a colleague, I'm even expensing the whole evening." He raised his glass. Gary was too sure of himself. The troubling thing was I liked it.

I raised my glass to his. "Well… we will see Gary, won't we?"

Being chauffeur driven twice in the one night was something I could get used to. I asked the driver to let me out at the beach, near the area where I used to teach surfing. This spot reminded me the most of Helen. I had a good night with Gary and was a little tipsy after drinking some of the best wine of my life. I didn't want to go home yet; I wanted to listen to the ocean and watch the waves in the moonlight.

There was a lot for me to process today and walking along the sand with no one around apart from the crash of the waves had always relaxed me since a young age. It's where I used to go to think about Mum when she was going through chemo, whether that was to cry or scream.

In the years after Mum's death, it was where Helen and I used to smoke drugs and bring guys, well the guys were mostly there for her. Even through it was warm tonight I could still feel the coolness of the sand between my toes. It made me feel alive. I sat down on a ridge of the sand close to the lap of the waves and placed my shoes next to me while I looked at the ocean.

"Wow Gary," I said out loud. A bit of a tool , but a tool that for some reason I liked. Also, Jane, Jesus, I could already see the arguments that we were going to have with each other. There were so many thoughts racing in my mind all at once it was hard to think straight.

I closed my eyes and shut all the noise out apart from the image of Helen. It was good seeing her today no matter how much it hurt at the same time. I placed my hands over my face while rubbing my eyes. When I opened my eyes, I saw the silhouette of a man standing a few feet away from me.

I sat for a couple of seconds making sure that I had the right focus, rubbing my eyes again.

"Hello Nevaeh, it's nice to meet you. I was going to say that I'm sorry to have startled you but that would be a lie, wouldn't it" the man said as though we were already acquaintances.

"Hi. Is there something I can help you with? Growing up on the beach I'm quite used to men trying to get the upper hand on me, so no, I don't scare easy." I said, not being afraid at all. I rarely was these days, even though I spent most of my waking life with vampires.

The man let out a loud laugh. "Well Nevaeh. Firstly, I am no man. I am a person of the dusk. I was born in darkness and that is where I must stay. I had heard through my contacts you are special and that has been proven to be correct."

"Have I met you at work?" I got to my feet. "Sorry I have met so many vampires I can't remember everyone. Can I help you?" this was becoming strange now.

"No, we have not met. I also know you remember every one of the vampires you meet as it is in your DNA. I recently made an offer for Helen the prison could not refuse and I am now the one who holds the bond and rights to Helen. You may call me Blake."

"Fuck," I said which bought a smile to his face. This was my chance to save Helen or at least try.

He slowly started walking towards me. As he moved into the light of the moon, I could finally see a dark haired, baby-faced vampire, he couldn't be much older than eighteen.

"I'm here to offer a trade. Helen's freedom for a name."

"Of course, mate, no problem. Would you like my Netflix login or maybe a kidney while you're at it?"

"No just one name please Nevaeh and your beautiful friend's neck is safe. Did I mention how sweet she tasted, like… mmm coconut."

"Is this how you interact with people who you want things from? Does this technique normally work?" My calm and flippant nature seemed to catch him off guard.

"Nevaeh, you really are not in any way wary of me, are you?" He moved ever so slightly closer. I gripped my shoe in my hand, ready to nail him in the head.

"I have been around a very long time and I have never been as surprised or as intrigued as I am right now. I have absolutely no indication of what you are thinking or what you're planning to do, this is unique for someone like me who is as old as your ancestors. It is clear that you cannot be intimidated."

"What is it you want Blake? I won't do anything illegal."

"Well Nevaeh, that's for you and your conscience to decide. One vampire is all I want. Once you hear their name I will need to know where they can be found. That is all."

Raising my voice "That's all? What are you going to do to this vampire?"

"Just one name Nevaeh." He seemed to be getting slowly closer.

"Alright! What fucking name?"

"Thomas Malcolm," he said softly.

16

Alfred

No more buzzing or ringing from work on my phone. Please no more. Everything seemed to be falling into place. I was so happy. I was taking charge of my future which meant Mum wasn't happy. "Why would you want to stay longer?" she said. She always seemed to have an innate ability to suppress my happiness. The not insignificant sums of money I sent her usually managed to stop the constant chatter of negativity, even if she didn't like the fact banks no longer used cheques. All of that was ok though because I was taking a gamble. I didn't see any reason why not, no matter how Mum whinged. I had no one I was close to back there.

It was the second friendly cricket game between the power company and the prison. Lucy from the prison arranged the games for charity. They were taking a leaf out of the companies of yesteryear, like the steel factory and the coal mines, who in their prime had employed a hefty percentage of the Hunter's male workforce. They used to arrange family days in an attempt to show they cared for their overworked and underpaid employees. Local rivalry ensured during games of cricket or soccer, originally arranged as a day of fun they often turned into bitter affairs. With the closure of the steel factory and huge layoffs at the mines the days of bringing workers together had faded into the past. But with the rise of the revitalised prison and our new shiny power station I was optimistic we could come together again as a community united. Hopefully tonight in the heart of the city, we could raise a lot of money for the area's impoverished families. It was a win for each institution involved. Some of the players were workers like me, who spent their days in the office, the others were engineers and front-line workers who ensured the power station ran safely and efficiently. The fact the station's CEO, the warden and the mayor had all come along made tonight's friendly game more of a star-studded event. The warden's confidence in front of a camera made it hard for anyone else to shine as brightly as he did.

What started as office jesting and teasing between loudmouth John and I now had the local media in a frenzy. John spoke with one of his mates who worked at the prison and they managed to get the game of the century together so the station could smash the prison's ass at cricket. Lucy, who was in charge of public relations at the prison, didn't take long to formulate a plan of action to get the most out of this occasion. She took charge of promotions and also set some rules, including only three vampires were allowed on each team at one time, to give some sort of balance to the proceedings. I thought the whole event sounded awesome and was keen to participate.

I was very excited about the whole affair until I got down to the part in the rules with those dreaded words for a constant loner like myself, 'plus one'. Instantly the self-doubt began to creep in. I think my assistant, Linda, read this on my face and said the kindest words I had heard from an older female for a long time;

"Alfred my dear, you're a nice young man and I know you don't think so, but a lot of your work colleagues, including myself, think you are quite the find. We are lucky you have led us to become the number one in efficiency in the state and we are well on the way to being in the top five in the world. I know I'm just good old Linda, who has more long service leave than some of the young workers have years, but I hear and see things happening. I've learnt long ago dear to never judge a book by its cover and I say go for it. We all have our quirks, and we deserve to be happy. Bring anyone you like Alfred and I do mean anyone. No one will judge, and if they attempt to, I will be on them in a flash."

It bought a tear to my eye to hear this. I realised she was taking in a lot more than just what I was saying. Linda also paid my expenses so would have a fair idea of where my earnings went. I was always thinking I was being judged by everyone and sometimes forgot to have an opinion of my own. I had put Linda into a bracket, for example, even before I met her. She would be too old and set in her ways and would hold me back. How wrong I was. Even loudmouth John and I were getting along, we would never be mates but that's ok, you can't be friends with everyone you meet. I touched the note I still had in my pocket from Samuel from our night in *The Great Gas*.

I had to be either brave or foolish to take Samuel up on his offer, time would tell. I met Samuel on our first official date for a quick drink at one of his favourite bars, it was unusual in that it was one of the unassuming establishments on The Vamp Strip. A little alleyway gem called *The Town Hall*, to the locals it was the *Townie*. It was behind the old council building, a heritage listed stone building that would have been a landmark in its day but now was completely rundown and dated.

When the influx of visitors and 'trashy' people like me arrived in vast numbers the locals had to hide somewhere where they could buy a schooner for less than nine dollars. This was the place, a place where vampires or humans could come after a long day at work. The bar was always open and the friendly staff did not judge those who worked on the strip, the sex workers, the chefs, the cleaners and other bar staff – the real underbelly of The Vamp Strip.

We slid ourselves onto the soft leather of a stylish wooden booth. I could not tear my eyes away from Samuel's majesty as we sipped at our cold beer. The bar's charm of being rough and ready appealed to me, as did the fact they had a choice of only three beers and two wines. I couldn't have asked for a more perfect evening.

That had been our first date, but tonight was a much bigger affair for me. I had told Samuel that it was a work function and rather than being deterred it only seemed to make him keener. I was worried but so far Samuel had not asked for anything from me, just my puny body and I was more than ok with that. I had some niggling doubts in the back of my mind I may be being used, yet I hoped the questions I dreaded wouldn't come, that being, "Alfie could you help me out?" or "Alfie can you get this one?"

Approaching the cricket ground, I couldn't help but notice the scope of tonight's event. Linda had said that there would be a lot of people here but I was flabbergasted. Tonight's event wasn't in the usual spot out near the power station but at a small local club ground in a suburb nearer the coast. The smell was different here, sweeter and less dry than that of the power station. The sea air mixed with the aroma of fresh cut grass relaxed me, and I held Samuel's hand as we got off the train. As we left the station we could see the stadium across the road, which was decked out to the nines.

This part of the city had not felt the influx of vampire money as of yet. While walking down the hill with other punters and players you were hit by the aroma of a sausage sizzle being put on by the club to raise funds.

Seeing as The Vamp Strip was out in the desert you didn't often find vampires here in the middle of suburbia, and with this area being in the vicinity of a school, vamps were usually not allowed within a five-kilometre radius. As the vampires were here for one night only, the children were prohibited from coming, all to make sure there was no repeat of the Sugar Reef incident of '65.

The original idea had been to hold a game of cricket every Thursday night as a team bonding exercise but morphed into something else entirely. The project I was implementing at the power station would cut down energy usage at the prison, thus saving them millions a year. As a result, the higher ups at the prison thought it would be a good idea to pump some of these savings back into the local community, including make a gala of the cricket. So, the weekly game became a grand event. When it came to generating good PR the prison didn't hesitate. The warden was making the most of it, his freckly face and wispy hair turned up everywhere. No matter how hard the mayor tried even he couldn't compete, Warwick was always first to be front and centre, working the crowds with his high-wattage smile, undoubtedly, we would see the same tonight.

I was looking forward to playing cricket against the prison as I had never met any of the employees from over there. I'd spoken to Lucy a few times, and a sour sounding person called Jane, who had provided me the prison's power usage data and helped me with the implementation process.

We arrived at the base of the hill and I stood there holding Samuel's hand, nervously looking at the crowd mingling together, I was beginning to wonder if this was good idea or not.

"It's ok Alfie, everything will be fine," Samuel said in his handsome Aussie way.

Smiling and nodding we made our way through the busy noisy crowd, past the many food trucks with their enticing smells to the VIP entrance where I showed my badge and we were admitted and shown to my team's area, some of whom were already there. I had never bought a partner before either, especially a male vampire partner, but I thought what the hell. I knew the person I was, how I appeared, and I was desperate to show off a little with who

I was bringing as my plus one.

We walked over to the roped off area with its tables and chairs. A makeshift tarpaulin had been set up as rain protection, which was pointless, as it almost never rained here.

I could see Linda and her partner as well as some new faces I hadn't seen before. The power station was a massive place where you could work for years and never see someone who had also worked there as long as you had. I was pretty sure that of all the players wearing our team's bright pink colours were of the highest calibre which meant, hopefully, I wouldn't have to show myself up too much.

As I introduced Samuel to my fellow work colleagues, I saw Linda look over and mouth the words, "Very nice," which made me relax. We mingled for a bit then I than heard the unmistakable voice of loudmouth John.

"It's ok, I'm finally here everyone, you can all take a breather now that the best player has arrived," he boasted. Unfortunately, I had heard that he was a very good wicketkeeper even though he was in his late forties and didn't look in tiptop condition, and he looked sturdier and stronger than myself. When Samuel looked at me, he made me feel six-feet-tall but the real truth of the matter was when I saw reflections of us together, I couldn't help but feel Samuel's tall broad body made my scrawny features stand out even more.

John walked over with his wife, who was a short but fit looking woman who didn't look at all like she belonged with someone as uncouth as John. But like I said before, who in this day and age could say what a couple should look like? Races, species and genders were blending together, it had taken long enough, especially where I hailed from.

My mum and her friends thought they meant well when they said things like, "I have no problem with gay people but I wouldn't wish that life on anyone," or "They're a lovely person, well, for someone who's black." I had heard that casual bigotry all my life but now I had found the courage to be myself I was not going to tolerate that behaviour anymore.

"Hello John," I said as he walked over with his arm out stretched to shake my hand. "I've heard from yourself, countless times, you're the best keeper in the state. Time to put your money where your mouth is as I think we will have our work cut out for us tonight, but it should be fun." I smiled and introduced myself to John's wife. John had been too busy to attend our first game, citing a chronic injury. After hearing we played very well his injury disappeared, as well as his excuses.

John shook my hand and slapped me on the back firmly. "You're kidding me aren't you Alfie? From the reports I've gathered from the power station you worked at back in Essex, you're a nifty little spinner, I have high hopes for us tonight." I was quite shocked that loud mouth John was complimenting me in public. Maybe he was on his best behaviour in front of his wife like I was in front of my Mum.

"I must say Alfie," John said rather loudly "you've done quite well for yourself with a tall strapping partner like Samuel. When I first saw you both together from behind, you looked like a schoolboy out after bedtime holding his dad's hand," he said laughing.

"Oh, do shut up for once," said Linda rather loudly, causing laughter. I saw John blush for the first time.

It all felt quite surreal and a bit like I was having an out of body experience, looking down on myself I couldn't believe I had a partner, well maybe, and was out with work colleagues who didn't seem to be judging me, on a social night I had organised. I had to pinch myself.

Getting ready I saw Samuel talking to a lady rather passionately. I instantly began to think the worst, that it was some ex-partner or something. I couldn't help but go to a dark place straight away.

He's a handsome man and it was bound to happen. There were no vampires within my work circles at the power station but of course there were plenty who worked in the plant itself. Being a vampire usually meant being exploited in the workplace. Due to humans' fear of the unknown work options were limited, with their strength, vampires found themselves only being offered low paid manual labour positions. Wanting to earn more money was why a lot of them worked in the sex industry instead. Imagine having a great job, a life you loved, then being turned into a vampire and your past, and all you achieved, just slips away. It's an enormous struggle vamps, like Samuel, find themselves dealing with every day.

Samuel made his way over to me while I was checking myself, and equipment, one final time.

"You know Alfie," he said, while playing with my collar. "You look quite hot in that pink outfit."

"Samuel," I said exasperated, "please try not to be so naughty around my workmates. I'll get in trouble."

"You're kidding Alfie, you've just gone from a five out of ten to at least a six and a half while hanging around with me," he said rather curtly.

Lowering my head and feeling a little taken aback, I said, "I was a five really even with my slick black hair."

Samuel let out a snort of laughter. "Oh Alfie, there's no need to be hurt, I'm here, aren't I?" He put his hand to my cheek. "And now you mention it wearing clay in your hair brings you down to a four out of ten."

"Oh, for god's sake Samuel it's an organic product!"

People were coyly looking at us while we teased each other, normally I wouldn't like it but tonight it was different. It was strange standing there with humans drinking beers and fancy cocktails while vampires drank ice-cold shots of blood, as casual as day, odd how it seemed normal, but now I suppose it was.

"I know we said that we would leave the past in the past but who is that you were just talking to?"

"Her name is Charlotte, Alfie. She's from the Red-Letter Alliance. They help workers like me in the industry. To be honest I was surprised to see her here. We were just having a chat about some vamp issues but nothing to worry about Alfie, everything is fine," he said flashing a smile at me.

"Issues? With *Blush*?"

"No Alfie," he said softly "About the murders that have been happening on The Vamp Strip. Wanting to know I had any info, but…" he looked away with sadness on his face that I hadn't seen before.

"Sorry I don't mean to pry. I don't really know what I'm doing as you can probably tell. I hadn't heard about any murders. Can I help in any way?"

Grasping my hand and squeezing tightly "No Alfie, just be the wonderful soul that you are."

The crowd was at its peak now, there was electricity in the air as our team were getting ready. The VIP area was full of dignitaries who I'd not seen before. I had never played cricket under the lights before and as our team entered the field of play to the sounds of 'Howzat' by *Sherbet* and scattered applause, I thought to myself, the night can't get much better.

17

Claire

I was so pleased to be running a food truck at the charity cricket match, serving gourmet sausage sandwiches, made using only fresh, local ingredients, with all proceeds going to our club. As a committee, we couldn't be more delighted. The pain of losing Tom was still there but nights like these, along with the support of my friends, colleagues and the community spirit of the club, was helping me get through this tough time. To think this club was just a bunch of misfits from all walks of life; teachers like me, business owners, tradies, and everything else in between. We were a family of sorts with the common goal helping others and supporting our community.

The prison liked to take centre stage, cementing its' position of power in the city, the self-christened new saviour. To be fair it was generating jobs, providing a steady income for families that had long suffered. Nights like this existed to show how much the prison could give, and to hide the things they may take. I see the very handsome, but untrustworthy, warden on TV and it sounds like he's running for mayor. He knows he has a stranglehold on the city and he has no intention of letting it go. His style is to butter us up with smiling speeches and by putting on events like this. The public image of the prison was obviously the driving force but the club would take any money we could to make us a better place for the community.

It was strange seeing vampires again for the first time in a while. I liked living near the coast and away from the dirty, dust ridden vampire town that had taken Tom away from me. I was beginning to feel like myself again, my psychologist wasn't so sure, but I was focused, I was doing the best I could by creating lists and checking then off as soon as possible.

At one point, while serving the hungry hoards from the side of the truck, I thought I saw my brother in the crowd. I had only seen him once, briefly, since Tom's funeral. We got on, but we were both so busy in our daily lives that we never had time to catch up. It's strange having a sibling that you are fond of but never really talk too, my brother had reached out more than once after Tom was taken away from me and even though I knew it was from a good place it felt hollow. So even though I saw him at the match I didn't call out.

We were one of only a few community AFL clubs up here in NSW, which made this sudden charity windfall all the more welcome, cash flow was always an issue. Even though tonight's gala event was cricket we would take what we can.

Thinking of the contract I had entered into with the vampires it finally felt like the last threads of guilt were slowly ebbing away from me. Of course, there was still some nagging remorse around being a co-conspirator in the demise of Tom's killers. Would there have been enough evidence for them to be found guilty of their crimes? Did I really need to take the law into my own hands? It's not like I needed the money I received for the vamp's death, but I took it anyway and the joy of their execution was an unexpected bonus. I guess at some level I will always question the decision I made but mostly I am at peace. Don't get me wrong, that overbearing vampire Thomas Malcolm had been a bit too pushy for my liking, he made it difficult to say no, no wonder he made a living doing what he does.

The money I received had helped to pay off some of the mortgage and make some home improvements, including added security for my sweet girls. Even through the grief I felt as though fortune was on my side in lots of small ways, doors just seemed to keep opening up for me. I was getting great job offers unsolicited and I got promoted at work and knowing how the school council worked it felt like someone was manipulating my life for the better. The death of Tom had made me less ruthless in how I now spoke and engaged with people, I felt like I had more empathy and that I could relate to others more. I was being less of a stuck-up bitch, which I knew I could be at times. The company Tom part owned paid out on a life insurance policy I didn't even know that Tom had taken out. If I had known all this before I agreed for those vampires to be killed, would I have still gone ahead with their deaths? I knew the answer and it scared me.

Looking around and seeing the smiling faces of people I did and didn't know I felt a familiar presence; I now knew the benefactor of my good fortune. We only encountered each other briefly, and even though I didn't possess the superpowers or skills of a vampire I still knew when someone was paying me attention.

As I handed out food to hungry punters, I could feel someone's gaze upon me. It felt like I could sense him even though I couldn't see him, which sounds ridiculous. Somehow, I just knew he was getting closer, I could feel him approaching, gliding through the throbbing crowd of people swirling around the food trucks? But how? And then, as I was handing out sandwich after sandwich to human hand after human hand it changed abruptly; a long slender graceful hand was before me, the hand of a vampire. The hand of Thomas Malcolm.

"Hello Claire, my dear, how are you tonight? Quite busy, aren't you?" his pompous European voice grated on my nerves.

18

Nevaeh

"Fuck me why am I even here? Why are you even here? And most importantly what the fuck are you wearing? It's a cricket game not some swanky polo game you play in some posh northern suburb of Sydney," I said rather abruptly.

"Well in fact, Nev, I think I look rather fetching in this sporting garb and to be honest this is similar to what I wore playing cricket for my private school." Gary said in jest, giving me a twirl.

"Oh, and one more thing Nev, I renew my polo membership every year my darling," he said trying to sound even more posh than he already did, which he instantly failed at.

"Oh, shut up, you wanker," laughing at him prancing around. He seemed to be able to make me smile, which I liked.

He even managed to look good in the emerald green cricket uniform that reminded me of the uniform the inmates wore. I think it was supposed to represent that we are all as one, the workers, the vampires and the victim. Bullshit! I didn't want to be tarnished with the same brush as the humans we had holed up at the prison and the more I got to know the warden and his annoying assistant Jane I didn't want to be associated with them either. I didn't trust them, there was definitely more going on at the prison than I knew. I was sure that the new VIP scheme I was helping set up was a front, but for what I didn't know.

This whole day felt like the storyline of a fairy tale. With the mysterious vampire Blake turning up unannounced like he did, me being offered a promotion out of the blue. Blake with his soft and precise words made me think this wasn't a coincidence. I think I intrigued him as much as he did me. I fucking knew there would be catch with all this good fortune. I had my eyes open but even this surprised me. I hadn't been able to find out anything about this Thomas Malcolm as of yet but I was hoping he would be easy to dislike and double cross. I didn't want to lose sleep over the fact I was going to have to give him up for Helen's freedom. It's why I couldn't commit to Gary, or anyone else for that matter, I didn't know who to trust, but I knew it wouldn't be that fucking old wind bag Jane.

"Well blow me down, Gary, I would never have guessed that you went to some private school mummy and daddy paid for. I've only heard a voice like yours on *Downton Abbey*," I said as I put on cricket pads and a helmet.

"That's harsh even for you Nev. What do you think you're doing right now?" he smirked.

"I told you," I said, raising my voice over the crowd noise, "I don't know what I'm doing, I've never even played this stupid game before."

He put his strong right hand gently on my sweaty arm. "It's ok Nev take a breath," he said calmly. "We're the tail-enders which means we bat last; we don't have to get ready until right at the end. We can just sit here in our cheap white plastic garden chairs and talk about work, the program and maybe us?"

He chuckled a low laugh when he saw me roll my eyes in the back of my head. I liked Gary but I wasn't ready yet. Work was completely crazy. I was doing two jobs; the day-to-day running of the feeding zone and setting up this reward system. Jane wanted a morning and evening briefing every day, there were no days off. Dave was told that I no longer worked for him, he totally understood but there was no one lined up to replace me. I couldn't leave him in the lurch like that. I had worked too hard to let my feeding zone go to shit; I was happy to stick around and help out.

I was under the pump and copping a lot of heat, which was mainly coming from Jane's direction, Gary's support was helping me implement the schedule I had created but it was a massive job. He thought I may be moving too fast but I saw a chance here to develop a first-class system where every vampire whose financial status met the guidelines would be receiving an invitation to our new club.

Gary was happy to take things slowly, but he was making it clear in his polite way that he was interested in me. At first, I thought he was joking and just wanted a bit of rough, and as soon as he swooned his way into my underwear, he would be off. I had worked my way up from the gift shop through hard work, not by with sleeping with anyone. I didn't want that to change with Gary. I knew how the situation would look to people like Jane but the opinions of others have never bothered me.

There had been hardly any boys in my life. I made no time for them. The truth be told I thought I was in love with Helen, but I had not had feelings for other women. Did it matter anymore? Why not just be happy with any soul who makes you happy no matter their race or gender? Telling Helen my feelings for her could have ruined our friendship and love for each other. When you have no one apart from your mother, who is then taken away from you, you crave love in any way possible and Helen and her dad had given me that.

"Gary you're very sweet, and even cute in those very tight revealing pants, but right now…"

"I know I know. I'm sorry Nev. Your good company and fun to

be around and I wouldn't want to jeopardise that right now," he said looking directly into my brown eyes. I felt very content standing there close to him.

"Don't tell anyone," I whispered "but you're a nice guy. I promise I won't tell a soul though."

Gary for once looked flustered and was fidgeting with his guard box, which made me laugh more. "Well, that's enough of that, would you like a drink to settle our nerves?" He said walking away to the open bar.

Gazing around the crowd of people attending tonight I couldn't believe I was here as VIP, how the hell did that happen? Lost in thought I didn't notice the person beside me.

"Hi Nevaeh, I'm Lucy it's nice to meet you," smiling as she reached out her hand.

"Sorry, I was in my own world. It's nice to finally meet you. I've heard so many good things." Our PR powerhouse was a tall and athletic woman with Mediterranean features, she reminded me of Helen, and had a firm grip as she shook my hand. Immaculate and fashionable she gave off the air of someone not to be messed with, there was something intriguing about her I just couldn't put my finger on.

"Are you managing to have fun? I'm never really able to switch off at events like these. Lots of the faces that are here are the same people that I have to wine and dine for the prison," Lucy said as more of as a statement rather than a complaint while looking over at the warden, who seemed to have a crowd of people and vampires under his spell while he told jokes and stories. The ever-present Jane was standing next to him diligently.

"To be honest Lucy, I have learnt to be myself no matter what the occasion from a young age. People have always looked at me with judgement but I don't let that stop me. So yes, even though I wouldn't normally be at a place like this I have adapted to be able roll with the punches. And for once the punches seem to be good, which let me tell you, hasn't always been the case."

Lucy gave a small smile like she knew where I was coming from, "You know, I've worked long and hard over the years to have absolute control of my life. I don't pander to anyone whether that's been at university or in the army, I have never been very good at talking to uptight pricks or condescending bitches like Jane."

That made me snort laugh like a pig, which bought glee to Lucy's face. "I'd rather be back fighting with the army in Fiji than at events like these. Even with the atrocities and evil I saw there at least I knew where I stood, unlike here." Looking at me intently she said, "How do you do it Nevaeh? Talk to vampires and not be repulsed like other humans?" She sipped her champagne while looking in the warden's direction again, but this time with contempt, I couldn't see who this was directed at.

"I don't get repulsed easily and I know more humans that are scum compared to the vampires I know. Vamps can sense they don't intimidate me and as result have always treated me with respect."

"That's very impressive. It's probably why you're so good at making vampires feel at ease at the prison. You know it's a shame that we haven't met sooner. Perhaps we can go out for a drink sometime so I can pick your brain a little?"

Lucy was right, it was nice talking to her and I hadn't really had a female friend since Helen. At that moment Gary re-joined me with drinks.

"Here you go Nev, sorry it took so long, I ran into some friends from my old polo days. Hi Lucy, good to see you again," he said as charming as ever.

"Polo friends? Could you be any posher Gary," which made them both laugh.

"I must go mingle, but I have your details Nevaeh, we will catch up, yes?"

"That would be great Lucy, see you soon," I said feeling quite happy.

"I tell you what Nev, people warm to you for who you are even after only meeting you briefly, it's almost like you're beginning to belong in this crowd. Before long I will be buying you a pink polo shirt," Gary said cheekily while passing me my drink.

"You think?" giving Gary a stern look while I sipped my beer.

"Alright enough jesting, tell me who's part of our team and who are the opposition?"

"You're the one with all the information, I have no idea who is on the other team. They're over the bridge near the sand dunes, I never go out that way."

"You know Nev, people are allowed to enjoy themselves and not everyone has an ulterior motive. This can be fun if you let it be, you're allowed to..."

"Wow you are so soppy," I said trying to change the subject as quickly as possible. I didn't like my feelings being on show. "Let's mingle after the game. I can see some vampires here that I haven't met before."

I think Mum would be proud now to see me standing here with a potential new boyfriend who was not only successful but also someone I'm sure she would find hot.

Looking up at all the people interacting with vampires, I couldn't believe this life existed and that I was part of it. Of course, they could rip us apart but for what purpose? The authorities seemed to be in control of this new coexistence, innocent civilians were no longer dying and the guilty were being punished. I could live with that.

19

Thomas Malcolm

As we drove along Jonathan was, as per usual, fidgeting with everything at his disposal. To be honest the more he fidgeted with his gadgets the happier it made me. After all, that's what I paid him for. I would worry if he were calm. Jonathan was in his mid-forties and I have never seen him look better in the ten years I have known him. Constantly on guard, loyal and quick-witted but what made him stand out from the others in his field I have met over the centuries was his kindness.

I have seen him kill and maim those who have threatened me, but it is only ever a last resort. Thomas Malcolm likes to be in the shadows, I don't want to stand out. To achieve this, I needed people that didn't seek out the adrenaline of violence. But Jonathan had told me he was tiring of this work and wanted to retire. It broke my heart. I respected his choices but it would be impossible to find anyone half as good as him. It had taken me eighty years to find someone as capable and talented as Jonathan. Feeling comfortable with someone, human or vampire was difficult, especially since my time with Claude. What fun we had discovering the world and each other but, no, I can't dwell on that period now.

The screams of a dying woman in Sydney's Kings Cross had led to me Jonathan. Following the screams to an alleyway behind a nightclub I saw her lying on the dirty cobblestones drenched in her own blood. Jonathan was next to her fighting bravely for his own life. It's often the case when vamps get carried away, they can tear a human apart. I had floated to the top of the buildings to get a better look. As I peered down from the rooftop, I saw him attempting to hold back three young, inexperienced and stupid vampires below. One vampire already lay dead on the ground, an impressive feat for any human. It would not be long before the other two tore the human apart. I could sense Jonathan was not afraid of the vampires, witnessing his fiancés death had brought out feelings of pure rage and revenge. He knew that he wasn't going to make it out of this situation alive but I could see there was still no way he was going to give up easily. The vampires slowly circling towards him were newly created with no regard for any type of life. It happens, the callousness of youth, out for a good time and feeling immortal, you think no one can touch you. It takes a good thirty to forty years before any type of empathy starts to creep into your soul (soul is a debatable reference Thomas Malcolm). With all of my years to hone my skills as a hunter they didn't stand a chance. I materialised behind them out of mist form and snapped two of their necks with a quick flick of the wrist. Jonathan jumped, startled to see me standing there. The other wild vamp didn't have a chance to even turn around before I made sure he was also dead. I took no joy in killing, to me it was just mundane and tedious.

These four dead vampires seemed almost still human to me. They had had no time to mature, to even understand a small amount of the power they could attain. I love all life, when you hold so much power in your hands, the power to create life that you can mould and shape can be very powerful. Only a fool, a young fool, creates vampires at the drop of a hat.

I will never forget sensing the feeling the loss that was evident in Jonathan's eyes. He looked sad to have survived rather than to have died alongside his poor Sophie. Understandably it took a while for Jonathan to trust me and to recover from his shock. Why had any of this happened? Why had they attacked him and his Sophie? Why had I intervened? Fate didn't exist from my point of view, but perhaps the wind had blown in the right direction allowing me to find Jonathan. We have been together ever since.

I try not to pry into too much into my employee's lives but I could feel that he wasn't ready to love anymore, until now that is. He was now ready to move on, to maybe start a family, he was a good man who deserved happiness.

The revenge quota I felt he needed to quench after the death of Sophie had been met. Killing is a gruesome business so I could understand why Jonathan may have had his fill. I wondered if there was a new path ahead for me, how would my company evolve after his departure? But for now, I was happy. I had heard of companies paying vampires to create more of our kind just so they could be experimented on. Whether you're human or not we can all be so cruel, that's the reason why I lost Claude. You never realise how much power you have until it's gone.

No matter the form I took I have never really cared deeply for anyone, including myself, I simply existed. Giving and taking as I saw fit. The powers attained differ between vampires. Generally, we can mind control almost all humans, only the very strong-minded can withstand someone like myself (oh Thomas Malcolm you're so powerful).

Many years ago, in Europe I was feared for my ability to transform into gas, a most helpful power for efficient killing and capture avoidance. It's so much easier being one of my kind these days as for the most part we are accepted. You didn't have to fear being randomly staked to death by an uneducated angry mob.

Once vampires and humans started working together it became all about making money. I liked to stay ahead of the curve with my business, but I had feared the vampire prison was an idea that might not take off. Still, it was the main reason why I chose to move here. I wanted to keep a watchful eye on what was happening at the prison and get in on the action if it was worth my while.

Observing the workings of the prison from the outside it was obvious it would be a difficult nut to crack. If you're on the outside too long you could become irrelevant and I had no plans to allow that to happen, which was why I had been at the cricket the previous evening.

I was in the back of the Rolls Royce and as we glided over the highest bridge in the city, I could see the mining mill to one side and the ocean and reflected lights of the city to the other. It was a truly remarkable place, to think it was once a road to nowhere but was now on everyone's destination list. The youthful charm of Australia intrigued me. What it lacked in terms of architecture and history it more than made up for with animals that could kill you. Being a vampire meant I was impervious to these creatures, but if I were still human, I would surely be in a constant state of fear.

It was strange not knowing what fear felt like anymore, I could only sense it in others by their heart rate or the dilation of their eyes. Through my necessity to feed I have seen fear many times, and it is no fun. It saddened me and I blamed my makers for my victims' pain. Of course, like any animal, I didn't want to die. The will to survive is ingrained in us all. So, I fought to live like everyone else, but at what cost? I was still trying to work that out (oh Thomas Malcolm you can be such a downer at times).

Still, it was game night tonight and I loved game night. Leaving the beach and heading into the city was fun. Usually there was no real reason for me to leave my humble abode with it's million-dollar water views, two fabulous restaurants and rooftop helipad (oh, you're so full of yourself). Through a contact Jonathan had found, I now had a way to view the prison's inner workings. Once

I had proved my wealth, which was very easy to do, I was granted access by the contact who worked as the prison's public relations liaison.

As we began to approach the city's CBD it was time to put my graceful yet intimidating self on show. There would be no hiding my power from the other vampires, they would instantly feel my presence when I entered a room and this could be intimidating. It could also be a hindrance as humans tend to notice when vampires are afraid of their own kind, it made staying in the shadows harder. A room full of the world's most powerful and wealthy vampires and Mr Thomas Malcolm walks in generating widespread fear, (you love it really – well yes, as a matter of fact I do darling.)

The rapidly developing city was a thirty-minute drive from prison town. It had been on the rise well before the influx of vampires, as humans had been moving from Sydney to find more affordable housing. Why not, I thought, why live in the middle of nowhere when you can be by the beach? But the city that holds my un-beating heart is Vienna, I will always be in awe of its beauty and it was also the place I fell in love.

I stood by the harbour and stared at the reflections of the apartments and restaurants in the water. I could hear Jonathan beavering behind, talking to the security detail of this exclusive event. Each vampire had their own entourage of security staff and hangers on. Vampires from all over the world were here to show their teeth.

I turned to watch these groups of pompous twats arrive. Why did some part of me think I still needed their approval when I spent much of my existence avoiding their kind.

I was thinking more like this lately, beginning to question the reasons why I choose to live the way I do. It was my choice not to be part of any vampire coven and now having no loving partner why was I holding on to that? When I lived in Vienna, I was pressured to join such organisations. Thomas Malcolm doesn't need to live in a class system where the older vampires are elite to the young bloods. I have met many of my kind that like to live in the presence of higher standing vampires as they valued the protection it offered. I, Thomas Malcolm follow no set rules, what protection do I need darling? With my power and flamboyance, I was always better off alone.

My thoughts were rudely interrupted by an unwelcome voice from the past.

"Oh TM, TM, I know you can hear me," screeched the staccato voice I had tried so hard to forget and never hear again. That classless woman it belonged to wouldn't know a real genuine piece of art no matter how many blow jobs she had given to curators over the years. Her name was Maggie, a remorseless vampire I had met many a moon ago in Rio de Janeiro.

Together we had fucked anything that moved or took our fancy, gorged on humans with no thought of regret and destroyed restaurants, bars and hotels with complete abandonment, all while being totally clueless and classless. We were the worst of the worst and managed to live in rampant opulence for over three years while feasting on everything we could get our teeth into. Maggie's bad influence changed me profoundly and affected me still to this day.

It was a crazy time in Rio back then, what with the civil unrest and the police sanctioned killings of homeless sewer dwelling orphans. The local people wore crosses around their necks while they murdered and raped their way through life, making a mockery of the statue of Jesus that watched over them. For us though it was a haze of passion, smoke and music. The annual carnival was a backdrop that hid the sins of the city, including what Maggie and Thomas Malcolm got up too. We danced, we drank, we did as we pleased.

I had loved the way Maggie made me feel back then.

Late one eventful evening we were in a small bar on top of Sugarloaf Mountain where couples and families enjoyed the view of Copacabana beach below. It was a hot and sultry night, not that either Maggie or myself could feel the heat, judging by the sweat glistening on human dancers they were enjoying themselves as much as we were.

I had only been with a few partners throughout my life, as a human and then a vampire. Male or female never mattered to me, which at times in history had been an issue. Sexual tolerance, I have found, swings aggressively one way, self-corrects, then goes the other way.

After a difficult and painful breakup with Claude I'd left Europe on a one-way ticket to Rio and I never looked back. Never run away from your problems they say, I would have flown away if that were one of my abilities back then. The joy of life was intoxicating, of people dancing, drinking and enjoying their young lives while they could. Hearing the music of Aquarela de Brazil even to this day bought back stirring memories of Maggie. The first few beats of that song always made me smile but then the sense of dread took over as I knew what had happened by the end of that night on top of Sugarloaf.

"For an uptight European, you can move your hips ok," Maggie had said as she grasped my tight firm buttocks tightly and dug her long green and yellow nails into my flesh. Maggie spoke many languages, as most of us vamps do, but when she spoke her native Portuguese through those luscious red lips in her low squeaky tone, she had me in her control. I stared into her brown dark eyes as we danced under the stars, fifty or so people were mingling around us having fun. Even as a vampire Maggie stood out with her bright red hair and petite, nimble body that always seem to be moving to some sort of beat, which the longer I knew her was mostly her own. I wasn't as pompous then as I am now, I was charming and handsome. Yet to be worn down by the burdens of work, the burdens of my own expectations of what I should and shouldn't achieve.

"Well, I certainly seem to be stiffer now I'm here with you."

She grabbed my private parts. "We are lucky enough to find each other at this state of our lives. We can take what we want, whenever we want TM. No one can stop us."

It was intoxicating being told you can, and should, take whatever you desire, to be confident at every turn, and never consider the word no. Maggie pushed me further and further into the unknown, I was so far in the darkness I couldn't escape, worst of all I didn't know I needed too.

As a vampire duo our hunting ways were subtle, taking our prey one by one in the shadows, mainly striking at more depraved and horrible human brings that were plentiful in that city of decadence. It wasn't surprising a lot of these evil individuals worked in the police force. A main source of our food were the police hit squads, whose methods made me truly squirm inside, even as a vampire. The blatancy of their killing was overwhelming. If our kind attempted such a thing the humans would attempt to wipe us out completely.

As the music played, we danced alongside families and couples, all of us feeling free and happy even if it was for a small moment in time.

I looked down at Maggie, "We have been doing anything and everything we want dear but I can't live like this forever. This life is thrilling but I need a deeper purpose. There will be a point where we need to settle down, now don't grimace Maggie, you know I'm right we can't just…"

"Can't what TM? Our powers as individuals are strong but when we work together, we are indestructible. We have enough force to do what we want without fear. I don't want to settle down. Don't make me show you what I'm capable of," she moved away from me. I couldn't hear the music or people in the background anymore, just Maggie. The conversation between us began to make me feel uneasy.

I reached for her hand, "Maggie what's wrong, we're just a couple, just talking. Come back to me," I said softly.

"We are a couple TM, but I'm in charge of both of us."

Maggie's actions to come on that night would cause traumatic ripples for vampires all over the world.

The most beautiful piece of music morphed into something horrific. I knew then what she was about to do. I lunged forward into the crowd of sweaty people swaying back and forth, scaring some of them away, too late though. At first, I could see looks of confusion on the faces of the people around us as they couldn't place where the high-pitched noise was coming from. It wasn't long before the confusion turned to pain as the pitch escalated into a loud and terrifying scream. The humans in Maggie's range fell to their knees and cried out in pain, blood ran down their noses and out of their ears, any attempts to protect themselves were futile.

Maggie was bent over, her body contorted as the scream left her small frame. The sound intensified as she taught me a lesson of control and anger that killed innocent humans around us. The music, screaming and cries of help had blended into one.

The lifeless bodies of men, women and children surrounded us. Those who had escaped the sound had run away in terror.

Gunshots filled the air and Maggie's screaming stopped. The police had us surrounded. As the shooting continued an injured Maggie somehow propelled her small frame over and behind the bar. I used my power to turn into mist and disappeared into the darkness of the night.

That's when I should have left, but I hovered around in the

darkness on the outskirts of the bar. I was horrified by the death and devastation Maggie had caused. The officers moved closer to where Maggie was hiding. She deserved what was coming but I couldn't let her die. One of the policemen raised a crude stake ready to despatch of Maggie. There had been too much blood but I was prepared, reluctantly, to add four more bodies to the count. I circled my targets and ended their lives as quickly and painlessly as possible. The only person who deserved to die was the one I saved. I walked over to Maggie; she was leaning up against a tree injured and exhausted she was trying to pull her blood-soaked hair away from her face.

"See my love, together we can do anything we want, we can…"

"No, not together."

That was the last time I had seen her. Hearing her voice calling me now and seeing her walk towards me with complete confidence knocked me visibly for six. Why her and why now? Not many people knew of my name, and no one had ever called me TM, apart from Maggie. As Maggie got closer to me, I could see Jonathan in the background reaching slowly for his gun, I waved him down with a subtle move of an eyebrow. I did love Jonathan, always ready.

Dressed tightly all in black her red hair shone brightly against the night sky. My God she was striking, I felt like I could possibly lose control of myself, and this evening. She opened her arms as she greeted me "TM you don't looked pleased to see me. Surely, you're not still holding a grudge about Brazil are you my dear?" She kissed my cheeks, (I hate her). "No, I'm not," I whispered.

"Sorry TM what was that you said? I sense you've changed, you're not the man you once were, you've become softer I feel," she was spitting out words like they were patronising Portuguese bullets. Maggie never rested on her laurels. The way she talked was like the samba itself always to a beat and moving swiftly with an elegant purpose, (Thomas Malcolm, I fucking hate her, let me kill her now).

"Well, yes, we all change and I'm guessing not for the better in your case, and just so we're clear, Maggie, don't ever touch me again. OK," I snarled. I was on my way to losing control already. It was the one of the powers Maggie possessed, even though I hated her I was still attracted to her. We couldn't shake each other off, as if it was in our DNA. Most vampires only have a few powers, but I had the feeling Maggie had many, most of which she had cleverly kept hidden from me.

"I didn't notice your name on the ledger for tonight's adventure TM, hiding yourself are you my dear? You still look as though you have a broom stuck up that pert bottom of yours."

"Don't call me TM, the name is Thomas Malcolm," I said starchily.

Maggie didn't listen to a single word I uttered, "Oh TM you're no fun."

She put her arm through mine and we walked towards the event entrance, Maggie's presence meant the evening would no longer be as enjoyable as I had hoped.

There would be a reason Maggie was here tonight, it would not be a mere coincidence. That night in Brazil would have something to do with it, for me it was the reason why I was now on this personal crusade to right my wrongs. Somewhere along the way I had found some courage, some morals.

Maggie on the hand wouldn't know what morals were. What was it about me that she wanted? The more I thought about it, the stronger the belief that I was being lured into someone else's plan. Although I hated Maggie, I also knew that I was responsible for my own actions on that night in Rio.

"I knew you weren't dead, my dear noble TM. After such a long time I was beginning to fear I would never see you again, but I am surprised to see you in Australia." Our credentials were checked at the door and Maggie's arm was still firmly on my own. I was starting to feel that she would never let go, surely Maggie hadn't been searching for me all this time?

"I looked all over the Greek, and Croatian islands; I swore to Jesus…" she said, completing the sign of the cross. No matter what we had done, Maggie remained strangely devoted to her religion, even though one of the games we used to play involved luring paedophile priests to their death.

"I always imagined you would be living in a villa somewhere collecting those antique treasures that you always liked."

I wondered if Maggie was still holding onto the past. I wasn't. I hadn't been back to South America since that fateful night. Neither had any vampire who didn't want to be killed. I wonder what feelings, if any, Maggie had on being banished from her homeland. Even for someone with my intelligence, (Oh Thomas Malcolm) living on this earth for so long it was hard to remember things, which is why I kept so much memorabilia, little trinkets of the past. Jonathan always found it peculiar I held treasures like photos, snuff boxes and glasses in a small, well secured room. The beginnings of a madman, I imagine he presumed. Fortunately, he never asked questions about my past.

It was hard to block out the constant garbage that kept coming out of Maggie's mouth. It was so distracting; tonight, was supposed to be fun. Ahead of us stood a smart dark-haired woman holding a tablet and surrounded by a few yes people. As we waited, I took in every detail of the room, this habit had often been a life saver. There was small bar to the left of the room where human waiters busily served blood-based cocktails to get the wealthy clientele in the mood.

The room itself was very similar to an auction room, not unlike Sotheby's in London. The only difference was there was a runway for our highly sort after dinner to parade down (love the word parade Thomas Malcolm).

The woman at the entrance introduced herself as Lucy, the prison's PR liaison, she checked us in and showed us to our seats, there was something familiar about her, but I couldn't quite put my finger on it.

"We have to be seated next to each other my darling TM; I don't want to miss out on all the fun. I am sure that's no problem for you Lucy?" Maggie said while tightening her grip on my arm.

Lucy nodded politely but I could sense my presence had thrown her.

"You know TM I can't wait for the auction to finish, there is someone so fantastic that I would like you meet afterwards. To be honest Mr Uptight, not only am I surprised to see you in Australia but also at one of these nights. I didn't think you drank fresh blood from humans anymore? I thought you were too high and mighty for that type of thing. Aren't you into some type of organic hippie product?"

Things weren't adding up. How would she know that if she'd only just discovered I was alive? And whom did she want me to meet?

"Well, my darling you know that we Europeans have rather higher standards than most and after Brazil it left a rather bad taste in my mouth," I said looking directly into Maggie's eyes. She didn't flinch once; she never was scared of me.

As we took our seats, I sized up my surroundings, it never hurt to be careful in new places, but it was hard to concentrate with Maggie's constant chatter. I was beginning to feel uneasy, something was unusual, I had never been in her presence while she had been nervous. She was giving off signals that I knew I needed to be aware of. I turned to Jonathon, warning him with my eyes to be ready.

The light began to dim and the vampires took their places as Lucy walked confidently and gracefully to her position with a distinct sense of purpose. I knew that she worked at the prison but I was surprised to see such a heavy influence on proceedings from the prison, they had their greedy fingers in all the strudels.

"Sooo TM who are you here for? What little delight did you venture out of your hole for? Have you changed your tastes? I would understand if you had after the way you acted in Brazil," Maggie said.

"Well, my darling if by hole you mean my luxury apartment, you should know that Thomas Malcolm was invited as a VIP, with regards to Brazil, well, the horror of that night broke me," she seemed surprised by my honesty. From behind the curtains, I sensed at least twenty human heartbeats racing as they were preparing to be paraded for our pleasure.

"Grow up TM," she said, "they were just human beings, little puppets for us to control."

"Maggie there were children lying dead on the floor in their own blood because of our first and only argument."

The show began and the humans started to walk down the runway one at a time, their skimpy prison green outfits showed off the bits that most piqued our interest. Well-groomed, fit and attractive they paraded up and down in front of us while Lucy read out each individual's statistics and the starting bid. Her voice was monotonous and cold, to me she seemed more dead than the rest of us, (oh Thomas Malcolm). The humans' heart rates were pumping at full speed now, which had the effect of making them even more appealing to us vampires. Seeing the veins pulse was like porn for all us bidders, (it has been so long Thomas Malcolm since we have tasted this).

I was enjoying the parade when Maggie interrupted, "TM, do you know what I went through that night in Rio, are you listening TM?" she said angrily. "You may have left me to die but someone else was kind enough to help me and he is here tonight."

I was on guard now; something was definitely wrong. Who was this man Maggie spoke of?

I look around and noticed a considerable increase in the number of vampire security staff surrounding us.

I now knew this evening was a trap. All the vampires around me were here for the auction and they were fixated on the parade. But it looked like my evening was going to be different.

"Oh, Maggie what have you done?" I said quietly.

Maggie smiled, "Did you think there wouldn't be repercussions for that night TM? Did you? I had to pay dearly to get my life back and tonight you will too, tonight is my night," she said smugly.

20

Nathan

Waking up in your own sweat never felt nice. I sat up in bed in the mostly dark room, only a few rays of light shone underneath the closed bedroom door, feeling my right side that was covered in bandages due to the cracked ribs from the commotion the night before. I didn't know what was scarier, being almost killed by vampires that were high on some drug we had never seen then watching them being burned alive by UV lights or the fact that a vampire was sitting in the corner of the room staring at my every move. Reaching out to the small bedside table I opened my bottle of room temperature water and popped some ibuprofen to ease the pain. I flipped over my phone to check the time. It was almost 3am.

"You're still here then, not bored yet?" I said, more irritated that the air con wasn't working than Gillian being in my bedroom.

"Nah mate, I love watching you sleep, you're quite beautiful rolling around like a sweaty pig, oink oink," he said laughing.

Swallowing the tablets with a dry throat while being mocked by someone was hard enough. To be fair to Gillian hadn't had it easy either, he was covered in burns to his hands and face that seemed to be fading now but it was difficult to tell with the lack of light. He did mention that the burns would make no difference to his ugly mug, that almost made me chuckle. I was annoyed I was feeling sorry for myself. I had never let myself feel that way and I didn't like it. Suffering a beating hadn't helped but the murders and the lack of a clear path to discovering what was going on was obviously getting to me. What would Gillian think? Since he had showed up the whole situation had gotten worse. I noticed Sam had texted; the mayor wanted to speak to me about the bedlam that had gone down at the *Glitter Ball*. Not great timing, I wasn't thinking straight and I didn't really feel like telling him that a suspect had apparently disappeared and while I was banged up at home there had been another victim.

"You know mate, sitting there feeling sorry for yourself isn't going to help."

"Is that one of your abilities, to be able tell people are upset after getting beaten to a pulp," I said sarcastically.

"Nah it's the way you sighed while reading your phone. It almost blew the house down my little piggy."

"If this is some sort therapy you've learnt to help us humans get motivated it's not working Gillian," I said dropping my tablets to the floor.

Quick as flash he was across the room catching the plastic container and placing them on the table in one smooth motion.

"You're right Nate, it's time to explain as much as I know, you're owed that."

"Thank you," I leaned back onto my pillows and pulled the sticky wet sheets off my body.

"Right mate, here goes," his usual cockney accent now sounded more like a BBC announcer.

"I've lived a long life and during that time I have had many personas, I am Gillian right now and was before you were even born. I don't remember my true self, like a lot of vampires, I always travel, always move on from place to place, dusk to dawn to gain new experiences, to see things I haven't seen and feel things I haven't felt before. Living as long as I have it's easy to forget what is part of my new persona and what is from my past. Have I been married before? No, I'll try that see what it's like, oh wait I've done that, a fragment of a memory pops into in my head. It becomes like Deja vu. The only way to remain sane is to focus on the present and make new memories.

"When you go on holidays you take a mental snapshot of the time you went fishing or when you caught a wave or met someone special, but once you fill that memory album up, they all become the same. How do you make an image or event stand out to be clear in your own mind so it doesn't blur or become fuzzy? You have to make that moment stand out somehow. So, you take a memento of that time, but you don't put it in a cupboard or hide it away as it will mean that memory will be hidden as well, it needs to be something that stands out and is unique, like the pendent around my neck.

"That's Jeff, within the chain that hangs around my neck. He was so loved by his community they created a statue in his honour but little did they know this would prevent Jeff from moving on. Humans are unable to comprehend they are pure energy. Over the years I have learned to control that energy and use it to great advantage. I am now training Jeff to use his powers.

"I used to collect material things to show my status to others and most importantly remind myself of that period of my life. See Nate there was once a time when all I could do was get lost inside how amazing I was. When people start telling you are amazing, the creator of eternal life, you never want that power to fade or disappear. But I became obnoxious, full of my own self-importance, I started commissioning oil paintings and statues of myself for god's sake.

"Some of my kind have the power to use the antiquities they have collected to travel back in time, one of these such vampires

gave me a 1920s pocket watch which I can use to take me back
to Paris where he obtained it. Travelling back in time started as
a hobby but I soon became obsessed with changing the past to
control my present. I had created this perfect being that people
were willing to follow blindly and throw their lives away for in
the search for immortality. But little did they know my image was
built on lies and deceit.

"I was trying to manipulate the past to control the present. As
wanky as that sounds, it's what I wanted to do."

"When I go back in time I am still physically here in the present
as it only equates to a fleeting second in present time. Although
for a day or so after time travelling, I am vulnerable. It can also be
very painful. But I've learned Nate that, no matter how small the
changes you make in the past are there are always consequences."

"In the late 1920's, when I was known as the vampire Claude,
I was forced to leave my Austrian lover Tom in order to save him
from another vampire Blake. I owed Blake money and he wanted
access to Tom as payment. I broke Tom's heart but I did it to save
him. To do so I had to leave my old self behind. I abandoned my
existence as Claude to become Antonio. I was heartbroken and
guilt ridden so I fled Europe for Mexico. I was in such a state of
emotion that I don't remember how I got on that flight. To get out
of my stupor I had to change not only my appearance, but also my
location and the belongings I had spent generations accumulating,
I also had to escape my own mind. And that's not easily done when
your mind is full of enough historical information to fill a library.

Anyway, to cut a long story short, I then became Antonio, the
vampire I was before Gillian, the difference being Antonio was
an utter twat. Feeling sorry for myself my personality went away
from the soft, caring Claude to the unpleasant selfish Antonio.
I was outlandish and charismatic and people were drawn to me, I
started to spout words and stories of fiction to them, telling them

I could live forever and whoever served me would have the same power and life I had. I found a small place along Tijuana Beach where I started my commune. It was just basically a fucking orgy of humans and vampires doing whatever they wanted. I eventually became so bored with it all that I started to mistreat my followers for entertainment. At first, I just played little tricks on them like making them clean my shoes with their tongues or getting them to run naked through the main street, all good fun. Then I found myself becoming mean and vindictive. I made them hurt and torture each other, so they could prove their love to me."

Gillian closed his eyes and started to shake his head in disapproval of his own self. He continued, "What scared me most was they all did this without question. They lusted after it, the more I got them to hurt and kill for me the more they revelled in it. It was like my fucking own version of the *Lord of the Flies*. One night we all went into town for a bit of fun. There were some locals on the beach drinking and playing music around a bonfire. My followers headed over to join in the festivities. It wasn't long before I cottoned on to the fact that their motives were not pure, I knew what they wanted, they wanted to kill these innocents in my name. It was then I realised how evil Antonio was and the memory of Claude came back to me and made me see the error of my ways. I saw what was going to happen, so I acted. I ripped my followers to pieces, both human and vampire. The innocents who witnessed this were horrified so I was forced to use my charm to calm them down. I disposed of what must have been at least twenty bodies and ran away to London and became who I am now, Gillian."

I was intrigued by one of the greatest stories I had ever heard but trying to remain awake on all this pain medication was hard. He was pouring his soul out to me and all I wanted to do was close my eyes. I quietly interrupted him, "Gillian, did people think you were a God?"

He smiled. "A lot of people followed me and died for me, so I guess in some ways you could say they did for a brief moment."

I nodded and let him continue.

"Shedding Antonio to become Gillian was painful and hard, it hurt a lot, I cried for days in self-pity not knowing how to escape the demon I'd created. But I have the ability to put my past personas in a box, which helped to stop me from going insane."

I could tell that this still haunted Gillian and I could feel his pain.

"Take Gillian for example, I am now him from head to toe in every way. I have to find a way in and the way in with Gillian was the punk era in late 1970s England. I was totally fascinated with the music and what that time stood for. That's how my transformations happen. I run away from a situation or a moment where I am maybe finding my old self again. You must know Nate time is of no consequence to me. There is no need for me to pay attention to it. I remember when being a punk vampire was a way of life not a choice, can you hear me mate, oh fuck me Nate you're asleep."

———————

I jolted awake. Sunlight was pouring in from where the blackout over the window had been removed. Rubbing my eyes and feeling less pain in my side I turned round to see if Gillian was still sitting in his chair looking after me. Thankfully he was gone, as I would expect at this time of day. I had fallen asleep while listening to Gillian do his best to explain what was going on. I had gotten a lot more information than I'd imagined, I had expected clues about the murders or maybe a theory, not the life story of Gillian.

There were many details that I was having trouble wrapping my mind round. The reason why we were attacked was still a mystery. Then there was the ferocity of the attack to start with. For vampires to purposely attack us while the UV light caused them pain, there had to be a very strong motivation. We had only gone there to follow up on a lead I had expected would be a dead end.

Add the fact that when Gillian had placed a pendant around my neck an elderly American man was able to communicate directly with my mind was confusing enough. When Jeff had spoken it was like a bold black headline of words from a newspaper. There was no need even to reply as he could read my thoughts. When Jeff spoke, I had no choice but to listen and stop what I was doing on the outside world, but maybe with practice I could develop this skill further?

There was also the matter of Gillian saying he was some sort of vampire god who travelled through time. I wasn't sure if this was due to the painkillers or me not understanding him clearly, or maybe both. Gillian had told me in the ambulance the mental strain of communicating with Jeff telepathically would be exhausting. Normally a person would build up to it with training and exercise. It felt like every individual bone had a small amount of pressure on it. It was beginning to wear off now though and it was time to get my mind back into matters of work. As I got up, I could hear rustling downstairs. It was almost lunchtime and perhaps Sam had come over again with Tim to make me some delicious (awful) kale soup. I put on an old t-shirt and some track pants and gingerly made my way down the corridor from the back of the house, leaning on the wall for support to take the weight off my left side. I smelled fresh coffee beans being blasted in my machine, which instantly put me into a better mood. Someone was humming an old song my mother used to sing when I was little. My first thought was, oh crap who has organised for my parents to come down from their holiday home in Forster. Their questions will go on forever and I won't be able to get any work done for their concern. But luckily it wasn't my mother humming, making coffee and ham and cheese jaffles.

"Wakey, wakey sleepy head," my sister said happily as she turned around. She came over to me and gave me a hug.

"Afternoon Claire."

Sitting back in my favourite bucket chair feeling full from the toasties and with my hands wrapped round a mug of coffee I felt safe and content. It wasn't often that I got to sit down in my chair, relax and feel real heat from the sun. I looked outside on to the small brown grass patch that was once a garden and waited for Claire to fill the dishwasher up and join me.

Having Claire in my home was stranger still, as we had never done anything like this, even with the passing of Tom. She had made it pretty clear that she wanted to be left alone.

"I haven't heard that song for a long time," I said. "It reminds me of Mum. I remember coming down the stairs early in the morning before my paper run and I would catch her scrubbing the kitchen floor while singing old songs to take her mind off things."

"By things you mean Dad," said Claire.

"No… well maybe a little, but Mum was always fun, always there for us, I hope we helped as much as we could. I mean they're both good together now but I think Dad has some regrets. But you're not here for that are you, sis?"

She nodded her head, took a long look at me and rolled her eyes.

"I'm ok, you know just cuts and bruises. It's nice you're here but to be honest I'm surprised to see you."

"Nathan, I heard you almost died. I spoke to Sam and she told me you were ok but that you and your partner, who is a vampire, which I'm pretty sure you didn't tell me about, were attacked. Also…" Here it comes I thought she can't help but lecture. "With Tom being taken away from me I have no choice but to be here. Just when I think I'm turning the corner I hear about you and before you start, I haven't told Mum or Dad yet." Claire sounded like she was explaining what two plus two is to one of her kindy kids.

"As of yet Claire? You know my job, you more than anyone know why I do what I do. The same with you, we both like to make a difference, to help people. It's just my job has gotten a little more dangerous over the years. Oh Claire, don't roll your eyes. What do you want me to say? I'm very sorry about Tom, he was an amazing man, it was such bad luck and eventually those vampires will get their come-uppance." A small unsettling smirk appeared at the bottom of her lip.

"I know we have a strained relationship but as callous as this sounds, I'm not just here about you but I need a favour if possible? I think you will find those particular vampires have disappeared and I'm ok with that."

I was taken a back a little, but I wasn't going to let her get away with her tone. "I have always loved your candour but isn't there somewhere else you have to be? Some list you need to check off?" I didn't want to sound mean, but I knew how Claire could be like. "I'm quite busy at the moment with the case, and other police matters you know I can't talk about."

"Oh, fuck off Nathan, I need someone found. It's someone you might know, who might be able to help you with your case."

"There's no need for the potty mouth. If you need a person found, I can take the details and pass them on to someone who can assist."

"No Nate, it has to be you, not that I think you could find him, it's more likely your new partner will be able to help."

"My partner? Gillian? How will he be able to help... wait your friend is a vampire? What's their name Claire?"

"It's Thomas Malcolm."

———ᰂᰂ———

I arrived at the police station before the nightshift came on and gave me grief for being back a day early. I needed to get a head start on the increasing number of problems that were piling up. I was too young to remember the days of piles of paper work, as some of the old timers liked to remind me, but I promised them that opening my emails and seeing over a hundred new messages everyday was just as overwhelming.

Tonight, I'd presumed there would be more, most of them coming from the mayor's office, and I was correct. If I were in his shoes, I would be wanting answers quickly too. It wasn't long before the mainstream press would get a hold of what had been happening over the last few months. The intensity of the situation was building and I could feel pressure. Seeing Claire had thrown me off my game. What was I supposed to do with that information? I didn't see how mentioning it to Gillian would help matters.

I was not often in the office as the sun set. The strip looked clean and hopeful before the darkness descended and both the street and people's demeanour changed considerably. The police station was different too, the skeleton crew who worked days mainly completed admin from the night before and dealt with missing partygoers who usually turn up when sober.

That's how the first murder had been discovered, a female sex worker had been found in a luxury hotel room with a young man who was out on his stag night. For this handsome and high-earning American a wild night of lust and vampires before tying the knot was alluring but turned deadly. The power of the strip was it made people feel superhuman, as if they are beyond reproach. People fly in from all the over the world thinking they are invincible and money will buy them everything they desire. All the client had to do was wake up and consume whatever it was they desire, indulging to their heart's content. Most partygoers would never imagine their trip would end in murder though.

I reply to as many emails as possible, trying to get my inbox under control, Claire would be proud of my efficiency. I was reviewing the report from the coroner. Earlier on the way to hospital after the incident at *Glitter* Gillian said we should request an autopsy on the vamps who had attacked us, as the way they had attacked us concerned him. The bodies had been sent to Sydney, as we didn't have the right equipment to open up vampires around here, this would only slow down the investigation further.

The sound of the door of my office being slammed shut in a dramatic manner woke me from my work trance. I looked up to see a smiling Gillian proffering me a cup of coffee in a get up Adam Ant would have been proud of.

"Alright guv, I knew you'd be back early and would be needing some black tar to get you through the night." I smiled.

"I'm sorry mate that I can't get in here early with ya, due to the fact that the sun might kill me and that."

"Is everything a joke?"

"How can you be such a delicate flower mate living in a country full of animals that scare even me?" He sat down on the edge of my desk and flicked through a file from the murder scene.

"This is not an episode of *Moonlighting* Gillian where you can just swoon in and do whatever you want."

"True guv but I found a present for you and it's all gift wrapped and waiting for you downstairs in one of the interview rooms," his big cheesy grin really showed off those teeth of his.

"Who is it?"

"I'll give you two guesses."

"Gillian!" I said impatiently.

"Ok, ok Nate down to business it is. Do you remember that fuck head vamp that got away from us the other night? Well, I found him, well what's left of him."

I couldn't believe it; this could be the break I, and the entire team, needed.

"Great work Gillian. Although, what do you mean, left of him?"

"No, it's not what you think I didn't rough him up. I got a tip from Mel, believe it or not, he'd heard what happened the other night and wanted to help. One of the employees at his night club had heard about a vampire being held up at some dodgy vamp hotel who was all burnt and badly beaten."

"I knew he had been burnt but you didn't assault him. So, when did this happen and by whom?"

"Exactly my old mate. What the hell happened to him after he escaped? Most of us vamps heal pretty quickly, one of the perks of being us. Shall we go downstairs and find out? Oh, by the way, do you want to be good cop or good cop 'cos there's no fucking way I'm going to be. By the way make sure you have Jeff with you."

At the mention of his name, Jeff pulsed and glowed showing Gillian that he was round my neck.

"Evening Jeff," Gillian said, taking a bow.

"You know he can't see you right?" I said laughing at the absurdity of it all.

"Jeff can do a lot more than you think me old mate."

From the way he was moving around my office Gillian was definitely pumped, he looked like he really enjoyed doing this sort of thing and I could see why, he was good at it. I started to get my jacket on and myself together before heading down for the interview.

"Oh, one more thing Gillian, we're going to need to talk to Mel about what he's up to as well."

"All ready on it guv. Sam's bringing him in for a friendly chat later."

"Well ok then, looks like I take one night off and things get done," I said jovially. "Oh, one more thing Gillian, my sister Claire popped over for a chat and she asked for some help in regards to a missing person, she thought you would be more equipped to assist, rather than myself."

He looked concerned, "She ok mate? You know I'm good at cracking skulls if need be." He mimed the motion rather heartily, scaring me a little.

"No, she isn't in danger from what I can gather, Claire has, since a young age, been able to look after herself. She has found it difficult to get back into the rhythm of her own life since the death of her husband Tom though. We don't talk much but we do care for each other and there is most definitely an edge to her that wasn't there before Tom's death."

"So, are you going to make me guess the person she wants found, is that part of the game?"

"Ok Gillian, you're full of it tonight. It's a vampire that she needs found and I'm apparently not up to the task. You're the one she wants."

"That's not always the case, humans can find vampires as well depending on age, so who is it Nate?"

"His name is Thomas Malcolm. Have you ever heard of him?"

He looked at me in shock "Fuck me," he said and walked out the office slamming the door shut in such a way everyone in the office took notice.

"So, I guess he does know him," I said to myself, intrigued.

21

Thomas Malcolm

Maggie didn't know my full power or the range of my abilities. She had only seen the fog once and to be honest I'm not sure if she was hiding behind the bar when that occurred. Now here I was upstairs from the auction room surrounded by vampires who possessed UV lights, wooden stakes, silver chains, guns and whatever else they thought they needed to stop Thomas Malcolm, they were fucking clueless (I could feel it starting mm hmm).

The vamps guarding me were young and puny compared to me. I was very intrigued why Maggie, and the powerful people she worked for, wanted me. They tried to intimidate me by burning me with silver and inserting shards of wood into various parts of my body. They also tortured Jonathan, but they had no idea he wasn't an insignificant and powerless human. We were sat across from each other and were asked ridiculous question after ridiculous question. We knew we both had each other's backs. The vampire interrogating us was starting to lose his mind. No matter what medieval methods he tried neither of us cried out in pain.

I kept up the charade of being under their control as I wanted to get as much information out of them before they became my *amuse bouche*, (oh Thomas Malcolm). Why go to this much trouble? I could hear Lucy arguing with Maggie out in the corridor.

Lucy was saying "this is not the way we do things," and "the warden won't be happy with what has happened this evening."

For the first time I sensed something different about Lucy, something not quite human, but that would have to wait for now.

The room that we were in had three solid concrete walls and a one-way mirror on the fourth, which I knew Maggie was standing behind, I could hear her irritating fucking laugh through the glass. I knew we were on the top floor of the building as the ceiling was glass. It was a perfect place to sit and watch the sun come up while being tied to a wooden chair with silver chains around my neck, wrist and ankles. In between being tortured, punched and stabbed I looked up at the beautiful stars of the southern hemisphere. It was so different to where I was from in Berlin where I became a vampire so many years ago.

Jonathan's body convulsed as electric shocks were sent through his naked body. They were taking turns in torturing us both, (it's almost time). "I know my dear shhh," I said.

"What was that old timer?" the supposedly toughest vampire said, leaning close to my face letting Jonathan's blood drip off his tongue on to my lips.

"Where are the artefacts, we want to know right now, you pompous old fuck!" he said slamming my head against the upright of the chair. "Time's running out, the sun always rises and I'll be out of here before then, I'm your only chance for freedom…"

"Oh, do shut up, you uncouth moron," I said tasting the blood on my lips. I had never tasted Jonathan before and my god he tasted good.

The idiot stood up ready to hit me again and as he did the light behind the one-way mirror came on and I could now see Maggie smiling with delight. Her red hair looked beautiful and she stood in stark contrast to the five men in the room with her, who all looked seriously ready to end my life. She leaned forward to grab a microphone then pressed her beautiful, red lips to its grill.

"Oh TM, TM, my dear old feeble-looking TM. I thought you had style and grace, but all you have is a weak fucking bodyguard. If you could see yourself now in a mirror you would be appalled at how pathetic you look. You wouldn't stand for this TM, you really wouldn't." Every word sounded like a mini laugh. She thought she finally had her prey in her grasp.

Please be careful my little Maggie, I thought, you need to look over your shoulder, not gloat with delight.

"Just tell me TM where are you holding the artefacts. You know you are both destined to die but I can make it less painless for your shitbag security guard and, luckily for you, you can die in my arms baby, as I suck the life out of you."

"Oh Maggie, I have never been anyone's baby, don't fool yourself."

I could tell that not having me still bothered her. Why would you turn Maggie down? The freedom she had offered was intoxicating. She was prancing around the room walking up and down with the face of someone listening intently to a voice in her ear.

"Who are you working with my dear? You and I both know being powerful is one of your strongest assets but planning is not your forte. Whom is the real brain behind this operation?" I said calmly.

"Why did you fuck it up so much TM? We understood each other. Why oh why? Fucking morals, tonight they are going to be the death of you. We could have had so much together and you chose the sadness of humans over me. For someone so uptight you are so stupid," she turned round in annoyance and flung her hands in the air, swearing in Portuguese, she then whispered to the guard beside her perhaps forgetting I could still hear.

"Who is Blake?" I said, (here it comes). I winked at Jonathan, hoping he would notice the signal.

Maggie spun round quickly.

"Oh, come on Maggie," I said sounding more aloof than I ever had, "I can hear everything you say."

She leant forward and shouted "You always thought being alone, away from your kind, away from the hierarchy made you stronger, but you were mistaken. Being part of a coven makes you stronger as you're about to fucking find out. We could have had it all, with our age and nobility we would have been top of the food chain. It's time TM, this is your last chance, tell me where the artefacts are or I swear to God, I will tear you apart."

It was time; I stood up, bursting through the silver chains, punched my hand through my torturer's chest and pulled out his heart. "Swear to what god Maggie? What do you think you're going to do?" I turned to Jonathan: "You know what to do." I released him and he walked into the corner and sat with his legs crossed yogi style facing the wall. Jonathan had seen this before and there was no reason for him to see it again.

The sheer panic in Maggie's eyes almost amused me. Did she think I would just sit there and take it? (It's my turn now Thomas Malcolm). Yes of course you're right, let me know when you're finished.

(Of course, I will, I observed the vampires in the viewing room scrambling to gather their thoughts as their minds went through their options, of course it was futile. I leapt through the unbreakable glass and Maggie fell back startled, she found her feet and ran through the door. Right, I thought to myself, let's get this party started.

Punching through one vamp's brains I felt the bone crunch on my hand, fucking awesome. Vampire two I picked up and rammed into the wall, squashing his head against the concrete with such force his eyes gushed out of their sockets, vampire three just stood there shitting himself and I ripped his fucking throat out with my bare hands. Right, who's fucking next I said to myself as I strode into the corridor. More of Maggie's entourage of vamps ran at me. One after another it was like swatting flies as I burst from mist to vampire form again and again. One second in front of my prey, one second behind them, teasing them, playing with them like putty in my blood-soaked hands, oh it feels so good to be out.

Your turn now Maggie.

I turned to mist and appeared in front of Maggie as she ran down the staircase, I grabbed her by the hair and threw her against the wall. Towering over her cowering frame I growled.)

"What are you?" she whimpered at the sight of the beast.

(Thomas Malcolm it's time for you to come back, I am tired now).

Jonathan arrived and restrained Maggie with silver chains.

"Maggie that is the part of me I kept from you and why I left you in Brazil."

I looked around. The beast had really had done a number on this place.

"Maggie, why couldn't you leave me alone? If only you had then none of this would have happened. I was content minding my own business and helping people get revenge on the humans and vampires who had done them wrong."

"I... I didn't know who you were, I knew that greatness was in you but I didn't know you had this wrath inside of you."

"Jonathan it's time for us to leave, Maggie will be joining us."

Jonathan placed a jacket over my naked body, I was disappointed, it wasn't often that I felt as free as I did right then.

"I'm sorry you had to see that again Jonathan, I know it's not very pleasant for you."

"It's ok boss," Jonathan said not looking the least bit frightened.

"It doesn't look too good, standing here, does it? But it wasn't as bad as last time, was it?"

"It's all relative boss," Jonathan stifled a smile.

Driving back with the sun chasing me after an eventful night was an experience that had not occurred for a generation or so, I never liked to cut it this late with the sun coming up but due to the surprising events of tonight there wasn't much choice. Maggie would be on the receiving end of some very intense interrogation as soon as we arrived back on safer ground. The team had been informed of what had happened tonight and a full risk assessment was being undertaken to ensure nothing like this could ever happen again.

As we crossed the high suspension bridge the moonlight hit the water and bounced across the city behind us. The beach would be nice and quiet at this time, maybe the odd keen early runner or a shift worker returning home. I owned all the buildings along that part of the strip so my team knew the comings and goings of almost every soul who was there.

The clock was fast approaching 4am, way past my bedtime but we weren't far from home. The night had been a thrill a minute, I hadn't had that much fun for a long time. I was usually repulsed by the loss of any life but if people who are sadists are attacking me, I just can't help myself. I had a good reason to let the inner demon out to play. There was no reason for me to hold back when I knew they deserved it.

Jonathan had seen the beast a few times and over the years he found meditating was the best way to keep calm and ready his mind for the atrocities that were about to commence. Jonathan was a human I truly admired. He was constantly putting his body on the line to protect me. I really needed to pay him more but he wouldn't take any more money. He said he has enough. He is unique, I think he might be the first human I've ever cared for since I became a vampire. After the escapades with Maggie, I think I am done with love. Maggie and whomever she was working with would never get near my artefacts, they could all go and fuck themselves.

As we pulled into the underground parking of my apartment block, I noticed Jonathan had fallen asleep from utter exhaustion. Danni, who was driving, was an ex-army medic so she could attend to Jonathan's needs. I looked rather worse for wear too but a pick-me-up shot of chilled possum blood would fix me right up. It was one of my fetishes, drinking animals' blood. Being here in this country of unique animals I loved trying new things. My team never questioned any of my motives and had complete trust in me, as did I in them, but a few eyebrows were raised when I asked for koala and quokka blood. I know they are cute and endangered but they also taste delicious, and cow or sheep blood can become rather tedious after a while. I had received a little taste of Jonathan's blood and forgotten how exhilarating human blood was. I could see why we killed for it, why we lusted for it and why we paid for the prison's service, but I was no savage.

The elevator opened, Frank was there with a little smile on his face, "Had too much fun tonight did we boss?" he said while handing me a soft velvet gown to cover myself in, it felt soft and soothing against my skin.

"You know me, Frank, always looking for a reason to be covered in blood. I presume everything is ready for tonight? I have an extra guest in the boot. Do you need any help to bring her up to the secure room?"

"Thanks for offering boss but you need to get to your crib as soon as you can, we have things under control and will have the full itinerary ready for you tonight when you wake up. Jonathan has put all the contingency plans in place and everything is in order. There is one more thing though, if it's ok to mention?"

Frank and myself were alone now, heading down below the carpark to my crypt where I had tunnels and safe rooms to escape to in case an evening like tonight ever occurred on home turf.

"Of course, Frank, I know I am the boss but I like to think you can tell me anything no matter what."

"There was confusion tonight with a woman arriving uninvited at the reception telling us that you had told her to come here for an interview. Is that correct sir?"

"Oh, fuck me Frank that is correct, I totally forget to mention it to anyone. Is she still here or did you send her home?"

"No sir she's still here in one of the guest rooms. Facial recognition showed we already had a file on her in the system. As far as I know boss, I didn't think we ever recruited from the people that we'd done jobs for. If I'm not too out of place I am slightly concerned, but of course you don't need to explain anything to me."

"Don't be silly Frank, my door is always open for discussion, I would die for each of you and I know you would do the same for me. To answer you, I have a feeling she can help the business."

Frank didn't seem impressed, "Sir, she's a teacher, I looked through her history and she's a do-gooder. Also, her brother is a policeman who is one of only a few honest cops in town. It could be more trouble than it's worth."

"Frank, you're just going to have to trust me on this one."

Finally, we reached the crypt, my humble abode. I liked this circular room with my luxury coffin in the centre, perched on top of a slab of Italian marble – yes very humble. The coffin was made of mahogany, much to the dismay of Jonathan, he wondered why on earth I would want a bed made of the same material humans carved into stakes to kill my kind. Because it's pretty, that's why.

I washed myself down quickly in French mineral water to remove the dried blood and wrapped my body in a black silk robe.

I was ready for a good well-deserved sleep. I had so much to attend to when I woke. Claire's aura intrigued me, there was something there. And of course, Maggie, there were many questions yet to be answered.

22

Jeff

Being a man with a large frame I had always been methodical with my movement, some would call it slow but there was no point going anywhere without thinking about things first. I didn't like wasting energy in any form. While most people thought that this was laziness, I considered it just being economical with one's energy. It's why I enjoyed being a mechanic, fixing machines was challenging but with experience and maturity I found I could always wait the problem out. Going in guns blazing often created more issues, whereas research and patience nearly always had a positive outcome, I had found this out pretty quickly as a young man in the US army.

Now having become pure energy of my former self, I was anything but slow. I still felt like human Jeff, at times I thought I could even fell the arthritis in my right knee, but my thoughts and spirit moved and acted much quicker than when I was alive. As humans we all have the normal senses that we take for granted. Death for me replaced the five senses with intuition and selective telepathy.

Meeting Gillian opened up my world and eased my fear of never-ending loneliness. He allowed me to plug straight into his own mind at the back of his lobe, just sitting there, watching and feeling. I could never interfere or force Gillian to speak or do anything physical but I could convey to him what I thought and felt but Gillian was too strong for me to force him to do anything against his will.

At first, I was just relieved to have found a way out of my prison inside the statue. I would have been happy with moving into a swamp frog or dragonfly, anything to get anyway from the passengers constantly complaining on that train platform about their privileged lives of freedom. Once I found myself linked to Gillian, I felt reassured and calm, it eased my loneliness and I was more content. Then the more I stayed inside of his mind the more I couldn't believe how lucky I was to find someone like Gillian, not only was he an experienced vampire but he was also willing to teach me how to use my own powers, powers I never knew I had. Like most men of my era, I had found it hard to ask for help, it's what Mary always complained about when we had our little tiffs, as she liked to call them. Mary would laugh with her friends saying that I would rather give away a kidney than talk about my own problems or confess that I was unhappy.

Gillian was offering to help by freeing me from that bronze copy of myself. As I was inside Gillian's consciousness I had access, with his consent, to rummage through his memories, but I could tell certain memories were missing. It felt like they had been erased, or maybe locked anyway in a place that Gillian himself was no longer aware of.

I knew Gillian was truthful and would fulfil his promise to get me back on earth or move me into the next realm. Unlike Gillian and the other travellers of this earth, I didn't want this existence, or whatever this was, to last forever. I had no desire to love again after Mary, I just knew that I didn't have it in me. I wanted the end that death hadn't yet given me, I wanted to transition to the next world. Gillian said that he could guide me and while I believed him, I had a feeling it would come at a cost. I was sure I could help Gillian and his partner Nathan but I couldn't help think there would be trouble along the way.

From a brief glimpse of Nathan's mind, I could tell was a good man who was sadly destined to have a fraught and miserable life. Nathan's human mind was very different to Gillian's. Of course, I should have suspected it to be different but it was confronting to be reminded how fragile human life was. To be honest, Gillian and Nathan were lucky to survive that night in the club and that scared me.

Abiding within a pendant was very different to being within the statue. Even though I couldn't be killed or destroyed I could be abandoned or lost, forgotten to time, which would be worse. Gillian's guidance had helped me to develop the skills necessary to communicate with any human or vampire in my vicinity, my success however depended on the intelligence and openness of my target. Gillian warned me that some would enjoy my company while others may reject me.

Nathan and I gelled right away. Saving Nathan's life generated a trust that most humans would never have with each other. The adrenaline and fear that was pumping through Nathans body felt so real to me that it was as though I was getting high on his endorphins kicking into overdrive, it was intense and exhilarating. Nathan was willing to trust and listen to me, which helped keep all of us alive. I felt more at home in Nathan than Gillian, whom I suspected knew this but didn't seem offended in any way. Unlike Gillian, I could manipulate Nathan physically to a small extent. Only time would tell if I could achieve more actions from within a human's mind. I wanted to be careful with Nathan, I liked what he stood for, even if he was white, privileged and a little idealistic. The most important thing was that he had a good soul and I was willing to work with that.

Being my first venture into a human's mind I wanted to do

my best to help Nathan in any way possible. I wanted to be up-front with Nathan in how I could support him and what we could achieve together, I was also mindful of how confusing this could be for Nathan.

During my years in the army, I witnessed a lot of death. I had even participated in the killing of others in the name of war. I fought alongside vampires as they were considered cheap labour as they could feed on the blood of our enemies. The US army was the first in the world to have vampires as part of its' infantry and they offered them citizenship if they enlisted. A vampire's worth was simple, they were efficient killing machines that fed on their victims as part of their payment. I had witnessed other platoons starve and humiliate their vampire troops into a frenzy so they would destroy a village of farmers without question.

Some of our platoon smoked pot and dabbled in other drugs, some even liked to taste each other's bloods as a sort of welcome pact with the vampires. I always liked to keep my mind and my eyes fully open and my only stimulant was coffee. I wanted to be alert and remember everything so I would appreciate my life from then on. Killing a man, a woman, or a child tore at your soul. Surviving that war and the monstrosities that came with it was enough of a burden for anyone, human or vampire. You could tell all the vampires in our platoon hated themselves for doing what they excelled at. Luckily, they couldn't see their reflection in a mirror. I could, and I despised what I saw.

Seeing into Gillian's past from within his mind was enlightening but I could sense that he was hiding from a part of himself that wasn't nice. Compared to Gillian I was generally a nice guy but I felt had achieved nothing with this. In the past Gillian had done some truly horrible things that would haunt most people for the rest of their lives but at least he had made an impact.

Nathan's mind showed me he had good intentions and he acted

on them. He made me realise this was something I wish I had done more often in the past. I didn't like to rock the boat though, Mary once told me she was being harassed at work and I didn't say anything, I didn't stand up and fight for the one I loved. Being around Nathan made me want to be a better person, his sense of right and wrong was impressive and his standards were high. How could I not help someone who was so noble.

Helping Nathan survive and take Vamps down one by one at *Glitter Ball* was exhilarating. It felt like I was ascending to a better place and that's why I wanted to continue helping Nathan. I had no such feeling with Gillian, he felt indestructible, almost too powerful, and to a certain degree he was. He had survived for so long and learned so many skills I think that his demise could only be at his own hands.

The question is am I helping Nathan for the greater good or for something more selfish? For the moment it was the good. Being inside someone else's mind and going against their own will I imagine would feel extremely powerful but it is not who I am right now, although I must admit helping Nathan destroy the vampires at the club was a little intoxicating.

I felt Gillian's training was unlocking something new inside of me, I felt more powerful every day. There was no judgement from Gillian, which meant I could do anything and feel anyway I wanted too. The idea of controlling a human started to be an attractive option. The line between good and bad, right and wrong was tangible.

I was free to explore, but with Nathan it was different. His human mind was much more constrained than a vampire. He never had a bad thought about anyone. His intentions were always true. Being inside a human mind I felt compassion like I used to when I was with Mary and I knew if I stayed with Gillian or another vampire that could change and I was in danger of losing my true self. But was I even Jeff anymore? His body was dust, long ago forgotten, yet holding on to his human emotions kept me on the side of good.

I spent so long in that goddamn statue listening to everyone's complaints and problems that I had grown tired of it all. It made me wonder did I care about anything anymore? For now, I did.

In a couple of weeks of being free, I had learned so much, including how to enter others people's minds without them knowing and how to manipulate their consciousness. Gillian said in time I would be able to touch and feel through those I inhabit and eventually I would be able to move objects. For now, mind control would just have to do.

Knowing that in the future I could travel from one being or object to another was freeing though as I couldn't die and had a choice of how I wanted to spend eternity.

At the moment that freedom meant being inside a circular blue and white pendant around Nathan's neck. Where had Gillian obtained this? I had no idea and it wasn't his style at all. Any normal person would still be in shock after coming into contact with a sentient being hanging around their neck but Nathan had taken it in his stride. Our first meeting had been so dangerous his instincts didn't any other option other than to accept me, it was either listen to a strong southern drawl in your head or die.

I wasn't sure what the future held but, for now, hanging here around Nathan's neck, I wanted to help.

23

Nevaeh

Sharing a room with vampires would petrify most humans but strangely I always felt at home. I didn't see what other humans saw when looking at vampires, nothing about them scared me. Regardless of their age, wealth or status I somehow found it easy to communicate with them and remain at ease. Throughout my time at the prison vampires would often request me by name as the human they wanted they wanted to work with. Colleagues would often comment how out of the ordinary this was.

I remember my first day working as a prison guard after I left the gift shop. I had applied to work there as soon as I could. I don't know what appealed to me about working with people who were guilty of crimes that the state thought deserved incarceration, maybe it was because I have never been afraid of anyone.

All I had to do was sign visitors into the prison, check their ID and make sure they had an appointment. It was easy. Helen said to me once that she didn't understand how I could handle all the crying and anger on a daily basis, I'd responded that she hadn't seen how it got in the caravan park.

I loved Helen but she could never understand how people without money or privilege often stuck together in times of desperate need. Too many times I saw men beat on their family and no one cared. Helen always told me to phone the police, like I never thought of that idea before. If the police ever did turn up, which was rare, they would take a report that I swear ended up in the bin. No matter how much noise or fanfare we made in our lowly caravan park we were totally ignored. That is until a white, blue-eyed reporter would interview one of us and say how bad the situation was and that we needed help. No one really cared though. People liked to think they do but when the lights went out and the alcohol started flowing, they ran a mile. Unless you were Helen's dad Maury, he was so trusting and good intentioned with people I don't know how he survived as long as he did, especially with those idiot sons of his. Without his support and love I wouldn't be who I am now. He, along with Helen, gave me the confidence to not be afraid to walk into a room with my head held high.

Working as a prison guard, spending much of my time looking through an unbreakable glass window at the visitors coming and going, had hardened me to despair. When a loved one is rightly or wrongly incarcerated it often left a trail of destruction for the whole family. When you added in the vampires, this pain increased tenfold as the added attention of the media, bloggers and spectators publicised the shame of being a criminal, not to mention the gore involved.

The first person to have their blood taken by a vampire live streamed across the world caused a media sensation. It was quite horrifying seeing someone have their blood sucked out of his body while screaming in fear and agony.

The first victim had to be an easy target to bring the public onside with viewing someone having the life sucked out of them. At first glance, all the ingredients had been there. A janitor at a local school had been accused of sexually assaulting a male student. He was an odd-looking lanky man who didn't quite fit into society. He was found guilty of this terrible act. The janitor and his wife protested his innocence but it fell on deaf ears. The court of public opinion had made its ruling. The janitor was perfect for the press and the haters jumped on it too for many reasons. His wife, work and friends all left him as soon as they could. It wasn't long after the vampire feeding that the janitor took his own life in his cell and when that happened, I felt a hole inside my heart. Soon after, the janitor's victim came forward and confessed that he had made up the whole incident. His death sent a mini shockwave throughout the prison. Not only had the whole system made a gigantic mistake but no one was willing to apologise for it. It was hushed up hurriedly. The media had hung him out to dry but they just moved on to the next story, barely acknowledging their wrongdoing.

Instead, more websites and forums popped up online to report on every movement of each new victim, analysing how they felt, their background and what crime they had committed. After the first feeding it was never filmed for television again. Seeing a human being having their blood sucked out by an invisible image just didn't work, it became a live viewing experience.

That's where radio and podcasting really came into its own. Vampires were treated like voice actors in the golden age of radio back in the 1940s. You couldn't look up pictures of them online so their voices were how they were recognised. Older generations were used to this but younger people like myself found it new and challenging. Listening to a vampire on the radio could let your imagination run wild. There were certain vampires who lived up to this and pandered to the desires of their audience.

A podcast called "*Late Night Feast*" was a homage to an old TV show called *Midnight Caller*. The host vampire was even called Cole but I was sure that wasn't his real name. The show talked about the feeding process from the vampire's point of view and Cole used to bait the audience with his over-the-top personality. It was a living stereotype of a classic vampire and the people loved it. He became a worldwide sensation and was on every radio chat show and news program you could think of. People emailed, texted and phoned in to give their opinions on the vamp prison. Cole was originally a guest on the show but due to his flamboyant behaviour and sense of humour he quickly took over as host. He would often interview vamps or victims so I had listened a couple of times, it was fun and silly but sometimes he would tease the victims too much which rather unsettled me. I had briefly met him at the charity game but he was far too busy to talk to some lowly prison worker.

Once the feedings found their rhythm, I quickly moved up the ranks. We now do thousands of tests runs of our equipment, establish due process and most importantly we only allow vampires with the right amount of restraint in, having vamps who wouldn't kill the victim was quite important. I remember standing in that small room pushing a button letting people in and out all day. It was a long and monotonous process. Once the prison cottoned on to the fact that I was the only person not freaking out during this hectic time, and that I looked bored out of my mind standing behind the battered safety glass, I was always rostered on to help. The first job I was given was to tend to one of the vampires who was helping us test out the facility. Andy was a local farmer who chose to keep living his old life after being made into a vampire. It took a while for his farm stock not to be intimidated by a walking killing machine. He had been turned into a vampire against his will when he was on the way home from his local pub one night. Being the thoughtful person that he was he didn't want to lose control and start feeding off his mates so instead he came to the prison. I spent a lot of time with Andy while setting up the new prison process so I got to know him very well. This is where I first noticed my ability to work with vampires. On paper a person being changed into a vampire was horrifying but when you got to know the person and who they actually were it was less sensational than you might think. I was able to put aside the fearsome fangs and the coldness of their aura and see the person that once lived inside.

Of course, not all vampires were like Andy, if you were a dick before being made it's more than likely you would remain one. The prison saw me handle Andy with ease and that was how I officially secured my role in the feeding zone.

Each time I had received a promotion at work it was unplanned. Taking the job at the gift shop I could have never thought that it would lead to where I was now and the money I was on. I had the chance to do something important with my life, and for the first time I felt like I was making my own path. The only issue was Helen. Helen had always been the high flyer; she'd had the power to manipulate her own future in a way I never felt I could. But Helen's circumstances had changed quite drastically and now I had the chance to help but I was feeling resistant. I could now afford a lawyer to assist her but at the same time I wanted to have some fun and plan for my own future.

"Are you paying attention Nevaeh?" Jane said with disdain that was plain for all to hear in the room. Sitting at a desk while she talked numbers was boring me to fucking tears. Jane had rudely informed me that this weekly meeting with the warden, Lucy, Jane and Gary was integral to the success of the prison. I couldn't see the point of saying the same thing every week when there was actual work to be done.

Jane remained the one person who seemed determined to undermine me. Did she think I was a threat to her? Or did she just have contempt for people who grew up in caravan parks? I turned my gaze from the window where I had been admiring the well-kept green grass that any gardener would be proud off in this dry heat.

"Of course, Jane, I was hanging on your every word," I said with courtly steel.

Jane didn't appreciate my flippant backchat. I loved seeing her annoyed with me.

"Well, there is no point in me continuing with these meetings if you're not going to listen is there Nevaeh?"

"You're right Jane but I am always listening. I heard your point that you feel we need to increase the number of vampires we are signing to the program but as I have said before I think we should work on the quality not quantity of new clients."

"Well, how are you planning to do that?" she asked, making it obvious to everyone in the room that she was pissed with me. As I was about to reply, I saw Gary give a small shake of his head as he knew I was about to antagonise Jane further.

"Jane," I said softly, trying to take the tension out of the room, "the report on the table in front of you outlines the new clients I have targeted. I have also informed Lucy and Gary whom I would like to meet, and they have also given me a list of names that shouldn't be too hard for me to attract." All eyes turned towards the door as Lucy had just arrived uncharacteristically late. I didn't know her well but I liked what I saw and I felt a certain kinship with her for some reason. I found her almost mesmerising. There seemed to be no pretence with her, no judgement, how you performed in your role was what mattered. Lucy always seemed unflappable to me but today I could sense tension as she took a seat.

"My apologies for being late, I'm afraid I have a serious incident to report. Unfortunately, last night didn't go at all to plan, a group of vamps breached security and held one of our guests hostage. The hostage eventually broke free and took lethal revenge on his captors. Our other guests and human prisoners all escaped shaken but unharmed. We have a crew completing a clean-up at the venue as we speak."

The warden looked livid. "This could be catastrophic Lucy; we pride ourselves on safety and control. It's going to cost us a fortune to keep this out of the press."

This was the most animated I had ever seen him. He spoke calmly compared to most people but I knew that he was vexed. The warden, as well as the prison program, prided itself on being discreet and professional at all times. Warwick was running the prison and its services more like a five-star hotel rather than a place that holds the worst of the worst perpetrators from all over the world. He never let emotion get in the way of decision-making, there was too much money at stake for that to be an option.

Lucy nodded, "I agree warden the situation is most dire."

"If this gets out Lucy it will set the program back years and it will be on your head. We cannot have these incidents happen with the goddamn media constantly holding a microscope up to us and not to mention the council, government and whoever else always looking for a financial hand out. Am I making myself clear?"

Lucy nodded, "I can assure you I am doing what needs to be done. I have just got off the phone with the personal assistant of the vampire who was taken hostage and he is willing to work with us to keep this under wraps. He may well end up being an extremely valuable asset as he is a very well-known and wealthy vampire by the name of Thomas Malcolm."

Oh, Christ that's the vamp Blake wants me to deliver. I had to remain calm in front of everyone but inside I was freaking out. The chance for me to rescue Helen was real and within reach. All I needed to do was listen and hope that Thomas Malcolm was a real prick so my conscience would have no problem in trading his life for Helen's.

"Thomas Malcolm has requested couple of conditions before he will agree to work with us though."

"That seems unusual Lucy, but considering the situation just get it done," the warden said,

Lucy straightened in her chair and responded, "The unusual part sir is that Thomas Malcolm has insisted on meeting with Nevaeh to discuss the prison program at the restaurant he owns in town."

"Sorry," I interrupted, "Did you say I will be meeting Thomas Malcolm? When's this going to happen?" I said feeling completely unprepared for this. True, it was my job to meet the new VIPs and welcome them with open arms. It's also true vampires don't scare me but if Lucy's account of the night was correct, I had a feeling this meeting might be more unpredictable than most.

Lucy turned her gaze to me. "I'm afraid Nevaeh, that you will be meeting Thomas Malcolm in," she looked at her smart watch, "three hours, so there is a lot of preparation to be done before then as he is unlike any vampire I have ever met." I was unnerved by not only the thought of meeting Thomas Malcolm but also by the intensity of Lucy's gaze.

"Can you enlighten us further, Lucy?" the warden said.

"I have spent a lot of time with vampires over the years and on occasion have seen some of their powers up close," she said seriously, "although most of the VIP's prefer to not to show their true selves. Regardless of their standing in public they know deep down they can appear terrifying to humans who are less progressive than us. Due to my experience in the Fijian civil war, it takes a lot to unsettle me but what I witnessed last night shook me to my core. He, Thomas Malcolm, became something else, like a monstrous hybrid of a vampire and a bat, it was hideous and disturbing to see."

I knew Lucy, who was roughly the same age as me, joined the army at an early age and had worked in The Fijian Islands. I didn't know what department she had worked for in the army but it was clear to me that she must have seen some terrible things. The war in Fiji had shown what vampires were capable of when they were trained and used by the army. The Australian government had decided to help the Fijians resolve a civil war that had already been going on for two years by sending over both human and vampire troops. This specialised force helped the locals destroy the dictatorship in the most brutal and bloody way. Lucy would have witnessed first-hand that vampires were efficient killing machines.

Warwick took a deep breath and walked over to the window.

"Well Lucy it seems like we have no option other than to work with Thomas Malcolm but he sounds both powerful and dangerous so we need to ensure we are prepared and that the health and safety of everyone involved is safeguarded. We have a lot of work to do before the meeting tonight I just hope this Thomas Malcolm is worth it."

Jane interrupted by placing her hand on the Warden's elbow, "We know of Lucy's experiences in the army and if what she saw scares her then it will petrify us, so Thomas Malcolm must be an influential vampire." As Jane spoke the tension ripples on his neck subsided. No wonder they had enjoyed working together for so long. I could feel the yin and the yang of their relationship playing out before me.

Jane took control of the meeting and for the first time I didn't want to strangle her. I now saw that she was good at this. The way she had diffused the situation was expertly done. "Gary, you start drawing up contracts for our new guest tonight."

Gary whispered to me, "She fucking loves this." As he leaned in, he touched my hand. Jane continued to talk.

"Lucy, you need to work on Nevaeh's game plan for tonight." She was being forthright with the both of us but in a more caring nurturing way, I didn't think Jane had it in her. I looked over at Lucy and she seemed unsettled, this worried me as the next couple of hours rested on me being ready for whatever was going to happen. None of them knew that this could be my chance to save

Helen.

"And Nevaeh, you and I need to work together and start prepping for tonight. Lucky you," she smiled at me for the first time. The world was really turning upside fucking down.

24

Nathan

Before interviewing any one, I liked to be prepared with as much information as possible and not to be rushed. Tonight, I was neither of these things, instead I had a very a pumped-up partner in Gillian who was desperate to interview our new guest. I told him to let me lead but Gillian had shown that he didn't follow protocol and liked to follow his own instinct. A background check on our prisoner had come up empty and I didn't expect anything else.

The suspect was housed in a small sandstone cell. This was no high-end police station, there was no two-way mirror. Bars covered a narrow window at the top of the three-metre wall, this was the only way air and light could enter this stale smelling room. The room felt claustrophobic with just one person occupying it, let alone three beings, one of which was a very bored vampire.

It was clear the vampire who was handcuffed to the chair was in no right state of mind. His lips were moving at a rapid pace yet no words were coming out. Glancing over at Gillian I shook my head in disappointment. I knew whatever evidence or confession we were going to get tonight would be tainted. We needed a psychiatrist here to decipher what we were about to hear.

"I'm Detective Jenkins and this is Detective Jacob." The words seemed to wash over the vampire's head, he didn't have a clue where he was.

I beckoned Gillian over to the corner of the room with my eyes and began to speak.

"I think that…"

Gillian instantly interrupted me with his hands. "Nate there's no point in whispering he's a vamp so he can hear every word we say regardless, we can use Jeff," he said winking.

I was annoyed with myself on two counts. Why I didn't think of this and why wasn't I getting used to vampire's abilities.

"Hi Nate," the American accent said in my head.

"Interesting as always Jeff," I said inside my own consciousness, which was still surreal.

"Hey can I join in?" said Gillian, "I love a threesome of any sorts." he chuckled.

"Oh my God Gillian, I don't think I can handle this if I get every uncontrolled word just being thrown out of your mind into mine."

"I tell you what mate, there is absolutely no difference to now or before."

Laughing out loud in the small room I must have looked like a mad man, standing in the corner just staring at Gillian then laughing, but it made no difference to our guest.

"I can read what's going through his mind," said Jeff. "A lot of it is gibberish but I think I can make out bits of it."

"Wow," said Gillian, "that is quick Jeff, to be able to jump into anyone's mind at will."

"I had a good teacher," he said sounding modest.

"What can you hear Jeff?" I interrupted trying to get us back on track.

"There are three words that are constant but in no order. Capture, time and trusted"

"Right?" I said sounding more puzzled than before.

"Can I start talking to him Nate, I have an idea?"

"As long as the idea is not to smash his face against the table, then go for it."

Gillian gave a big smile as he grabbed the metal chair in front of the zoned-out vamp, span the chair round and sat on it with his arms leaning on the back of the chair. I don't know if he tried to look cool or it just came naturally.

"So, mate, do you have a name? I can sense that you're lost, that you've had no guidance, no maker, for whatever its worth I'm sorry. To come into this world with no help and no light to assist you when all you want to do is feed is a painful burden."

Gillian's tone was soft and caring. The vampire made eye contact, looking less crazed.

"Looking for a bed, a place to rest, a place to feed when you haven't been taught is torture. Never knowing what dusk will be your last. It's easy to be manipulated mate. My guess is someone promised you safety and unlimited food for just one meaningless task. Someone you trusted used you and left you on the streets to die." Gillian leaned back outstretching his arms, "How long have you been a Dusk Traveller?"

"Around six months," the vamp said staring down at the table.

"You're pretty powerful for a young vampire, how did you get to this point."

"I was out drinking with a few friends. We had been working hard at one of my friends' farms. I had never seen a vampire before. We thought it would fun to spend the night."

Looking more closely I realised he was just a kid of eighteen if not younger. The burns from the UV lights and the beating had made him appear older. What the hell had happened to this kid?

"Do you know who turned you and what they want? Or maybe how you became so strong?"

"A friend had heard that if we wanted to get lucky our best

chances were at *The Glitter Ball*. We were just drinking and having fun. My mates wanted to move on to somewhere else to watch the Knights play but I like that type of music so I stayed. I couldn't shake off the feeling that someone was watching me. When I looked around, I saw him across the room staring at me, the most mesmerising vampire I had ever seen. Before I knew it, he was by my side and paying for my drinks. The rest of the night was a haze and when I woke, I was a vampire." Small tears formed from the realisation of what had happened ran down his cheeks.

"Any idea what he looked like?" Gillian said sounding like he already knew the answer.

The beaten vampire started to rock in his seat and stare vacantly at the wall at this question, it was obvious that the last few nights had traumatised him. Gillian got up and walked over to me.

"I don't think we're going to get any further Nate."

"Maybe that's not true," interjected Jeff. "The words 'baby blue' and 'time' are being repeated in his thoughts. He is saying them over and over. Now it's 'capture the Austrian man', again and again."

Gillian slammed his hand against the wall. "Nate and Jeff from that I think we're fucked."

The fear in Gillian's eyes was real.

"Do you remember the other night Nate when I told you about the man I ran from. The man I hid Thomas Malcolm from. Well, from what Jeff has just told us he's here, which means Thomas Malcolm must also be close. Fuck!" he shouted which made the whole room sit up.

"You sure Gillian? It seems like a long shot."

"Come on Nate open your eyes. First your sister mentions Thomas Malcolm's name, then the spate of killings. From the repeated mentioning of baby blues, it's got to be Blake, I know it.

We both turned to a knock on the door. Charlie entered the

room. "Sir the accused's representation is here and they insist we cease the interview. Also, I haven't heard from Sam for a while and she's not answering her phone."

I beckoned for us all to leave the room and talk in the corridor, "No one knows the accused is here, did they say who they are?"

"Yes sir, one of them said her name is Lucy Thea and she works for the prison."

"Prison? What the hell? And what's going on with Sam?"

"She didn't report in on her scheduled check in. The last location we have is from her car outside *Smash* nightclub."

"Fuck Nate, that's where one of the last murders was. This doesn't feel right mate, this can't be a mere coincidence. I have a bad feeling something ominous is upon us and it all seems to be leading up to tonight. I'm worried, Nate"

"Ok, right," I said out loud but mainly to compose myself. "Charlie run a search on any farm hands who have gone missing in the area, start with people under the age of twenty. Also, Charlie do not let anyone related to this leave no matter what, do you hear me? Right let's go Gillian," I said as we both moved swiftly down the corridor, the pain from the battle the other night seemingly replaced by adrenaline.

"Nate, shit's about to get real and for God's sake find out where your sister is, if she's with Thomas Malcolm she's in danger."

25

Claire

He asked for me to come and like an obedient dog I agreed. I had proven to myself and to other people that I only do what suits my family and myself. I don't just drop my focus or my goals for no one, not even Tom, so why was I here? He was the pompous one, the one who looked down at us with all his European aloofness. Perhaps he was using his charisma on me but I didn't think that was the case.

Ever since that first meeting with Thomas Malcolm I knew that our paths would cross again and it gave me butterflies. After watching the death of Tom's killers, I thought that I would suffer some type of guilt, which would be expected, the scary thing was I didn't. Even though they were vampires they were once human so in some small way I had been complicit in murder, for money.

The money was an added bonus but insignificant for me, it would help with looking after the foster kids but honestly, I had enough money saved from teaching. The real reward had been the excitement I felt after he approached me while I was working at the charity cricket game. The initial glimpse of him took my breath away. It had felt like my world was about to change.

I had spent so much time on that fucking treadmill planning my whole existence to within an inch and I had been happy with that, until Tom was killed. I had lost a loved one, and I had also lost the restraint that comes from being in a relationship where you have to think of your partner and your family before you think of yourself. I felt liberated and guilty with these new thoughts. A vampire had decided to take something away from me on a whim, and that was not going to happen again.

I had been waiting for Thomas Malcolm in one of his immaculate guest rooms. I had no idea why he had requested my company but I had been there for hours. Who the hell did he think he was? At around 4am there was a loud commotion, people screaming and banging. On phoning reception, one of Thomas Malcolm's many handlers assured me everything was ok. Although hearing a female scream, "I will fucking kill you TM," in a Portuguese accent did make me question why I was here. But much to my surprise I fell asleep with no worries in my head.

I could never afford the view that I had right now looking out from the balcony. People below me were starting to traverse the promenade looking for places to eat. The sun was setting gently over the ocean and this meant my host or whatever you could call him, was about to materialise from his daily slumber. When the sun disappeared and darkness fell, I couldn't help but wonder how vampires lived like this. The idea of the night sky being what I woke to every day for the rest of my life would depress me greatly.

I lived for daylight; it's why I rose early to run on my friend the treadmill. Every step I pounded into that machine; every bead of sweat helped turn darkness into light. I did my best to greet each day with a positive outlook and this along with the reward of working with children every day is what kept me from losing my mind after Tom passed. If I woke each day to darkness, I don't think I could go on living.

Exercise and sunshine were as important to me as my lists, they all made life more bearable. I never accept anything less than someone's best effort and I know this can make me hard to be around. I guess my high standards can make me seem like a well-intentioned know it all. It's hard to change though.

The balcony I was sitting on was stylish, and elegant, like the rest of the apartment. The simple and modern décor was purposefully put together to make you feel relaxed and calm. I didn't know why Thomas Malcolm had extended me an invitation. He was aloof and confounding but there was something about him that attracted me to his presence. He intrigued me, and in my organised life of lists this was something I couldn't plan or predict.

The lapping of the waves mixed with the chatter of people floated up from below. I was lost and didn't hear the apartment door open. I sensed something behind me and I was startled to see a tall broad woman standing there with a kind, but reserved, face. The black, fitted suit she wore with a white shirt emphasised her impressive frame.

"Hi Claire, I'm Danni, one of the security guards that work for Thomas Malcolm," she said softly, defying her imposing appearance. All of Malcolm's staff looked as though they could be part of one those 1980s action films Nathan was obsessed with when we were younger.

"I didn't mean to frighten you but I came to check that you have everything you need and to let you know that Mr Malcolm is ready to see you at your convenience."

For fuck's sake Thomas Malcolm was so up himself he even got his staff to speak like him, at your convenience, does he think he is part of some monarchy? I sipped some extravagantly expensive sparkling water and smiled and nodded at Danni.

"Thank you, everything is wonderful. It's like being on a mini break to an expensive resort," I said jokily.

"Thomas Malcolm will be pleased; he likes all his guests to feel relaxed and happy. If you are ready to see him, I will take you to his chamber."

Saying the word chamber made me feel anxious. Was I being led into a trap where he would feast on me? If so, there was no way to stop him. Still, a fluttering feeling in my stomach was pushing me forward, deeper into this impressive building that Thomas Malcolm had made his home.

I followed Danni down the corridor to the same lift that had brought me from the carpark. My face in the mirrored walls was tense as I watched the numbers descend well below ground level.

This was a well-guarded fortified vampire home on the coast of Australia, which bore no resemblance to the Transylvanian castle described in folklore. Still the countless corridors, mirrors and uniformed staff made it hard to get my bearings. The lift finally reached its destination with a chime. The doors opened to a well-lit white corridor that was more like a hospital than part of the luxurious apartment above.

As I stepped out of the lift Danni moved towards me reaching out her hand. "Please Claire let me take your bag." Her smile was deliberately reassuring, which made me think I must have looked tenser than I thought. "Jonathan will meet you at the end of corridor and he will take you in to see Mr Malcolm, good luck," she said, stepping back into the lift. The mirrored doors closed leaving me standing there staring at a face full of worry.

There was no apparent need for me to feel threatened, I had been treated as a very special guest, yet still I had no idea what I was walking into and why. I walked along the corridor and could see Jonathan standing at the end talking to yet another guard. He seemed rather stern as he looked at a tablet. On hearing me approach he looked up with tired brown eyes that gave mine a run for their money. He wasn't an intimidating man in size, unlike his counterpart, and his frame reminded me slightly of Tom. He definitely didn't look like a man in charge of a highly trained group of vampire kidnappers but maybe that was the point.

As I got closer the unmistakable smell of bleach hit me, I wondered what they had been cleaning up after. Not that I was one to judge, I had to remember that I was a part of this operation too, even if only a small one.

"Hello Claire, I'm Jonathan, head of operations here." His manner was curt and to the point.

"Hello, nice to meet you," I said. "You definitely take security seriously here."

"We do Claire, the boss is just finishing up an interview with a new guest, he will join us shortly…"

A door on my left opened and a rather pleased with himself looking Thomas Malcolm walked out of the room smiling devilishly ear to ear. He walked towards me and reached out his hand in greeting. In the background, before the door was closed, I glimpsed what I looked like a small red-haired vampire crouching in a metal cage with two other vampires circling around her.

"Don't be alarmed my dear Claire," said Thomas Malcolm. "The lady you saw, if you can call her that, threatened me and is a danger to my very existence, trust me she is not a good person, but we are not here for that tonight."

He opened another door and we left Jonathan and the hospital corridor behind. I found myself in a large circular room that was decorated with objects, trinkets and artefacts from all over the world. It was breathtakingly beautiful and not what I had expected at all. It was like a well-curated exhibition, full to the brim with art even I recognised and pieces of what looked like ancient Japanese armour. I had no doubt the treasures were genuine. There was a small plaque next to each item describing where it was from and when it had been found.

I was fascinated, just the effect Thomas Malcolm wanted, as he walked over to a small lounge area with a bar and chairs and sat down. I could see he was very pleased with himself. One of his staff entered the room and began preparing drinks, bottles were opened and ice clinked into glasses, it was all very theatrical. Thomas Malcolm allowed me to wander around the room at my leisure. Did he know I studied history as part of my education degree? There was no way he could have obtained all of these objects just to impress me. This sort of collection took centuries to put together. Of course, I knew the pompous bastard was enjoying every minute of my fawning over it. I could see he was drinking a blood-coloured cocktail and my favourite drink, a passionfruit martini, was waiting for me next to the chair he was sitting in. He knows everything about me, I thought. It felt very surreal, like I was being stalked. Maybe he thought it was cute or reassuring that he was looking after a guest. I found it creepy.

After taking in as much detail as possible I walked over to Thomas Malcolm and sat down next to him. "Thomas Malcolm, I don't like being manipulated, or being stalked. You may consider it part of your service but it makes me feel like you are trying to control me and I don't work that way, even with all this expensive extravagance surrounding me."

"Claire. I, Thomas Malcolm, do not control the people you see here working for me, but it's true I am capable of persuasion. It is no cause for alarm though, I don't use mind control on my family. And this is what this is Claire, a family, a family that has taken a long time to come together. There are many perks for those working for me and I can be involved with your life as much or as little as you feel is appropriate."

I was confused as to what he was saying and I knew he could tell that.

"No matter how powerful I have become or how long I have lived, I have learned that it never pays to force anyone to do what I desire out of fear. Everyone here including myself, no matter how much I try to hide it, I was once like you Claire."

For once his words weren't filled with condescension, I sensed real emotion, although I couldn't tell for sure whether I was being manipulated or not.

"Do you know why I've asked you here Claire?"

"No, but you already know that, right? I thought I might be in trouble because of what happened with the business surrounding my late husband."

"No Claire you are not in trouble, from the moment I first met you I felt the is something different about you, don't scoff, it's true and it's not a line."

He seemed to be speaking from the heart. But how could I ever be sure?

"I find it hard to trust anything you say Thomas Malcolm, because of who you are."

"Claire I am not somebody who lies. I have never lied to those who work for me, trust is imperative and it is my hope you will become part of my team."

It seemed that Thomas Malcolm himself was nervous, even anxious. There was no need for him to speak so openly with me. I automatically picked up the cocktail to calm my nerves. The smell of fresh passionfruit reminded me of growing up with Nate, picking fruit from the garden and stuffing our faces until we could eat no more. God nostalgia tasted good. As I drank, I was annoyed at myself that I may be just falling into whatever trap he had set up.

He smiled at me with those whiter than white teeth but this time it didn't feel like an act. He looked less like a dangerous and intimidating vampire and more like the rest of us, aging and tired, tired of life with nowhere else to go. He almost looked lost.

"Claire the first moment I saw you I judged you in the same way everyone judges me, I saw a wife who had cruelly had her husband taken away from her far too soon. Just another weak human, who like most, would come and go and leave no imprint in this world, but I was wrong. When I saw you at the cricket match, I sensed you had powers you are unaware of and with your permission I would like to help you harness those powers."

I was confused yet also a small part of me knew he could be right.

Thomas Malcolm continued, "We both have something inside of us we need to control, for me it's a dangerous beast which resides in me but I don't let it define me. Claire you are using your power right now and you are not even aware of it."

It registered with me Thomas Malcolm was no longer moving his lips but I could still hear his words. As the realisation of what was happening began to sink in, I jumped up from my seat. My glass dropped and shattered on the grey polished concrete floor. How was this happening? I started to back away from Thomas Malcolm towards the door. He remained where he was, smiling.

"Just breathe Claire, I'm here to help. I had an inkling of our connection at our first meeting and then it was more pronounced at the cricket ground. It was as though you were calling to me."

"Here to help? You're reading my goddamn mind without my permission," I shouted, tears of fear ran down my cheeks, "how dare you take advantage of me. I won't be treated this way."

"Claire my dear, I'm not reading your mind, you're reading mine."

26

Alfred

I don't normally like surprises but Samuel was quite insistent he wanted to spoil me as a thank you for allowing him to stay with me for so long. I didn't know why he felt like he had to repay me for anything. I knew this was puppy love and that it was bound to end in tears for me but I was truly happy. Samuel is someone I would usually consider unattainable and out of my league but in reality, he is caring and considerate. It was nice to have a man about the house. I've never felt manly, but that was starting to change with the help and confidence of my work colleagues and the choices I was now making.

I was at the *Great Gas* waiting for Samuel to pick me up, even though this club was brash and loud, and maybe even a little vulgar for my taste, it reminded me of freedom and I would always have a fondness for it. As I sipped on my cocktail, I found myself thinking of Samuel and I could be more.

I saw Samuel making his way through the busy crowd, people stared at his beauty as he passed, this was commonplace. Their faces turned from awe to shock when they saw him kiss scrawny old me with affection and kindness but I was becoming used to that and not caring as much. Samuel sat down looking impeccable in fitted beige pants and a tight white shirt that showed his impressive physique. I didn't know what was more shocking, the fact I was dating a vampire or that I was dating a hipster vampire.

"So why are we here?" I said playfully, happy to see him after finishing a busy week of work and looking forward to the week-end. As he sculled a blood shot, he had picked up from the bar I noticed he looked slightly off kilter.

"I have a surprise for my little Alfie," he said while beckoning for another drink.

"Everything ok Samuel? You look a little off?" He gave me a smile and ruffled my hair, which he knows I don't like.

"Of course, it is, I'm just excited for you to see what I have planned for you tonight. I've booked a swanky apartment for the night and was thinking maybe we can get a little wild." His next drink arrived and he sculled it again, this wasn't like him.

"Samuel, you don't have to do buy me gifts or do things like this. You're more than I could ever hope for," I was trying not to sound too corny.

He gave me a big kiss on the lips. "Oh Alfie" he said looking into my eyes, "I think I've fallen for you, haven't I."

"Well good, I feel the same way." I pulled him closer to me, "We should go right now!" I had never been happier.

I put down my drink and took Samuel's hand as we left the club, it was so crowded it took us about ten minutes to leave. It was around midnight, peak time on the strip. I couldn't believe how quickly I'd adjusted my body clock to being awake at all hours during the weekend. If I wanted to continue this lifestyle, I had no choice. Samuel was leading me across the road full of punters and pedestrians to Smashed, the bar he worked at.

"I thought that we were going to a nice apartment?" I asked.

"We are, it's just above the club, and I didn't even know it was here until yesterday. The staff behind the bar tell me it's an exclu-sive apartment only high rollers know about."

Samuel scanned us through a non-descript door that surprisingly led to a room full of elegant period features. The door shut out all the hustle and bustle of the club as it closed behind us. Wow, I thought, you would never know this place was here. The beauty and elegance of this place was such a contrast to the madness outside.

Entering the first room of the apartment I couldn't get over how serene and stylish everything was. There was a dinner trolley in the middle of the apartment with two flutes of champagne sitting there waiting for us. A smartly dressed vampire was preparing food in the open plan kitchen. Smiling from ear to ear I turned to Samuel, "This is fantastic, it feels like our own private villa, we even have a room attendant".

Samuel had gone quiet and when I turned towards him, he looked anxious.

"What's wrong darling?" holding his hand.

"Alfie my dear," he said slowly, "I think I've made a terrible mistake. I need to get us out of here. I need to get you out of here. Just give me second. Do you trust me?" He looked panicked and scared.

"Yes, yes of course I do but you're scaring me a little. What's going on?'

As Samuel headed back towards the barkeeper an attractive male walked out of the bedroom dressed in nothing but a pair of black speedos, I thought I might have seen him at *Blush* before but I couldn't be sure.

"Well, hello everyone. What do we have here?" he announced while giving Samuel and I a look up and down. "Yum yum, aren't we going to have some fun tonight," he said before walking over to me and grasping my groin. My heart sank a little, I didn't want to share Samuel with anyone and especially not with someone as confident as him.

"What's your name honey pie?" he said in a broad American accent.

I knew I must look flustered. I was about to answer when I could hear shouting from behind the bar from Samuel and the vampire preparing drinks.

"You can't do this; you will get us all killed!" the tall scared looking vampire said trying to reason with Samuel. Samuel was heading swiftly my way.

"He won't stand for this, once he finds out he will kill you and your precious meat bag."

"Fuck off," Samuel retorted back angrily.

"Whoa, calm down," said black speedo man as he inhaled a line of white powder off the kitchen counter. "Why don't we all just try to have some fun? I know am."

"We are leaving Alfie, right now," Samuel put his arm round me and guided me to the front door.

"Samuel, you're scaring me."

"I know, I'm sorry, just know that I love you, I'll explain once we get out of here," before we could leave the apartment door opened and a youthful-looking vampire stood before us.

"Tut tut, Samuel, don't make a decision which would let me down," he said softly and ominously.

"Fuck." Samuel placed his arm in front of me and started pushing me backwards. "You can't have him. I won't let you do this."

The young vamp walked purposefully through the door followed by two much larger vampires, instantly my hair stood on end.

"You don't have any choice; I give you everything you need and this is how you treat me?" he truly looked upset with Samuel.

The male escort interjected, "Look everyone, no need to argue, let's all just have a good time." The young vampire waved his hand dismissively towards him, and with that one of the big vampires flashed across the apartment and snapped his neck like you would a twig, his body fell to the ground with a thud.

"Jesus Christ Blake!" shouted Samuel, "Run to the bathroom Alfie and lock yourself in until you hear my voice."

"No, that won't be happening," Blake said calmly, "I had big plans for Alfred but if you are going to stand in my way then both of you are of no use to me. To say I'm disappointed is an understatement."

I ran towards the bathroom while the vamp behind the bar tried to make his escape behind Blake's back. Blake was a good few feet away from the barman but he moved so fast that before anyone knew what was happening, he surged towards him and ripped out his throat with one hand. He just stood there holding a hunk of flesh in his hand while blood sprayed across the room from the now dead vampire's neck.

I locked the bathroom door as fast as I could with fumbling fingers. What the hell is happening? What does this Blake want with me and what has Samuel done? Sweat was running down my forehead that left my hair dangling in my face. I didn't know what to do.

I could hear Samuel screaming my name through the door. The commotion of the apartment getting torn apart was getting closer and closer. I staggered back to the wall of the shower screen door feeling trapped. There was no escape. The door exploded inwards, pieces of wood flew everywhere and I instinctively put my arms up to protect my face. When I looked up, Blake was standing in the doorframe his piercing baby blue eyes staring at me coldly. Behind him I could see Samuel being held down on the floor by Blake's two imposing offsiders, he was beaten and bloody. One of the vampires had Samuel in a headlock, angling his face in my direction.

"This is what happens when someone betrays me Samuel, you now get to watch your lover die!"

"Please don't do this!" Samuel screamed as tears ran down his face.

"Samuel?" I said in a whimper, his eyes were filled with a mixture of love and fear. I couldn't move, I was frozen, petrified, I began to wet myself as Blake walked towards me with outstretched hands, showing me the full array of his teeth.

"It's nothing personal," he said coldly as he leant towards my neck.

27

Nevaeh

As I sat looking out at the ocean with the busy promenade behind me, I couldn't help but think tonight's meeting with Thomas Malcolm was going to be a challenge. After the bedlam of the other night at the auction house Thomas Malcolm's team had understandably insisted meeting on their turf.

Lucy was supposed to accompany me but she had been called away at the last moment. I couldn't imagine what she would consider more important than this. Jane had seemed concerned for my safety and wanted to postpone but while it wasn't ideal, I told her I could handle it. I appreciated her insistence on allocating a driver to me for the night though, yet still I felt no fear towards the vampires

Thomas Malcolm's personal bodyguard Jonathan had scheduled the meeting at Claude's, as apparently Thomas owned the restaurant. Of course, he owns the place I thought to myself, just another fucking status symbol, vampire or not rich white people were all the same. Why the hell would a vampire as old as Thomas Malcolm need a bodyguard though? More posturing I assume. The more I had gotten to know vampires the more I became aware they like to collect a wide variety of items, mainly so they can show them off to others of their kind. They didn't just settle for houses, cars and other material objects, they also liked to own people, not that different to the human powers that be.

Nothing I had heard so far would stop me from giving Thomas Malcolm's whereabouts to Blake to save Helen. The idea of Blake sucking the life out of Helen compelled me forward this evening but I needed to remain professional; I couldn't afford to blow it. I was hoping the meeting with Thomas Malcolm tonight would go quickly and uneventfully but deep inside I knew that was nonsense.

Many of today's revelations had been surprising but the most by far was when Jane replaced her usually patronising tone with pleasantries. At first, I thought that she was trying to humour me but I must have passed some invisible test that she had set for me. I thought she was just another one of the racist baby boomers that seemed to be multiplying by their thousands in this town.

The brief moment I had with Jane felt real and genuine but as I had been burned in the past, I still had my guard up with most people at this prison, including handsome Gary. Jane had told me that I was doing a great job and I shouldn't lose focus on what is important to me and to the future of the prison. I was pretty sure she was warning me off Gary but it was only a feeling. Jane was far too well seasoned not to see what was happening around her, I had begun to admire her for it.

As I finished my ice cream here in the moonlight it made me realise how much I missed being outside at night, being able to feel the humid air on my skin. Working night shift for the last year and a bit had robbed me of these simple pleasures. My desire to prove my worth and succeed in my career meant living in the world of the vampires and tonight was no exception. I heard people approaching from behind me, I turned to see a man and a woman heading in my direction. The man had a similar build and shape to Gary but looked as though he'd had a much harder life, he must be the bodyguard, Jonathan, I thought to myself. A handsome man,

I'm sure, but the combination of deep wrinkles and darkness round his eyes would have seen him fit right in where I grew up, a little rough around the edges. One glance at Jonathan I could see the aura of toughness that people who have lost someone close have, not unlike myself.

"Hello Nevaeh," he said walking purposefully to me, he reached out his hand for a firm but professional handshake. "I'm Jonathan, Thomas Malcolm's head of security."

I nodded politely with a small smile and looked at the woman beside him, she seemed refined and younger than Jonathan, closer to my age.

"This is my colleague, Claire; she will be accompanying us this evening." This was said as a statement more than as a request.

"Good to meet you Jonathan and Claire. How is everyone recovering from last night?" I asked trying to find out how bad the situation was.

Jonathan seemed to look me up and down, trying to gather what my angle is before answering, "The other night was an utter disaster on many fronts, but that's why you're here, isn't it? To smooth over proceedings and to get back in my boss's good books."

Staring back directly at Jonathan, "You're correct, from the briefing I have had the other night was utter chaos, which has damaged the reputation of both your boss and the prison." I thought I saw Jonathan flinch a little at this comment. "I am here at the request of Thomas Malcolm but I am also here to work with you to repair the damage from last night's incident."

There was an edge to our conversation, which was only just bordering on civil. That's when I noticed his partner Claire was looking at me with a strange befuddled expression on her face, I found this concerning, I glanced at Jonathan and saw the concern on his face.

"You ok Claire?" Jonathan asked, but she just continued to stare at me until the ringing of her phone woke her from her weird day trance. Claire quickly took her phone from her pocket and gave it a quick glance, turning it off right away.

"Claire?" Jonathan repeated.

"Sorry it's my brother, he won't stop calling me, I'll sort it out later. My apologies that won't happen again," Claire said sounding a little distracted.

"Fine," Jonathan said but I could tell be wasn't happy.

"So," I said. "Shall we get to it?"

Surprisingly Jonathan appeared to give me a smirk.

"You're right," he said. "Let's head over to the restaurant shall we," he gestured across the road.

As we headed over to see this Thomas Malcolm, I suddenly realised that I had been to Claude's only recently but tonight was very different, walking up the stairs, I couldn't help but notice no one else was here. Upon reaching the restaurant I realised it was devoid from all human life apart from the three of us.

Jonathan led me into the beautiful open-air dining area, Thomas Malcolm was at a table in the middle surrounded by tea lights which twinkled like the stars of the Milky Way. He stood to greet me, a very tall and graceful vampire who European-ness oozed from every pore. He was dressed in an all-white suit, with a matching cravat and he gave me a huge smile that appeared genuine, but I was dubious.

He moved quickly and smoothly towards me, as if he was floating above the floor and before I knew it, he was kissing me lightly on each cheek. "Oh, this is wonderful, it's so good to finally meet you Nevaeh."

Thomas Malcolm took a step back from me and smiled again.

"Well, my dear, aren't you quite a surprise. I underestimated how unique you are!"

"Excuse me?" I replied, this tall lean vampire who looked like he was dressed from the last century had me totally confused. I turned to face Jonathan.

"What is happening? This isn't very professional." I said in frustration.

"Boss. This is Nevaeh from the prison. You do remember, right boss?"

"Yes, yes. Come all, sit down my darlings, we are all in for a treat and I will explain everything." He looked almost giddy.

I could see Claire shifting uncomfortably beside me.

"I have no interest in sitting down and playing happy families until you explain to me what is going on," Claire said sternly with her arms folded across her chest sounding like one of my old school teachers when I had done something wrong. "I feel nothing about her and I know you can't too. Her mind is blank! I need some answers." It was obvious that Claire was stressed and that Thomas Malcolm's eccentricity wasn't helping her demeanour.

"Claire," Thomas Malcolm said in a low tone, moving closer and looking as though he was trying to console her.

"The reason you are unable read Nevaeh's mind is because she is of true blood. Nevaeh my dear I'm sure you have found you are able to converse with my brethren without fear. Your ancestors are the oldest civilisation on this planet, older than we vampires. Your kind were there to witness the birth of our kind. Most vampires are not old enough to have knowledge of this, but this is the reason why you feel so at ease in our presence. We cannot harm you."

"What do you mean Claire can read minds? My mind. Since when?" Jonathan said, sounding like it was the first time in a while he didn't know the answer to a question.

"Oh, Jonathan my most loyal friend, is it so hard to believe that a human would possess similar abilities to we vampires? I only had an inkling of this until recently. In all my years of existence I have not had the pleasure of meeting any humans with powers and now delightfully there are two in my very presence." He was moving to the jazz music as he spoke, which I found strangely amusing.

"Boss," Jonathan said with intensity "give us a straight answer please, no more of this aloofness and ambiguity." I sensed that this remark hurt Thomas Malcolm, which surprised me.

"Fine, I guess I owe you some answers." he turned around dramatically and sat down at the table and poured himself a wineglass of blood.

Drawing the situation out theatrically, he made a slurping noise as he drank, licking his fangs with his tongue to savour the ruby red liquid

"Very well my dear Jonathan, my most trusted confidant. Meet Nevaeh who is here with us as she has no idea of the power she possesses over we vampires yet, and secondly," he said with glee in his voice. "Meet Claire who has joined our team because of her mindreading abilities, but who is at the moment is rather annoyed that she cannot read Nevaeh's thoughts."

"Happy now everyone?" he said as he drank.

"No," Jonathan and Claire said in unison, which made the star of the show roll his eyes.

"Oh, don't be like that, this is something that will change all of our lives for the better." Thomas Malcolm said giddily.

I was intrigued by what I was hearing, Thomas Malcolm was saying things that deep down I felt I already knew. When I had met Blake the other night, I was more than willing to trade Thomas Malcolm to save my beloved Helen, but now for some reason, I couldn't betray Thomas Malcolm, I felt an affinity for him and couldn't throw him to the wolves. I needed to know more. My gut instinct was now telling me to side with Thomas Malcolm, suddenly I knew deep within my soul Blake was not to be trusted. Is this what an epiphany feels like?

"Thomas Malcolm," I said nervously, which was a first for me.

"I think I may have made a mistake."

"What is it my dear child?" he said while beckoning me to sit next to him.

"I fear I may have put you in grave danger. What you have said resonates with me. I didn't know until right now that I should work with you rather than against you."

Jonathan was immediately on guard, "What do you mean, danger?" he said worriedly, Thomas Malcolm waved him down.

"Jonathan, let Nevaeh speak."

"Recently I was approached by a vampire requesting I give him your whereabouts in exchange for my best friends release from prison. At the time I agreed but now after meeting you and hearing what you have had to say I just can't do it. I feel compelled to keep you safe." I said earnestly.

Thomas Malcolm stood up and approached me and he took my hand in his, "Tell me this vampire's name please Nevaeh?" he said gently.

Drawing a long breath I replied, "His name is Blake." Upon hearing this name Jonathan sprang into action radioing his people to prepare for an imminent ambush.

("It's fucking time!") This loud booming voice came from Thomas Malcolm but didn't sound like him at all. ("Ladies please excuse me while I transform into the beast,") he said as his white suit ripped off his contorting limbs.

Thomas Malcolm fell to his knees and his body began to writhe and transform in front of our very eyes. I could hear the sounds of his bones cracking as what appeared to be wings grew from beneath his arms. His eyes gleamed red and his face look pained as it began to take on the characteristics of a bat. The beast that was Thomas Malcolm rose to his feet, spread his wings and revealed strength and power that left no doubt he was ready for battle. Claire gasped in horror.

I on the other hand couldn't help but think this was the most beautiful and intriguing creature I had ever encountered.

28

Nathan

I ran down the packed street from the police station sweating profusely and dodging the punters as best as I could. Gillian's warning about something going down tonight had me on high alert, with Sam missing in action and Claire not responding to my calls my stress levels were rising rapidly. Jeff was constantly talking to me in my head, telling me to relax and focus on the task ahead, he was correct but I had to admit I was finding it difficult. It had taken an age to get anywhere near *Smash* nightclub through all the other sweaty bodies out for the night.

"Nate something's happening up ahead. I can sense it." Just as the words came out of Gillian's mouth, hundreds of people came swarming out of *Smash*. People and vampires were screaming and covered in blood, it was chaos. I was reminded this was the first place Gillian and I visited upon his arrival. We both instantly took out our guns out and headed to the entrance. It was hard to think with music blaring from the speakers outside the club. I looked through the darkened windows but the blinding neon lights made it impossible to see what was going on inside. Jeff was telling me that he couldn't sense any vampires within the club.

"There are two human heart beats inside, one very faint. They are both next to each other. It feels as though one's life has just passed but I can't be sure," Jeff told us both.

Gillian entered through the heavy stainless-steel doors on the left and I headed to the right with my back against the wall. As we entered you couldn't but help notice the blood dripping from the countless TVs as world sport continued to play beneath the splatter. Tables and chairs were upturned over the floor as if a stampede of buffalo had just run through. I could see two security staff on the floor, their bodies lifeless.

"Hello? Is there anyone here?" I shouted above the music. "This is Detective Jenkins, we are here to help."

"I can hear a faint female voice towards the rear," Gillian said to Jeff and me. I nodded and we both carefully made our way to the side of the bar. A blood-soaked corridor led to offices out back.

Mel's body was in the office doorway, he was cold to the touch and had been ripped to shreds, his wounds were deep and claw like. The look on his face showed he had been petrified when the attacked had taken place.

"In here," I heard a familiar but weak voice.

I put my gun away and rushed over to Charlotte who was trying her best to save Sam, her hands desperately tried to stop the blood flowing from her neck.

"What the hell Charlotte? What happened?"

"A vampire murdered Mel right in front of my eyes. Sam did what she could but didn't stand a chance. I will never forget that vamp's cold baby blue eyes." Charlotte was covered in blood and obviously traumatised.

"Gillian, behind the bar, there should be a first aid kit, someone call an ambulance," I yelled.

Charlotte was in shock from whatever had just occurred. Visibly shaking and holding Sam's hand tightly as my colleague held on for her life.

Gillian returned in a flash with the first aid box, "What do you need?"

"Bandages, lots of them." Sam's eyes were open and I could see there was recognition but she was only barely holding on. All the years of training for moments like these kicked into gear. I had to stop the bleeding but I was more than worried we were too late.

Gillian spoke to me via Jeff, "Nate, we're going to lose her." The sadness from Gillian was palpable.

Gillian moved next to me, holding Sam's other hand, while I frantically tried to stop the blood, it was useless though, the wound was just too deep. Sam's breathing was getting shallower by the second.

"Sweet Sam," Gillian said softly and caringly. "You can't leave me I've only just gotten to know you."

Sam turned her head to him and a small smile crossed her tired face. Her large blue eyes were starting to lose their colour.

"Gillian," Sam said barely audible. Gillian moved his head closer to her mouth. "Why do people hate vampires?" Blood was coming out of her mouth now, "Because they suck."

Sam's eyes closed and she let go of Gillian's hand. Tears were running down Gillian's face, he stood up, shouted "FUCK!" and smashed his fists against the wall. I was frozen in shock I just couldn't believe…

"Nate, Nate you need to regain control," Jeff said.

"Can't I have one goddamn minute?" I shouted aloud, which startled those in the room.

"No, I'm afraid you cannot Detective Jenkins. There is someone else in the apartment upstairs who needs your help. There are also multiple vampires up there, I can sense it."

Upon hearing this, Gillian snapped out of his stupor and turned and walked out the door, "Let's go crack some skulls Nate. I am going to rip that cunt Blake in fucking half!" Which I knew he meant literally.

Gillian and I left the club and headed onto the main strip, I could hear the sirens of our back up and the ambulance for Sam that was already too late. I couldn't believe Sam was gone, for the first time I could feel hatred and anger at those who had done this taking over, Jeff reminded me, "Time to focus Nate."

I took off my jacket and drew my vampire gun, "You know what Jeff I don't need your fu…"

Gillian placed his hand on my shoulder, while looking me in the eyes, "Nate, you need Jeff right now. Save the emotion until after we get these scumbags, if you don't it could kill us all. We need to be on our A game, we have no idea what nasty surprises wait for us."

"There are four vampires, one of whom is incredibly powerful," reported Jeff.

Gillian and I turned to each other. Gillian walked up to the door of the apartment that was the scene of the last murder and kicked it down effortlessly. He bounded up the stairs while I followed as quickly as possible doing my best to recall the layout of the apartment.

When we arrived on the landing, it was obvious which room the screams were coming from as blood was seeping out from under the door.

Gillian leaned against the door and carefully looked in.

"Nate," he said through Jeff. "There's a body of vampire to the left and a body of a human directly in front. I can hear struggling from the bedroom. I'll go along the wall on the right but I need you to get to the kitchen counter and cover me. When you shoot aim for the heart, ok mate? We go on three." I took a deep breath.

Gillian counted "1, 2, 3." A loud anguished scream came from inside the apartment as Gillian crept in. I crouched as low as possible and snuck behind the kitchen counter, Gillian was hiding behind a column, ready to pounce.

"You killed him, you killed Alfie!" I could hear the loud desperate cry of a loved one. There were two huge vampires holding another down on the floor, he was sobbing uncontrollably, "Kill me," he kept saying. "Please, kill me!"

"Tut-tut Samuel, you are truly pathetic," said a small young-looking vampire as he walked out of the bathroom wiping blood from his mouth. "You don't get to play me. No one ever has or ever will. We wanted to use Alfred to control the power station and ultimately control this city but you let emotions get in the way. I must say your lover tasted rather sweet," he said as he licked his fangs, "I can see why you enjoyed him so." The anguish on the vampire's face was heart breaking.

"Is that fucking so Blake?" Gillian said walking out into the open like the rock star he is. The young blue-eyed vamp appeared surprised, as he looked Gillian up and down, "Is that you Claude? You really have let yourself go," he chuckled nastily.

"You've always been an obnoxious twat, Blake. Shall we just get this over with?" Although I hadn't known Gillian for long, I could tell that he was worried.

"Why? Do you have a death wish? To think of the decades my partner Lucille and I have spent travelling, searching for you, and then you and the elusive Thomas Malcolm turn up at the same location at the same time." Upon hearing the name Lucille, I could see fear spread across Gillian's face.

"Fuck off Blake," Gillian said in anguish. "Lucille is a legend, a whisper in the night. What would she be doing around someone like you?"

A self-righteous smirk appeared on Blake's face, "Lucille knows a good thing when she sees it, she will be so pleased you have landed here on our doorstep." Blake stood his ground and stared Gillian straight in the eye, "I've known all along what you sacrificed back in Santorini to save your lover Thomas Malcolm."

Gillian snarled, "Blake once I dispose of these two buffoons, I promise you will be next!"

I was intrigued by Gillian and Blake's conversation when I heard what sounded like an arrow and then saw the vampire Samuel drop to the floor limp and bleeding from his chest, which I could see had been penetrated by a wooden stake. I heard a familiar female voice from the entrance of the apartment.

"It's been a long time since I saw you in Greece Gillian," I could see a statuesque, well-kept woman holding a crossbow. "Threatening Blake would not be in your best interests as you know very well what I am capable of."

"Hello Lucille, my guiding light," Blake said affectionately.

Blake moved to stand alongside the woman he called Lucille and as he did, I could sense Gillian's fear pour into me through Jeff.

"Hello Detective," Lucille said turning to my hiding spot. "You may as well show yourself, I can sense you there, as well as a very impressive presence hanging around your neck." She removed her glasses and addressed Gillian, "You have changed an awful lot from the vampire Claude who kept Thomas Malcolm from me in Santorini."

Jeff's voice entered my mind, "This Lucy is a powerful being, I can't get a read on her and it disturbs me and I can tell Gillian is frightened." I was more than worried about the situation at hand.

"Claude it's time for you to tell me where Thomas Malcolm is," Lucille demanded.

"You know you must do as Lucille says Gillian," Blake said, "You cannot deny the power of our first light, our curator, our mother."

"I won't do that," Gillian replied, his voice strained and the words coming out of his mouth slowly, as if he was trying to fight off some form of internal attack.

"It's too late for you and your ex-lover," Lucille said staring at Gillian. "If only you had just given Thomas Malcolm up all those years ago then we wouldn't be in the situation we now find ourselves. I have spent many a century manipulating people in positions of power and influence. Slowly and inconspicuously over time I exerted my control over them and used them for my own gains. I have chosen my pawns for small yet crucial roles and when their influence is combined, I will be able to change the world to the way I want it to be run, away from the control of the patriarchy. There have been many men that have exerted their power over the weak, the fallible, the women and the children. I have been bringing men to justice for centuries, Nero, Vlad the Impaler, Pol Pot to name but a few. In the past it was easier to spot the men of evil and the atrocities they carried out from the past, now they are billionaires who hide behind their corporations. My plan is to control this city and utilise the access it has to powerful vampires around the world, manipulating them to use their influence to do my bidding. It's time to overthrow the governments and create a new world order.

"Thomas Malcolm is an integral part of this plan, his ability to move across time will allow me to change history. I know how you feel about him Gillian and I simply cannot have you in my way. One way or another I will have the power Thomas Malcolm possesses but sadly you and your partner will not be alive to see it."

Gillian appeared to be in shock and unable to speak or move. I could see his panic so I took the opportunity to haul him over the counter, which seemed to shake him from the trance he was in.

"Fuck Nate we need to get out of here," Gillian said frantically.

"They're coming," Jeff warned us.

Gillian grabbed the handgun from my belt and fired off a couple of rounds at the two large vampires moving quickly towards us.

"We won't be able to shoot or fight our way out of this one Nate. Blake is too strong and Lucille is untouchable." Gillian continued to shoot while he spoke doing his best to keep them back,

"She has evolved into something extraordinary and I am power-less against her."

"But she seems human to me?" I said getting my stake ready for action.

"I assure you she definitely isn't," Jeff communicated. "She's try-ing to enter my mind, trying to control me. She's reading all of our goddamn thoughts; we haven't got long so we need to get out of here!" The panic from Jeff was spreading throughout my body. The situation felt grim.

"Right," Gillian said firing off his last round directly into the heart of one of the burly vampires, exploding him into dust. "What can we do Jeff, 'cos I'm all out?"

"I can pulse Nathan out of here, but you would be on your own," Jeff sounded like he was being pulled apart, spitting out the words quickly, leaving me feeling dazed.

I fired off a shot at the other vampire but missed completely.

"Right-o mate," Gillian grimaced "I didn't know you could pulse. Go back to the place where I first met Thomas Malcolm."

I could hear Lucy shouting angrily at the vampires.

"She knows our plan you need to go now; I'll delay them as long as possible. I'll find you Nate, I promise," Gillian said. And with that he jumped over the counter, and used the element of surprise to tear the throat out of the remaining vampire bodyguard. Blake was on to Gillian in a flash knocking him to the ground with the weight of his body. I took aim at Blake but Jeff had other ideas. I began to shudder and could see my arms shimmering; I had no idea what was happening. My hands around the gun looked trans-lucent and it felt like I was beginning to leave this plane behind.

"Breathe Nate or I can't move us through time," Jeff said breath-lessly

"You what?" I screamed.

"Blake!" Lucy commanded, "Get the detective, NOW!"

My head was spinning, it was difficult to keep my eyes open. As Blake went for me, I saw Gillian give me a cheeky wink then launch himself out of the window sending shards of glass everywhere.

I tried shooting at Blake but I had no idea if I hit him. He was so close to my face, the room was spinning, my breath felt laboured. Blake's hands were around my neck. "Relax!" Jeff was screaming in my mind as I placed my hands to my head and neck to stop the pain. I looked at Lucy but then she was gone.

29

The shock of seeing a body catapult out of a window from a two-floor apartment caught the police officers and paramedics standing on the kerb below off guard. The club had been taped off and most people who were out on The Vamp Strip for a good time had dispersed. When the jumper stood up it was clear to see that it was actually an older looking vampire dressed in '80s metal attire. Blood poured from his head and he had shards of glass and bruises all over his rough and ready exterior.

He gained his composure, dusted himself down and started hobbling towards a police car while looking over his shoulder towards the window he just came from, like he was expecting to be followed.

A young officer ran up to the vampire, flustered, "Gillian you, ok?"

"Yeah, I'm fucking great Charlie, what do you do think?" he said dryly. "You're going to need to secure the area I just came from. You'll need some back up as there is an extremely dangerous vampire called Blake up there, and also Lucy, that woman from the prison, who just killed someone with a crossbow."

Charlie looked perplexed as Gillian got into the car and started the engine.

"Where are you going?" the officer said worriedly.

Starting the police siren and putting on his seat belt he looked up at Charlie.

"I need to save Nate and to do that I have to find a pompous twat called Thomas Malcolm."

And with that he put the pedal to the metal and sped off into the night.

The End

Acknowledgements

I couldn't have finished my book without the following people who have always been there for me and picked me up when I needed it most. For this I will be forever grateful.

My sister Lisa, for lifting me up and telling me I can do anything, and for encouraging me to keep writing whenever I got stuck and who is officially the best sister in the world.

My Mum and Dad, for being proud of me no matter what, who have always loved and supported me and been there when I needed them most without asking for anything in return.

Steve, for giving me the confidence to push my writing further and follow through with my ideas and who gave me constructive criticism and help when I needed it.

Eamonn, for always making me laugh and being there when I need to talk, no matter what the time, especially when I was at my lowest.

Viv, for being a friend and for allowing me to be myself through the years.

Paul, for walking beside me and helping me get my head together again after cancer and who is always there for a therapeutic chat when I need it.

Megan, for helping me sort through design ideas and for giving me great advice and most importantly, supporting me when I was ill and for being a fantastic auntie to my boys.

Belinda, for being my cheerleader and believing in me from early conception, never judging and being truly inspiring.

Andy, for keeping the humour flowing and for bringing me a tray of mangoes when I was at my sickest.

Chris and his wonderful family, for listening, understanding and keeping me going through the tough times.

My wonderful boys Sebastian and Otis, who I am so very lucky to be spending quality time with while they are growing up. Two totally different and unique individuals who in their own ways make me laugh and also make me proud.

Most of all my wife Justine, who not only got me through cancer without complaint but edited the first draft of *Dusk Travellers*, night after night, red line after red line, whose support and love is invaluable and helps me make sense of it all.

Milton Keynes UK
Ingram Content Group UK Ltd.
UKHW020850260124
436746UK00013B/392

9 780645 309126